AN AMERICAN DREAM

War hero, ex-Congressman, television personality and husband of the rich and beautiful Deborah ('a girl who would have been bored by a diamond as big as the Ritz'), Stephen Rojack lived the American Dream. But his enviable life concealed a strange tension, the constant 'itch to jump', and when one day he finally cracks and strangles his luscious wife, he unleashes a personality of undreamt-of ferocity.

A wanted murderer, Rojack is suddenly catapulted into an alien world of gangsters, crumbling tenements and downtown bars. Here, he meets Cherry, a small-time singer who ekes out her living in sleazy night-clubs, waiting for a break. She's the woman Rojack falls for, dangerously, desperately, tragically . . .

NORMAN MAILER was born in New Jersey in 1923. During the Second World War, Mailer served in the Philippines, an experience which formed the basis of his famous debut novel, the bestselling *The Naked and the Dead*. A powerful exploration of one man's quest for depravity, Mailer's *An American Dream* shocked the USA on first publication in 1965 with its graphic depictions of sex and violence. One of the key works of twentieth-century American literature, the novel's white-hot prose makes it, for many, Mailer's finest achievement.

flamingo sixties classic

Norman Mailer

AN AMERICAN DREAM

Flamingo
An Imprint of HarperCollins*Publishers*

Flamingo
An imprint of HarperCollins*Publishers*
77–85 Fulham Palace Road,
Hammersmith, London w6 8jb

Flamingo is a registered trade mark of HarperCollins Publishers Ltd.

www.fireandwater.com

This Flamingo Sixties Classic edition published 2001
9 8 7 6 5 4 3 2 1

First published in Great Britain by André Deutsch Ltd 1965

isbn 0 00 711528 8

Set in Monotype Apollo and Optima Display by
Rowland Phototypesetting Ltd
Bury St Edmunds, Suffolk

Printed and bound in Great Britain by
Clays Ltd, St Ives plc

ACKNOWLEDGEMENTS

'Deep Purple' – music by Peter DeRose, lyrics by Mitchell Parish. Copyright 1934 (renewed) by Robbins Music Corporation, New York. Used by permission of copyright proprietor.

Variant of the original lyrics of 'Hong Kong Blues', copyright 1939 Larry Spier, Inc. by permission of Larry Spier, Inc.

'Love for Sale', copyright 1930 by Harms Inc. Copyright renewed. Used by permission.

'That's Why the Lady is a Tramp', copyright 1937 by Chappell & Co., Inc., New York. Used by permission.

CONTENTS

1

The Harbors of the Moon

I met Jack Kennedy in November, 1946. We were both war heroes, and both of us had just been elected to Congress. We went out one night on a double date and it turned out to be a fair evening for me. I seduced a girl who would have been bored by a diamond as big as the Ritz.

She was Deborah Caughlin Mangaravidi Kelly, of the Caughlins first, English-Irish bankers, financiers and priests; the Mangaravidis, a Sicilian issue from the Bourbons and the Hapsburgs; Kelly's family was just Kelly; but he had made a million two hundred times. So there was a vision of treasure, far-off blood, and fear. The night I met her we had a wild ninety minutes in the back seat of my car parked behind a trailer truck on a deserted factory street in Alexandria, Virginia. Since Kelly owned part of the third largest trucking firm in the Midwest and West, I may have had a speck of genius to try for his daughter where I did. Forgive me. I thought the road to President might begin at the entrance to her Irish heart. She heard the snake rustle however in *my* heart; on the telephone next morning she told me I was evil, awful and evil, and took herself back to the convent in London where she had lived at times before. I did not know as yet that ogres stand on guard before the portal of an heiress. Now in retrospect I can say with cheer: that was the closest I came to being President. (By the time I found Deborah again –

all of seven years later in Paris — she was no longer her father's delight, and we were married in a week. Like any tale which could take ten books, it is best to quit it by a parenthesis — less than ten volumes might be untrue.)

Of course Jack has gone on a bit since those days, and I have traveled up and I have voyaged down and I've gone up and down, but I remember a full moon the night we had our double date, and to be phenomenologically precise, there was also a full moon on the night I led my patrol to the top of a particular hill in Italy, and a full moon the night I met another girl, and a full moon . . . There are times when I like to think I still have my card in the intellectual's guild, but I seem to be joining the company with that horde of the mediocre and the mad who listen to popular songs and act upon coincidence. The real difference between the President and myself may be that I ended with too large an appreciation of the moon, for I looked down the abyss on the first night I killed: four men, four very separate Germans, dead under a full moon — whereas Jack, for all I know, never saw the abyss.

Of course, I did not have any illusion that my heroism was the equal of his. I got good for one night. I was a stiff, overburdened, nervous young Second Lieutenant, fresh from Harvard, graduated a year behind Prince Jack (we never met — not there). I had gone into the Army with a sweaty near-adolescent style, Harvard on the half-shell ('Raw-Jock' Rojack was the sporting name bestowed on me in House Football) and I had been a humdrum athlete and, as a student, excessively bright: Phi Beta Kappa, *summa cum laude*, Government.

Small wonder I was thus busy working to keep some government among the hard-nosed Southerners and young Mafiosos from the Bronx who made up the double nucleus of my platoon, working so busily that death this night first appeared to me as a possibility considerably more agreeable than my status in some further disorder. I really didn't care much longer whether I stayed alive. When I steered us up the hill therefore to get pinned down in a long, bad line, one hundred feet from the summit, a modest twin dome, a double hill with a German machine gun on one knoll and a German machine gun on the other, I was so ready to die in atonement I was not even scared.

Trapped beneath a rusty sputter – the guns had not quite found me nor any of the others – the full moon giving a fine stain to the salient of our mood (which was fear and funk and a sniff of the grave), I could nonetheless feel danger withdraw from me like an angel, withdraw like a retreating wave over a quiet sea, sinking quietly into the sand, and I stood and then I ran, I ran up the hill into the aisle of safety I felt opening for me which is part of what captured that large decoration later, because the route I took was under the separate fire of each of those guns and the two together could stitch you to a pulp. Their fire was jagged, however, it was startled, and as I ran, I threw my carbine away, out ten yards to the front of me, crossed my arms to pull a grenade from each shirt pocket, pulled the rings with my teeth, which I had hardly been able to do in practice (much too hard on the teeth), released the spoon handles, the fuse now lit, and spitting, and shot my arms out like the wings of the letter Y. The grenades sailed away in separate flights and I had time to stop, turn around, and dive back for my carbine which I had overrun.

Years later I read *Zen in the Art of Archery* and understood the book. Because I did not throw the grenades on that night on the hill under the moon, *it* threw them, and *it* did a near-perfect job. The grenades went off somewhere between five and ten yards over each machine gun, *blast, blast*, like a boxer's tattoo, one-two, and I was exploded in the butt from a piece of my own shrapnel, whacked with a delicious pain clean as a mistress' sharp teeth going 'Yummy' in your rump, and then the barrel of my carbine swung around like a long fine antenna and pointed itself at the machine-gun hole on my right where a great bloody sweet German face, a healthy spoiled overspoiled young beauty of a face, mother-love all over its making, possessor of that overcurved mouth which only great fat sweet young faggots can have when their rectum is tuned and entertained from adolescence on, came crying, sliding, smiling up over the edge of the hole, 'Hello death!' blood and mud like the herald of sodomy upon his chest, and I pulled the trigger as if I were squeezing the softest breast of the softest pigeon which ever flew, still a woman's breast takes me now and then to the pigeon on that trigger, and the shot cracked like a birth twig across my palm, *whop!* and the round went in at the base of his nose and spread and I saw his face sucked in backward upon the gouge of the bullet, he looked suddenly like an old man, toothless, sly, reminiscent of lechery. Then he whimpered '*Mutter*,' one yelp from the first memory of the womb, and down he went into his own blood just in time, timed like the interval in a shooting gallery, for the next was up, his hole-mate, a hard avenging specter with a pistol in his hand and one arm off, blown off, rectitude like a stringer of saliva across the straight edge of his lip, the straightest lip I ever saw, German-Protestant rectitude. *Whap!* went my carbine and the hole was in his heart and he folded back the long arm with the pistol, back across his chest to cover his new hole and went down straight and with a clown's deep gloom as if he were sliding down a long thin pipe, and then I turned, feeling something tear in my wound, nice in its pain, a good blood at liberty, and I took on the other two coming out of the other hole, one short stocky ape-like wretch with his back all askew, as if he'd had a false stuffed hump which shrapnel had disgorged beyond his shoulder blade: I fired at him and he went down and I never knew where it hit nor quite saw his face; then the last stood up straight with a bayonet in his hand and invited me to advance. He was bleeding below his belt. Neat and clean

4

was his shirt, level the line of his helmet, and nothing but blood and carnage below the belt. I started to rise. I wanted to charge as if that were our contract, and held, for I could not face his eyes, they now contained all of it, the two grenades, the blood on my thigh, the fat faggot, the ghost with the pistol, the hunchback, the blood, those bloody screams that never sounded, it was all in his eyes, he had eyes I was to see once later on an autopsy table in a small town in Missouri, eyes belonging to a redneck farmer from a deep road in the Ozarks, eyes of blue, so perfectly blue and mad they go all the way in deep into celestial vaults of sky, eyes which go back all the way to God is the way I think I heard it said once in the South, and I faltered before that stare, clear as ice in the moonlight, and hung on one knee, not knowing if I could push my wound, and suddenly it was all gone, the clean presence of *it*, the grace, *it* had deserted me in the instant I hesitated, and now I had no stomach to go, I could charge his bayonet no more. So I fired. And missed. And fired again. And missed. Then he threw his bayonet at me. It did not reach. He was too weak. It struck a stone instead and made a quivering whanging sound like the yowl of a tomcat on the jump. Then it stopped between us. The light was going out in his eye. It started to collect, to coagulate into the thick jelly which forms on the pupil of a just-dead dog, and he died then, and fell over. Like a noble tree with rotten roots. And the platoon was up around me, shooting a storm into those two holes, and they were cheering, buzzing, kissing my mouth (one of the Italians for certain), pounding my back. 'Get off him, he's wounded,' shouted somebody, the Sergeant, and I felt like a halfback who has caught a fifty-yard pass and run another forty-eight for the longest touchdown in the history of the school, except that the final excellence of it was smuggled away since the ball squiggled out of my arms as I ran it out past the end zone. I had scored, but no football in my belly at the end, just six points. And those blue eyes kept staring into the new flesh of my memory until I went over with a thud, a wave from the wound carrying me back, forcing my head to the ground with some desire of its own. 'Medics,' I heard a man yell.

I was carried out later on a stretcher, an X-ray showed a minor crack and small split in the girdle of the pelvis. I was evacuated to a base hospital, then sent to New York where I was given a Distinguished Service Cross, not anything less, and was used for the last year to bring good public relations for the Army. Which I did, showing the trace of a distinguished limp. A hero in mid-'44, a hero for all of '45, surviving even V-J Day, I had my pick of opportunities and used them. I went around for a time speaking with Mrs Roosevelt at one honorable drive after another, and she liked me. She encouraged me to think of politics. Those became the years when the gears worked together, the contacts and the insights, the style and the manufacture of oneself. It all turned together very well, I was a curiosity after all, a most special product: I was the one intellectual in America's history with a DSC and I spoke in public with a modest warrior's charm.

About the time the Party machine in New York County was sorting through its culls and giving me odd off-hand invitations to lunch with the Cardinal and the Bishop ('One question, son,' asked the first Eminence, 'do you believe in God?' 'Yes, your Eminence') Mrs Roosevelt was introducing me to Protestant gentry and Jewish gentry and, yes, it all began to fit and fit so well I came out, by the end, a candidate for Congress, and was then elected. Congressman Stephen Richards Rojack, Democrat from New York.

Now, I could go into more detail about the precise sequence of steps which left me a young Congressman in 1946 at the age of twenty-six – the moves were not automatic after all, but that would merely describe the

adventures of the part which I as a young actor was playing. There are any number of movie stars who capture the
love of women they have never seen; the poor husbands
of those women are in competition with a man they cannot
meet. But I think of those particular few movie stars who
are not only profiles for a great lover, but homosexual and
private in their life. They must live with insanity on every
breath. And something which could correspond to this was
true for me. Where many another young athlete or hero
might have had a vast and continuing recreation with sex,
I was lost in a private kaleidoscope of death. I could not
forget the fourth soldier. His eyes had come to see what
was waiting on the other side, and they told me then that
death was a creation more dangerous than life. I could have
had a career in politics if only I had been able to think
that death was zero, death was everyone's emptiness. But
I knew it was not. I remained an actor. My personality
was built upon a void. Thus I quit my place in politics
almost as quickly as I gained it, for by '48 I chose to bolt
the Democratic Party and run for office on the Progressive
ticket. Henry Wallace, Glen Taylor, and me. I had reasons
for the choice, some honorable, some spurious, but one
motive now seems clear – I wanted to depart from politics
before I was separated from myself forever by the distance
between my public appearance which had become vital on
television, indeed nearly robust, and my secret frightened
romance with the phases of the moon. About the month
you decide not to make a speech because it is the week of
the full lunar face you also know if still you are sane that
politics is not for you and you are not for politics.

Now, that was a long time ago. Since then I had, as I
say, gone up, and I had certainly gone down, and I had
gone up and down. I was now at a university in New
York, a professor of existential psychology with the not
inconsiderable thesis that magic, dread, and the perception
of death were the roots of motivation; I was a personality

on television and an author of sorts: I had had one popular book published, *The Psychology of the Hangman*, a psychological study of the styles of execution in different states and nations – death by guillotine, firing squad, by rope, by electric chair, by gas pellets – an interesting book. I had also – as I indicated – become the husband of an heiress, and I had been most unsuccessful at that. In fact I had come to the end of a very long street. Call it an avenue. For I had come to decide I was finally a failure.

I had had a bad year this last year, and for a while it got very bad; I may as well admit that for the first time in my life I had come to understand there was suicide in me. (Murder I had known was there for a long time.) It was the worst of discoveries, this suicide. Murder, after all, has exhilaration within it. I do not mean it is a state to entertain; the tension which develops in your body makes you sicken over a period, and I had my fill of walking about with a chest full of hatred and a brain jammed to burst, but there is something manly about containing your rage, it is so difficult, it is like carrying a two-hundred-pound safe up a cast-iron hill. The exhilaration comes I suppose from possessing such strength. Besides, murder offers the promise of vast relief. It is never unsexual.

But there is little which is sexual about suicide. It is a lonely landscape with the pale light of a dream and something is calling to you, a voice on the wind. Certain nights I would go leaden with dread because I could hear the chamber music tuning up, tuning up and near to pitch. (Yes, murder sounds like a symphony in your head, and suicide is a pure quartet.) I was approaching my forty-fourth year, but for the first time I knew why some of my friends, and so many of the women I had thought I understood, could not bear to be alone at night.

I had spent the last year parting company with my wife. We had been married most intimately and often most unhappily for eight years, and for the last five I had been trying to evacuate my expeditionary army, that force of hopes, all-out need, plain virile desire and commitment which I had spent on her. It was a losing war, and I wanted to withdraw, count my dead, and look for love in another land, but she was a great bitch, Deborah, a lioness of the species: unconditional surrender was her only raw meat. A Great Bitch has losses to calculate after all if the gent gets away. For ideally a Great Bitch delivers extermination to any bucko brave enough to take carnal knowledge of her. She somehow *fails in her role* (as psychoanalysts, those frustrated stage directors, might say) if the lover escapes without being maimed to the nines or nailed to the mast. And Deborah had gotten her hooks into me, eight years ago she had clinched the hooks and they had given birth to other hooks. Living with her I was murderous; attempting to separate, suicide came into me. Some psychic bombardment of the will to live had begun, a new particle of love's mysterious atom had been discovered – the itch to jump. I had been on a balcony ten stories high talking to my host, the cock-tail party was done, and we stood looking down on Sutton Place, not talking about Deborah – what else was there not to talk about this last long year? – and I was wondering, as indeed often I did, whether this old buddy, comfortably drunk with me, a pleasant-looking stud of forty-six, with a waist kept trim by squash at the New York A.C. and a rogue's look in the eye kept alive by corners he cut making his little brokerage prosper (not to speak of women he met for lunch – he had a flair, this buddy), well, wondering whether his concern was so true for me as the timbre of his voice, now sincere, now so place-your-bets sincere, or if he'd been banging my blessed Deborah five times a year, five times each of the last eight years, forty glorious bang-eroos upon the unconscious horror of my back (something so hot they could hardly contain themselves, and kept it down to five each twelve-month out of delicacy, out of a neatness which recognized that if ever they let themselves go, it would all go crash and boom) well, as I say, I stood there, not knowing if Old Buddy was in the Carnal Delights, or a true sword and friend, or even both – there was a wife or two after all with whom I had done the five times eight years bit, and sweet was the prize – no offering like a wife so determined to claw her man that months of hatred are converted to Instant Sweet for the passing stud in the hay, and I felt all the stirrings of real compassion talking to *her* husband next time out. So all was possible – either this guy before me now suffered conceivably a true concern for an old friend and his difficult wife, or was part of the difficulty, or indeed yes was both, both, precisely like me so many times, and before the straight-out complexity of this, the simple incalculable difficulty of ever knowing what is true with an interesting woman, I was lost. I tell you in shame that for those eight years, I could point with certainty to only five bonafide confessed infidelities by Deborah; she had indeed announced each of them to me, each an accent, a transition, a concrete step in the descent of our marriage, a curtain to each act in a five-act play: but beyond this, in the great unknown, were anywhere from two hundred to precisely no infidelities, for Deborah was an artist in that great dialectic of uncertainty where lies lead to truth, and truth begets the shimmering of lies – 'Are you *mad*?' she would ask when I would disclose my suspicions of a particular gentleman or lad, 'Why, he's a boy,' or 'Don't you know he's *repulsive* to me,' which she always said in her best London voice, five years of Catholic schooling in England contributing much to the patrician parts of her American tongue. Yes, before the uncertainty of this, feeling like a scientist of love whose instruments of detection were either wholly inaccurate or unverifiably acute, I stood up in the middle of my conversation with old friend rogue, and simply heaved my cakes, all the gin-and-tonics, anchovy paste, pigs-in-blankets, shrimp cum cocktail sauce, and last six belts of bourbon zip over his balcony and down in a burning cascade of glob and glottle, a thundering herd of love's poisoned hoofs.

'Oh, my God,' said the friend, out-rogued for once.

'Stow it,' I grunted.

'My God,' he repeated, 'it's dropped on the second floor.'

We had both expected as a matter of course – the seizure was so pure – that my paint would land on the doorman's ears. Instead, some tenant would soon complain. The sheer mechanics of it had me next to laughter – how did one send an awning to the cleaners?

'I suppose I've got to tell them,' said the friend.

'Let the rain wash away what the moonlight fails to bless,' said I, in a tone I had come to abhor, a sort of boozed Connecticut gentry in the voice, putting together poetic phrases which were unpoetic, part of the product of living with Deborah's near-English lilts and lecturing too many classes over too many unfulfilled hours. 'In fact, old buddy, leave me. If you can bear it.'

So I stood on the balcony by myself and stared at the moon which was full and very low. I had a moment then. For the moon spoke back to me. By which I do not mean that I heard voices, or Luna and I indulged in the whimsy of a dialogue, no, truly it was worse than that. Something in the deep of that full moon, some tender and not so innocent radiance traveled fast as the thought of lightning across our night sky, out from the depths of the dead in those caverns of the moon, out and a leap through space and into me. And suddenly I understood the moon. Believe it if you will. The only true journey of knowledge is from the depth of one being to the heart of another and I was nothing but open raw depths at that instant alone on the balcony, looking down on Sutton Place, the spirits of the food and drink I had ingested wrenched out of my belly and upper gut, leaving me in raw Being, there were clefts

and rents which cut like geological faults right through all
the lead and concrete and kapok and leather of my ego,
that mutilated piece of insulation, I could feel my Being,
ridiculous enough, what! I could feel lights shifting inside
myself, drifting like vapors over the broken rocks of my
ego while a forest of small nerves jumped up, foul in their
odor, smelling for all the world like the rotten, carious
shudder of a decayed tooth. Half-drunk, half-sick, half on
the balcony, half off, for I had put my leg over the balustrade as if I were able better to breathe with one toe
pointing at the moon, I looked into my Being, all that
lovely light and rotting nerve, and proceeded to listen.
Which is to say, I looked out deep into that shimmer of
past death and new madness, that platinum lady with her
silver light, and she was in my ear, I could hear her music:
'Come to me,' she was saying, 'Come now. Now!' and I
could feel my other foot go over the balustrade, and I was
standing on the wrong side of the railing, only my fingers
(since my thumbs were up and pointing like horns at the
moon), only my eight fingers to hold me from the plunge.
But it was worse than that. Because I knew I would fly.
My body would drop like a sack, down with it, bag of
clothes, bones, and all, but I would rise, the part of me
which spoke and thought and had its glimpses of the landscape of my Being, would soar, would rise, would leap the
miles of darkness to that moon. Like a lion would I join
the legions of the past and share their power. 'Come now,'
said the moon, 'now is your moment. What joy in the
flight.' And I actually let one hand go. It was my left.
Instinct was telling me to die.

Which instinct and where? The right hand tightened in
its grip, and I whipped half-around to the balcony, almost
banging into the rail with my breast, my back now to the
street and the sky. Only if I turned my head could I see
the Lady.

'Drop,' she said one more time, but the moment had

gone. Now if I dropped, all of me passed down. There would be no trip.

'You can't die yet,' said the formal part of my brain, 'you haven't done your work.'

'Yes,' said the moon, 'you haven't done your work, but you've lived your life, and you are dead with it.' 'Let me be not all dead,' I cried to myself, and slipped back over the rail, and dropped into a chair. I was sick. I assure you I was sick in a way I had never been sick before. Deep in a fever, or bumping through the rapids of a bad nausea, one's soul could always speak to one, 'Look what this illness is doing to us, you coward,' that voice might say and one would shake or twist in the fever, but that at least was a nightmare. This illness now, huddling in the deck chair, was an extinction. I could feel what was good in me going away, going away perhaps forever, rising after all to the moon, my courage, my wit, ambition and hope. Nothing but sickness and dung remained in the sack of my torso. And the moon looked back, baleful in her radiance now. Will you understand me if I say that at that moment I felt the other illness come to me, that I knew then if it took twenty years or forty for my death, that if I died from a revolt of the cells, a growth against the design of my organs, that this was the moment it all began, this was the hour when the cells took their leap? Never have I known such a sickening – the retaliation of the moon was complete. What an utter suffocation of my faculties, as if I had disappointed a lady and now must eat the cold tapeworm of her displeasure. Nothing noble seemed to remain of me.

Well, I got up from that deck chair and back to the living room which felt like an indoor pool. So steamy was the air on my stomach, just so ultra-violet seemed the light. I must have been in some far-gone state because there was an aureole about each electric light, each bulb stood out like a personage, and I remember thinking: of course, this is how they appeared to Van Gogh at the end.

'You don't look too well,' said the host.

'Well, buddy, I feel worse than I look. Give me a drop of blood, will you?'

The bourbon tasted like linseed oil and lit a low smoke in the liverish caverns of my belly. I could feel some effulgence of the moon glowing through the windows and dread came back like a hoot from a bully on the street outside.

'It's a great night for the race,' I said.

'What race?' said my host. It was obvious he wished me to be gone.

'The human race. Ho. Ho. Ho,' I said.

'Steve!'

'I'm on my way.'

My hand offered him the glass as if it were the gift of a shiny apple, and then I strolled, closing my host's door so carefully it failed to shut. I turned around to jam it once again and felt a force on me as palpable as a magnetic field. 'Get out of here,' said a voice in my brain. The elevator took too long. I rang, and rang again, but there was not a sound from the cable or the cage. I broke into a galloping sweat. 'If you're not out of here in thirty seconds,' said the same voice, 'your new disease takes another step. Metastases are made of moments like this, lover-man.' So I bolted down the stairs. It was ten flights taken in two banks each, twenty banks of concrete steps, cement-block walls painted guacamole-green, blood-iron railing made of pipe, and I flew down pursued by panic, because I had lost my sense of being alive and here on earth, it was more as if I had died and did not altogether know it, this might be the way it was for the first hour of death if you chose to die in bed – you could blunder through some endless repetition believing your life was still here.

The door to the lobby was locked. Of course. I tired of beating on it with my hands – I was half certain I was really gone – and shifted to one foot, took off a shoe, began to whang away. The doorman opened in a pet. 'What's going

on?' he asked. 'I go up in the elevator and you ain't there.'
He was Italian, some stout dull lump of rejection from the
Mafia – they had assigned him to this job about the time they
decided he was hopeless for waiting on tables in a hopeless
bar. 'Ain't you got any consideration?' he asked.

'Up your ass, friend.' I put on my shoe and walked past
him. As I was going to the street he muttered behind me,
'Up yours too.'

Walking fast I was two blocks away before I saw I had
forgotten my overcoat. It was a night in late March, it was
cold, it was much colder now than it had been on the
balcony, and I shivered from the realization, the wind
reaching in to the forest of nerves on my gut. I could feel
those nerves wriggling now like a hive of worms; they
were flinching as the wind rode by. A familiar misery was
on me. I was separated from Deborah as much as a week
or two at a time, but there would come a moment, there
would always come a moment, after everything else had
gone, when it was impossible not to call her. At moments
like that I would feel as if I had committed hari-kari and
was walking about with my chest separated from my groin.
It was a moment which was physically insupportable, it
was the remains of my love for her, love draining from the
wound, leaving behind its sense of desolation as if all the
love I possessed were being lost and some doom whose
dimensions I could hardly glimpse was getting ready on
the consequence. I hated her more than not by now, my
life with her had been a series of successes cancelled by
quick failures, and I knew so far as I could still keep any
confidence that she had done her best to birth each loss,
she was an artist at sucking the marrow from a broken
bone, she worked each side of the street with a skill shared
only in common by the best of streetwalkers and the most
professional of heiresses. Once, for an instance, at a party,
a friend of hers, a man I was never able to like, a man who
never liked me, had proceeded to beat on me so well for

'celebrity' on television that he was carried away. He invited me to box. Well, we were both drunk. But when it came to boxing I was a good *torero de salón*. I was not bad with four drinks and furniture to circle about. So we sparred to the grim amusement and wild consternation of the ladies, the sober evaluation of the gents. I was feeling mean. I roughed him up a hitch or two in the clinches, I slapped him at will with my jab, holding my hand open but swinging the slaps in, he was such an ass, and after it went on for a minute, he was beginning in compensation to throw his punches as hard (and wild) as he could, whereas I was deepening into concentration. Which is the first reward of the ring. I was sliding my moves off the look in his eye and the shift of his fists, I had settled into the calm of a pregnant typhoon, the kill was sweet and up in me, I could feel it twenty moves away, he was going to finish with three slugs to the belly and his arms apart, that is what it would take, his eye was sweaty and I was going keen. Just then his wife broke in. 'Stop!' she cried, 'absolutely stop!' and came between us.

He was a bad type. 'Why'd you stop it?' he asked. 'It was getting to be fun.'

'Fun!' she said, 'you were going to get killed.'

Well, the point to the story is that when I turned around to wink at Deborah – she had heard me talk much about boxing but had never seen me fight – I discovered she had quit the room.

'Of course I left,' she said later, 'it was a sight, bullying that poor man.'

'Poor? He's bigger than I am.'

'And ten years older.'

That took the taste away. Next time some passing friend invited me to spar at a party – not until a year later I believe, not *all* the parties ended in a bout – I refused. He filed the needle to a point. I still refused. When we got home, she told me I was afraid.

It was worth little to refer to the first episode. 'This man, at least,' she said, 'was younger than you.'

'I could have taken him.'

'I don't believe it. Your mouth was weak, and you were perspiring.'

When I looked into myself I was not certain any longer that there had been no fear. So it took on prominence for me. I did not know any longer.

One could multiply that little puncture by a thousand; Deborah was an artist with the needle, and never pinked you twice on the same spot. (Unless it had turned to ulcer.) So I hated her, yes indeed I did, but my hatred was a cage which wired my love, and I did not know if I had the force to find my way free. Marriage to her was the armature of my ego; remove the armature and I might topple like clay. When I was altogether depressed by myself it seemed as if she were the only achievement to which I could point – I finally had been the man whom Deborah Caughlin Mangaravidi Kelly had lived with in marriage, and since she'd been notorious in her day, picking and choosing among a gallery of beaux: politicians of the first rank, racing drivers, tycoons, and her fair share of the more certified playboys of the Western world, she had been my entry to the big league. I had loved her with the fury of my ego, that way I loved her still, but I loved her the way a drum majorette loved the power of the band for the swell it gave to each little strut. If I was a war hero, an ex-Congressman, a professor of popular but somewhat notorious reputation, and a star of sorts on a television show which I cannot here even bear to explain, if I also had a major work on existential psychology, a herculean endeavor of six to twenty volumes which would (ideally) turn Freud on his head (but remained still in my own head) I had also the secret ambition to return to politics. I had the idea of running some day for Senator, an operation which would not be possible without the vast connections of Deborah's clan. Of course there had never been a cent from *them* — we lived on the money *I* made even if Deborah had the accumulated tastes and habits of the money Barney Oswald Kelly had made. She claimed he had cut her off when she married me — which is possible — but I always thought she lied. It was more probable she did not trust me enough to show the buried loot. Heiresses have a scale: they surrender their heart a quarter-century before they open the purse. I did not care about the money itself, I half hated it, in fact I might have despised the money if it had not become the manifest of how unconsummated and unmasculine was the core of my force. It was like being married to a woman who would not relinquish her first lover.

At any rate, such were my parts. Without Deborah they did not add to any more than another name for the bars and gossip columns of New York. With her beside me, I had leverage, however, I was one of the more active figures of the city — no one could be certain finally that nothing large would ever come from me. But for myself the evidence made no good case: probably I did not have the strength to stand alone.

The difficulty is that I have given an undue portrait of Deborah, and so reduce myself. She had, at her best, a winner's force, and when she loved me (which may be averaged out somewhere between every other day to one day in three) her strength seemed then to pass to mine and I was live with wit, I had vitality, I could depend on stamina, I possessed my style. It was just that the gift was only up for loan. The instant she stopped loving me — which could be for a fault so severe as failing to open the door with a touch of éclat, thereby reminding her of all the swords, humors, and arbiters who had opened doors for her on better nights — why then my psyche was whisked from the stage and stuffed in a pit. A devil's contract, and during all of this last year, not living with her and yet never separated, for though a week might go by or two weeks in which I hardly thought of her at all, I would nonetheless be dropped suddenly into an hour where all of my substance fell out of me and I had to see her. I had a physical need to see her as direct as an addict's panic waiting for his drug – if too many more minutes must be endured, who knows what intolerable damage can be done?

It was like this now. Walking the street just this cold night in March, the horrors were beginning. On these occasions when I had to see her, my instinct gave the warning that if I waited another half hour, even another ten minutes, I might lose her forever. It made no sense, I was almost always wrong in my anticipation of her mood, I was too rattled these months ever to divine what her mood might be, and yet I knew that the way I would probably lose her in the end was by waiting too long on some exceptional night when she might be hoping I would call. For once a certain moment was passed, once Deborah ever said to herself, 'I am rid of him, I am rid of him now finally and forever,' then it would all be gone. She was nothing if not final, she took forever to form her mind, but come the moment and she would not look back.

So I went into an outdoor booth, and shivering in the trapped cold air, I phoned her apartment. She was home – there were agonies on those nights I phoned and she was out – but she was home this night, and she was cordial. Which was a very bad sign.

'Darling,' she said, 'where have you been? You must rush over.' She was a handsome woman, Deborah, she was big. With high heels she stood at least an inch over me. She had a huge mass of black hair and striking green eyes sufficiently arrogant and upon occasion sufficiently amused to belong to a queen. She had a large Irish nose and a wide mouth which took many shapes, but her complexion was her claim to beauty, for the skin was cream-white and her cheeks were colored with a fine rose, centuries of Irish mist had produced that complexion. It was her voice however which seduced one first. Her face was large and all-but-honest; her voice was a masterwork of treachery. Clear as a bell, yet slithery with innuendo, it leaped like a deer, slipped like a snake. She could not utter a sentence for giving a tinkle of value to some innocent word. It may have been the voice of a woman you would not trust for an instant, but I did not know if I could forget it.

'I'll be right over,' I said.

'Run. You must *run*.'

When we separated, she was the one who had moved out. Our marriage had been a war, a good eighteenth-century war, fought by many rules, most of them broken if the prize to be gained was bright enough, but we had developed the cheerful respect of one enemy general for another. So I had been able to admire the strategic splendor of leaving me in our apartment. It *stifled* her, she explained to me, it was a source of much misery. If we were to separate, there was small logic for her to remain behind in an apartment she did not like, no, it was better for her to leave me there, I was fond of the apartment after all. I was not, I had never been, but I had pretended to be fond. Therefore I inherited her misery. Now the apartment, the empty stadium of our marriage, stifled *me*, but I had not the pluck, the time, nor the clean desperation to move. I used it as a place to drop my dirty shirts. Meanwhile, she hopped from one fine suite to another; there was always a friend leaving for Europe, and no one was ready to remind Deborah she was very behind on the rent. (What cowards were her friends!) I would get the bill finally, it would be a knockout, $2700 for three months' rent – I would hold it, no question of paying. Part of the attrition on my military reserves had been the expenses. Deborah got four hundred dollars a week – it was senseless to give her less, she would merely run up her bills, and I had been scuffling and humping, taking three hundred dollars for a spot appearance on a television show, and seven hundred fifty for a spiced-up lecture to some Ladies Auxiliary in Long Island – 'The Existential Approach to Sex.' Yes, debt was grinding me bad. I was something like $16,000 in the hole already and probably worse – I did not care to count.

The apartment she had now was a small duplex suspended some hundred or more feet above the East River Drive, and every vertical surface within was covered with flock, which must have gone for twenty-five dollars a yard; a hot-house of flat velvet flowers, royal, sinister, cultivated in their twinings, breathed at one from all four walls, upstairs and down. It had the specific density of a jungle conceived by Rousseau, and Deborah liked it the best of her purloined pads. 'I feel warm in here,' she would say, 'nice and *warm*.'

The maid let me in. 'Madame is upstairs in the bedroom,' she said with a smile. She was a young German maid who must have had an interesting life in the ruins of Berlin from the age of five, for nothing missed her attention. She had taken lately to smiling at me with a droll mocking compassionate and very wound-up spite which promised portfolios of detail if I were ever rich enough to turn her tongue just once. I was sometimes tempted to start, to grab her in the hall and take her spiced mouth, lay my tongue on hers and rustle up with a stroke those overtones of malicious music she could sing. What Madame did with me she knew too well because I might still spend a night with Deborah from time to time, but what Madame did with others . . . that would have to be bought.

I ascended the stairway, a padded perfumed aisle up a wall of flowers. Deborah was in bed. Her body was not only large but lazy and she hopped into bed whenever she did not know what else to do.

'My God,' she said, 'you look awful.' Her mouth turned fond at the corners. She never disliked me so much as when I came to see her looking my best. 'You really are a contemptible-looking creature this evening.'

Did she know about the balcony? Sometimes I was convinced I was mad, because it seemed not at all exceptional to me that Deborah had been in touch with the moon and now had the word. She had powers, my Deborah, she was psychic to the worst degree, and she had the power to lay a curse. Once after a fight with her, I had been given traffic tickets three times in fifteen minutes, once for going down a one-way street, once for jumping a red light, and once because the policeman in the last car did not like my eye and decided I was drunk. That had all been in the form of a warning from Deborah, I was certain of that. I could see her waiting alone in bed, waving her long fingers languidly to spark the obedient diabolisms and traffic officers at her command.

'It was a bad party,' I said.

'How is Philippe?'

'Looking well.'

'He's a *very* attractive man. Don't you think so?' said Deborah.

'Everyone we know is attractive,' I said to annoy her.

'Except you, pet. You look as if you've used up your liver for keeps this time.'

'I'm not very happy,' I said.

'Well, come *here* and live. There's no reason why you can't move back with me.'

Her invitation was open. She wanted me to dispose of my apartment, sell our furniture, move in with her. After a month she would move out again, leaving me with the velvet flock.

'If you'd come this afternoon,' she went on, 'you could have seen Deirdre. Now she's off to school. You are a swine not to have seen her.' Deirdre was her daughter, my step-daughter. Deborah's first husband had been a French count. He had died of a lingering illness after a year of marriage, and Deirdre, so far as I knew, had been the child of that marriage, a delicate haunted girl with eyes which contained a promise she would learn everything about you if she looked too long, and so chose not to look. I adored her, I had realized for years that being step-father to Deirdre was the most agreeable part of our marriage; for that reason I tried to see her as little as possible now.

'Is she pleased at going back to school this trip?'

'She would have been more pleased if you had come by.' Deborah's complexion was mottling with red. When she became angry a red flush, raw as a rash, spotted her neck. 'You pretended to love that child for so long, and now you give her no attention.'

'It's too painful,' I said.

'God, you're a whimperer,' said Deborah. 'Sometimes I lie here and wonder how you ever became a hero. You're such a bloody whimperer. I suppose the Germans were whimpering even worse than you. It must have been quite a sight. You whimpering and they whimpering, and you going pop pop pop with your little gun.'

Never had she gone quite so far before. 'How do you tell that story these days?' Deborah went on.

'I don't tell it.'

'Except when you're too drunk to remember.'

'I'm never too drunk to remember.'

'I can't get over the way you look,' Deborah exclaimed. 'I mean you really look like some poor peddler from the Lower East Side.'

'I'm descended from peddlers.'

'Don't I know it, honey-one,' said Deborah. 'All those poor materialistic grabby little people.'

'Well, they never hurt anyone particularly.' This was a reference to her father.

'No, they didn't, and they didn't have the guts to do anything else either. Except to make your father brainy enough to make your mother and then make you.' She said this with such a stir of fury that I moved uneasily. Deborah was violent. I had a bad scar on my ear. People thought it came from the ring, but the truth was less presentable – Deborah had once bitten it half-through in a fight.

'Go easy,' I said.

'You're fragile tonight, aren't you?' She nodded, her face almost gentle, almost attentive, as if she were listening to the echo of an event. 'I know something happened to you.'

'I don't want to talk about it.' Which was in effect a counter-attack. Deborah could not bear not to know.

'I thought you were dead,' said Deborah. 'Isn't that funny. I was certain you were dead.'

'Were you sorry?'

'Oh, I felt a great woe.' She smiled. 'I thought you were dead and you'd left a will that you wished to be cremated. I was going to keep your ashes in an urn. There – right by the window table. Each morning I was going to take a handful of your dust and drop it on the East River Drive. In time, who knows, you might have been *strewn* all over New York.'

'I would have done my best to haunt you.'

'Can't, pet. Not when you're cremated. That atomizes the soul. Didn't you know?' Her green eyes had a particularly bad light. 'Come here, darling, and give a kiss.'

'I'd rather not.'

'Tell me why not.'

'Because I threw up a while ago and my breath is foul.'

'Bad smells never bother me.'

'Well, they bother me. And you've been drinking rum. You smell Godawful.' It was true. When she drank too much, a stench of sweet rot lifted from her. 'The Irish were never meant to go near rum,' I said, 'it brings out the odor of their fat.'

'Do you talk this way to all your little girls?'

She did not know what I did with the days and weeks I spent away from her. This was forever agitating her rage.

Once, years ago, she uncovered an affair I had been keeping in a corner. It had been with a rather ordinary young lady who (for compensation, no doubt) had been a burning wizard in bed. Otherwise, the girl was undeniably plain. Somehow, Deborah learned about her. The subsequent details are vicious, private detectives, so forth, but the indigestible issue was that Deborah had gone with the private detective to a restaurant where the girl always had lunch and studied her through a meal, all through a long meal the poor girl ate by herself. What a scene followed!

'I don't think I've been quite so marooned in all my beloved life,' Deborah had said. 'I mean, *figure-toi*, pet, I had to keep up a conversation with the detective, a *horrible* man, and he was laughing at me. All that money spent on fees, and for what, a poor wet little mouse. She was even afraid of the *waitresses*, and this was a *tea*-room. What a big boy you must be to take up with a sparrow.'

The real part of her fury was that no intrigue had ensued; if the affair had been with one of her friends, or with some other woman of parts, then Deborah could have gone to war and fought one of her grand campaigns, hook and eye, tooth and talon, a series of parties with exquisite confrontations; but I had merely been piddling and that was the unforgivable sin. Since that time Deborah spoke only of my *little girls*.

'What do you say to them, pet?' asked Deborah now, 'do you say, "Please stop drinking so much because you smell like a piece of fat," or do you say, "Oh God, darling, I love your stink?"'

The mottling had spread in ugly smears and patches upon her neck, her shoulders, and what I could see of her breast. They radiated a detestation so palpable that my body began to race as if a foreign element, a poison altogether suffocating, were beginning to seep through me. Did you ever feel the malignity which rises from a swamp? It is real, I could swear it, and some whisper of ominous calm, that heavy air one breathes in the hours before a hurricane, now came to rest between us. I was afraid of her. She was not incapable of murdering me. There are killers one is ready to welcome, I suppose. They offer a clean death and free passage to one's soul. The moon had spoken to me as just such an assassin. But Deborah promised bad burial. One would go down in one's death, and muck would wash over the last of one's wind. She did not wish to tear the body, she was out to spoil the light, and in an epidemic of fear, as if her face – that wide mouth, fullfleshed nose, and pointed green eyes, pointed as arrows – would be my first view of eternity, as if she were ministering angel (ministering devil) I knelt beside her and tried to take her hand. It was soft now as a jellyfish, and almost as repugnant – the touch shot my palm with a thousand needles which stung into my arm exactly as if I had been swimming at night and lashed onto a Portuguese man o' war.

'Your hand feels nice,' she said in a sudden turn of mood.

There was a period when we held hands often. She had become pregnant after three years of marriage, a ticklish pregnancy to conserve, for there had been something malformed about her uterus – she was never explicit – and her ducts had suffered from a chronic inflammation since Deirdre had been born. But we had succeeded, we wanted a child, there was genius between us we believed, and we held hands for the first six months. Then we crashed. After a black night of drink and a quarrel beyond dimension, she lost the baby, it came brokenly to birth, in terror, I always thought, of the womb which was shaping it, came out and went back in again to death, tearing by this miscarriage the hope of any other child for Deborah. What it left behind was a heart-land of revenge. Now, cohabiting with Deborah was like sitting to dinner in an empty castle with no more for host than a butler and his curse. Yes,

I knelt in fear, and my skin lived on thin wire, this side of a profound shudder. All the while she stroked my hand.

But compassion, the trapped bird of compassion, struggled up from my chest and flew to my throat. 'Deborah, I love you,' I said. I did not know at that instant if I meant it truly, or was some monster of deception, hiding myself from myself. And having said it, knew the mistake. For all feeling departed from her hand, even that tingling so evil to my flesh, and left a cool empty touch. I could have been holding a tiny casket in my palm.

'Do you love me, pet?' she asked.

'Yes.'

'It must be awful. Because you know I don't love you any more at all.'

She said it so quietly, with such a nice finality, that I thought again of the moon and the promise of extinction which had descended on me. I had opened a void — I was now without center. Can you understand? I did not belong to myself any longer. Deborah had occupied my center.

'Yes, you're looking awful again,' said Deborah. 'You began to look all right for a little while, but now you look awful again.'

'You don't love me.'

'Oh, not in the least.'

'Do you know what it's like to look at someone you love and see no love come back?'

'It must be awful,' said Deborah.

'It's unendurable,' I said. Yes, the center was gone. In another minute I would begin to grovel.

'It is unendurable,' she said.

'You do know?'

'Yes, I do.'

'You have felt it?'

'There was a man I loved very much,' she said, 'and he didn't love me.'

'You never told me that before.'

'No, I didn't.'

Before we married, she told me everything. She confessed every last lover – it had been her heritage from the
convent: she had done more than tell me, she had gone to
detail – we would giggle in the dark while she tapped my
shoulder with one cultivated and very learned finger, giving me a sense of the roll and snap and lurch and grace
(or lack of it) in each of her lovers, she had even given me
a sense of what was good in the best of them, and I had
loved her for it, painful as the news had sometimes been,
for I had known at least what I was up against, and how
many husbands could ever say that? It was the warrant of
our love; whatever our marriage had been, that was our
covenant, that had been her way of saying I was more
valuable than the others.

And now she was inside me, fused at my center, ready
to blow the rails.

'You don't mean it,' I said.

'I do. There was one man I never told you about. I never
told anyone about him. Although once, somebody guessed.'

'Who was the man?'

'He was a bullfighter. Marvelous ripe man.'

'You're lying.'

'Have it your way.'

'It wasn't a bullfighter.'

'No, it wasn't. It was someone far better than a bullfighter, far greater.' Her face had turned plump with mal-
ice, and the red mottling had begun to fade. 'As a matter
of fact, it was the finest and most extraordinary man I ever
knew. Delicious. Just a marvelous wild feast of things. I
tried to make him jealous once and lost him.'

'Who could it be?' I asked.

'Don't bother to hop on one foot and then the other like
a three-year-old who's got to go to the Lou. I'm not going
to tell you.' She took a sip of her rum, and jiggled the
tumbler not indelicately, as if the tender circles of the

liquor might transmit a message to some distant force, or – better – receive one. 'It's going to be a bore not having you here once in a while.'

'You want a divorce,' I said.

'I think so.'

'Like that.'

'Not like *that*, darling. *After* all that.' She yawned prettily and looked for the moment like a fifteen-year-old Irish maid. 'When you didn't come by today to say good-bye to Deirdre . . .'

'I didn't know she was leaving.'

'Of course you didn't know. How could you know? You haven't called in two weeks. You've been nuzzling and nipping with your little girls.' She did not know that at the moment I had no girl.

'They're not so little any more.' A fire had begun to spread in me. It was burning now in my stomach and my lungs were dry as old leaves, my heart had a herded pressure which gave promise to explode. 'Give us a bit of the rum,' I said.

She handed over the bottle. 'Well, they may not be so little any more, but I doubt that, pet. Besides I don't care. Because I made a vow this afternoon. I said to myself that I would never . . .' and then she did not speak the rest of the sentence, but she was talking about something she had done with me and never with anyone else. 'No,' said Deborah, 'I thought: There's no need for that any more. Never again. Not with Steve.'

I had taught it to her, but she had developed a pro-nounced royal taste of her own for that little act. Likely it had become the first of her pleasures.

'Not ever again?' I asked.

'Never. The thought – at least in relation to you, dear sweet – makes me brush my gums with peroxide.'

'Well, goodbye to all that. You don't do it so famously if the truth be told.'

'Not so famously as your little girls?'

'Not nearly as well as five I could name.'

The mottling came back to her neck and shoulders. A powerful odor of rot and musk and something much more violent came from her. It was like the scent of the carnivore in a zoo. This last odor was fearful – it had the breath of burning rubber.

'Isn't that odd?' asked Deborah. 'I haven't heard a word of complaint from any new beau.'

From the day of our separation she had admitted to no lover. Not until this moment. A sharp sad pain, almost pleasurable, thrust into me. It was replaced immediately by a fine horror.

'How many do you have?' I asked.

'At the moment, pet, just three.'

'And you . . .' But I couldn't ask it.

'Yes, darling. Every last little thing. I can't tell you how shocked they were when I began. One of them said: "Where did you ever learn to root about like that? Didn't know such things went on outside a Mexican whorehouse."'

'Shut your fucking mouth,' I said.

'Lately I've had the most famous practice.'

I struck her open-handed across the face. I had meant – some last calm intention of my mind had meant – to make it no more than a slap, but my body was speaking faster than my brain, and the blow caught her on the side of the ear and knocked her half out of bed. She was up like a bull and like a bull she charged. Her head struck me in the stomach (setting off a flash in that forest of nerves) and then she drove one powerful knee at my groin (she fought like a prep-school bully) and missing that, she reached with both hands, tried to find my root and mangle me.

That blew it out. I struck her a blow on the back of the neck, a dead cold chop which dropped her to a knee, and then hooked an arm about her head and put a pressure on her throat. She was strong, I had always known she was strong, but now her strength was huge. For a moment I did not know if I could hold her down, she had almost the strength to force herself up to her feet and lift me in the air, which in that position is exceptional strength even for a wrestler. For ten or twenty seconds she strained in balance, and then her strength began to pass, it passed over to me, and I felt my arm tightening about her neck. My eyes were closed. I had the mental image I was pushing with my shoulder against an enormous door which would give inch by inch to the effort.

One of her hands fluttered up to my shoulder and tapped it gently. Like a gladiator admitting defeat. I released the pressure on her throat, and the door I had been opening began to close. But I had had a view of what was on the other side of the door, and heaven was there, some quiver of jeweled cities shining in the glow of a tropical dusk, and I thrust against the door once more and hardly felt her hand leave my shoulder, I was driving now with force against that door: spasms began to open in me, and my mind cried out then, 'Hold back! you're going too far, hold back!' I could feel a series of orders whip like tracers of light from my head to my arm, I was ready to obey. I was trying to stop, but pulse packed behind pulse in a pressure up to thunderhead; some blackbiled lust, some desire to go ahead not unlike the instant one comes in a woman against her cry that she is without protection came bursting with rage from out of me and my mind exploded in a fireworks of rockets, stars, and hurtling embers, the arm about her neck leaped against the whisper I could still feel murmuring in her throat, and *crack* I choked her harder, and *crack* I choked her again, and *crack* I gave her payment – never halt now – and *crack* the door flew open and the wire tore in her throat, and I was through the door, hatred passing from me in wave after wave, illness as well, rot and pestilence, nausea, a bleak string of salts. I was floating. I was as far into myself as I had ever been and universes wheeled in a dream. To my closed eyes Deborah's face seemed to float off from her body and stare at me in darkness. She gave one malevolent look which said: 'There are dimensions to evil which reach beyond the light,' and then she smiled like a milkmaid and floated away and was gone. And in the midst of that Oriental splendor of landscape, I felt the lost touch of her finger on my shoulder, radiating some faint but ineradicable pulse of detestation into the new grace. I opened my eyes. I was weary with a most honorable fatigue, and my flesh seemed new. I had not felt so nice since I was twelve. It seemed inconceivable at this instant that anything in life could fail to please. But there was Deborah, dead beside me on the flowered carpet of the floor, and there was no question of that. She was dead, indeed she was dead.

2

A Runner from the Gaming Room

On that night sixteen years ago when I made love to Deborah in the back seat of my car, she looked up when we were done, smiling with a misty somewhat bewildered look, and said, 'You're not Catholic, are you?'

'No.'

'I was hoping perhaps you were Polish Catholic. Rojack, you know.'

'I'm half Jewish.'

'What is the other half?'

'Protestant. Nothing really.'

'Nothing really,' she said. 'Come, take me home.' And she was depressed.

It took eight years for me to find out why, seven years of living my own life and a first year of being married to her. It took all of that first year for me to understand that Deborah had prejudices which were as complex and attractive as passions. Her detestation of Jewish Protestants and Gentile Jews was complete. 'They know nothing about grace,' she finally explained to me.

Like any other exceptional Catholic, Deborah was steeped in her idea of grace. Grace was a robber bridegroom, grace was the specter in our marriage bed. When things went badly, she would say sorrowfully, even remotely, 'I used to be filled with grace, and now I'm not.' When she had been pregnant, grace had come to her again. 'I don't think God is so annoyed at me any more,' she said.

And indeed a tenderness rose from her at moments like that, a warm full-bodied balm to my nerves but for the purity of it: Deborah's grace always offered its intimation of the grave. I would be content she loved me, and yet at such moments my mind drifted out to the empty peak of a mountaintop or prepared to drop down the sheer gray face of a ten-foot wave in a storm at sea. That was love with Deborah and it was separate from making love to Deborah; no doubt she classified the two as Grace and Lust. When she felt love, she was formidable; making love she left you with no uncertain memory of having passed through a carnal transaction with a caged animal. It was not just her odor (that smell with the white gloves off) of the wild boar full of rot, that hot odor from a gallery of the zoo, no, there was something other, her perfume perhaps, a hint of sanctity, something as calculating and full of guile as high finance, that was it – she smelled like a bank, Christ she would have been too much for any man, there was something so sly at the center of her, some snake, I used literally to conceive of a snake guarding the cave which opened to the treasure, the riches, the filthy-lucred wealth of all the world, and rare was the instant I could pay my dues without feeling a high pinch of pain as if fangs had sunk into me. The afterbreath, lying on her body, floated on a current of low heavy fire, a sullen poisonous fire, an oil on flame which went out of her and took me in. Invariably a groan came out of me like the clanking of chains, my mouth on hers, not sobbing but groping for air. I always felt as if I had torn free some promise of my soul and paid it over in ransom.

'You're wonderful,' she would say then.

Yes, I had come to believe in grace and the lack of it, in the long finger of God and the swish of the Devil, I had come to give my scientific apprehension to the reality of witches. Deborah believed in demons. It was Celtic blood, she had once been ready to explain, the Celts were in tune with the spirits, made love with them, hunted with the spirits. And in fact she was an exceptional hunter. She had gone on safari with her first husband and killed a wounded lion charging ten feet from her throat, she dropped an Alaskan bear with two shots to the heart (30/06 Winchester), I suspect she finally lost her nerve. She hinted once that she had broken from an animal and the guide had been forced to take it. But that I didn't know – she was not definite. I offered to go hunting with her, to Kodiak, to the Congo, I did not care where: in the first two years of our marriage I would have been willing to go to war with any expert, guide, or champion – she took pains to separate me from that romantic heart. 'But darling, I could never go hunting with you,' she said. 'Pamphli' – the almost unpronounceable nickname of her first husband – 'was a superb hunter. It was the best thing we had together. You don't think I want to spoil that memory by smashing about with you? That would do none of us any good. No, I'll never hunt big ones again. Not unless I should fall in love with somebody who's divine as a hunter.' Like most of her friends, she had an aristocratic indifference to the development of talent. One enjoyed what was in flower, one devoured it if it were good for one, but one left the planting to others.

Finally she took me on a hunt – for moles and woodchucks. I was shown the distance of my place from her beloved Pamphli, but even on this hunt, a casual walk through the Vermont woods near a house we were renting for a season, I saw how good she was. She did not see a forest like others. No, out of the cool and the damp, the scent of forest odor aromatic and soft with rot, Deborah drew a mood – she knew the spirit which created attention in the grove, she told me once she could sense that spirit watching her, and when it was replaced by something else, also watching, well, *there* was an animal. And so there was. Some small thing would leap from concealment and

Deborah would pot him with her .22. She could flush more
small animals than any hunter I ever saw. Often as not she
fired from the hip, as nicely as pointing a finger. And many
of the creatures she allowed to escape. 'You take him,' she
would say, and sometimes I would miss. Which elicited a
laugh of gentle contempt altogether sinister. 'Buy a shot-
gun, darling,' she would whisper. We hunted only a few
times but by the end I knew I would never go hunting
again. Not with her. Because Deborah went for the most
beautiful and the most ugly of the animals she flushed. She
knocked down squirrels with exquisite faces, tender as a
doe in their dying swoon, and she blasted the hindquarters
off groundhogs whose grimace at death was as carved in
stone as a gargoyle's horn. No patch of forest was quite
the same once she had hunted there. 'You see,' she told
me once at night, late, when the booze had left her in the
rarest of moods, not violent, not vicious, not amorous, but
simply reflective, an air circling in on itself, 'I know that
I am more good and more evil than anyone alive, but which
was I born with, and what came into me?'

'You shift allegiance from day to day.'

'No. I just pretend to.' She smiled. 'I'm evil if truth be
told. But I despise it, truly I do. It's just that evil has
power.'

Which was a way of saying goodness was imprisoned
by evil. After nine years of marriage to her I did not have
a clue myself. I had learned to speak in a world which
believed in the *New York Times*: Experts Divided on Fluori-
dation, Diplomat Attacks Council Text, Self-Rule Near for
Bantu Province, Chancellor Outlines Purpose of Talks, New
Drive for Health Care for Aged. I had lost my faith in all
of that by now: now I swam in the well of Deborah's
intuitions; they were nearer to my memory of the four
Germans than anything encountered before or since. But
what I did not know was which of us imprisoned the other,
and how? It was horror this edge of madness to lie beside

Deborah in a marriage bed and wonder who was respon-
sible for the cloud of foul intent which lifted on the ming-
ling of our breath. Yes, I had come to believe in spirits and
demons, in devils, warlocks, omens, wizards and fiends, in
incubi and succubi; more than once had I sat up in a
strange woman's bed feeling claws on my chest, a familiar
bad odor above the liquor on my tongue and Deborah's
green eyes staring at me in the dark, an oppression close
to strangling on my throat. She was evil, I would decide,
and then think next that goodness could come on a visit
to evil only in the disguise of evil: yes, evil would know
that goodness had come only by the power of its force. I
might be the one who was therefore evil, and Deborah was
trapped with me. Or was I blind? For now I remembered
that I was where I was and no place else and she was dead.
It was odd. I had to remind my mind of that. It seemed as
if she were not so much dead as no longer quite living.

Well, I came to myself then, and recognized I had been
lying in a half sleep, resting beside Deborah's body for a
minute or two, or could it be ten or more? I still felt good.
I felt very good but I had an intimation I must not think
of Deborah now, certainly not now, and so I got up from
the floor and went to the bathroom and washed my hands.
Have you ever taken peyote? – the bathroom tile was quivering with a violet light, and at the edge of my vision was
a rainbow curving out to the horizon of the tile. I had only
to close my eyes and a fall of velvet rain red as the drapery
in a carmine box ran back into my retina. My hands were
tingling in the water. I had a recollection then of Deborah's
fingers on my shoulder and I stripped my shirt and washed
my upper arm. As I put down the soap, its weight in my
palm was alive; the soap made a low sticky sound as it
settled back to the dish. I was ready to spend an hour
contemplating that sound. But the towel was in my hand,
and my hands could have been picking up the crisp powder
of autumn leaves as they crumbled in my fingers. So it

went with the shirt. Something was demonstrating to me that I had never understood the nature of a shirt. Each of its odors (those particular separate molecules) was scattered through the linen like a school of dead fish on the beach, their decay, the intimate whiff of their decay a thread of connection leading back to the hidden heart of the sea. Yes, I returned this shirt to my body with the devotion of a cardinal fixing his hat – then I fixed my tie. A simple black knit tie, but I might have been snugging a ship to the wharf; the tie felt huge, a run of one-inch Manila long enough to please the requirements of a difficult knot – my fingers ran in and out of the interstices of this Windsor double-hitch like mice through the rigging. Speak of a state of grace – I had never known such calm. Have you ever heard a silence in a room at night or a great silence alone in the middle of a wood? Listen: for beneath the silence is a world where each separate silence takes up its pitch. I stood in that bathroom, water off, and listened to the silence of the tile. Somewhere deep in the stories of this apartment building a fan turned on, a refrigerator clicked: they had started like beasts out of some quickened response to the silence which came from me. I looked into the mirror, searching once again into the riddle of my face; I had never seen a face more handsome. It was the truth. It was exactly the sort of truth one discovers by turning a corner and colliding with a stranger. My hair was alive and my eyes had the blue of a mirror held between the ocean and the sky – they were eyes to equal at last the eyes of the German who stood before me with a bayonet – one moment of fright flew like a comet across the harbor of my calm, and I looked deeper into the eyes in the mirror as if they were keyholes to a gate which gave on a palace, and asked myself, 'Am I now good? Am I evil forever?' – it seemed a simple indispensable question to ask – but the lights went down suddenly in the bathroom, then flickered up. Someone had tipped a salute. And now the eyes in the mirror were merry and a touch blank. I could not believe I was studying them.

I quit the bathroom then, and returned to look at Deborah. But she was lying on her stomach, her face to the rug. I did not want to turn her over just yet. The calm I contained seemed delicate. It was enough to stand near her body and look about the room. We had made little mess. The bedspread and the blankets had slipped to the floor, and one of the pillows was sprawling at her foot. An armchair had been pushed to the side; it had pulled a fold in the carpet. That was all. The rum was still standing in its bottles and its glasses, no lamps were overturned, no pictures were off the hook, nothing broken, no debris. A quiet scene − an empty field with a Civil War cannon: it has fired some minutes ago and a last curl of smoke issues like a snake from its barrel, is beheaded in the breeze. Quiet as that. I walked to the window and looked down ten flights to the East River Drive where traffic was going by at a good full clip. Should I jump? But the question had no force: there was a decision to be made inside the room. I could pick up the phone and call the police. Or I could wait. (I was taking a pleasure in each step which gave hint of the grace a ballerina might know in her feet.) Yes, I could go to prison, spend ten or twenty years, and if I were good enough I could try to write that huge work which had all but atrophied in my brain over the years of booze and Deborah's games. That was the honorable course and yet I felt no more than a wistful muted impulse to show such honor; no, there was something other working at the base of my brain, a scheme, some desire − I was feeling good, as if my life had just begun. 'Wait,' said my head very directly to me.

But I was uneasy. When I closed my eyes I saw again the luminous full moon − would I never be free of her? I almost picked up the phone.

The voice in my brain said, 'Look first at Deborah's face.'

I knelt to turn her over. Her body made some rustling sound of protest, a muted whimper. She was bad in death. A beast stared back at me. Her teeth showed, the point of light in her eye was violent, and her mouth was open. It looked like a cave. I could hear some wind which reached down to the cellars of a sunless earth. A little line of spit came from the corner of her mouth, and at an angle from her nose one green seed had floated its small distance on an abortive rill of blood. I did not feel a thing. Which is not to say that nothing was happening to me. Like ghosts, emotions were passing invisibly through the aisles of my body. I knew I would mourn her on some distant day, and I would fear her. I had a certainty this instant that Deborah had been divided by death – by whatever fraction, what was good in her had been willed to me (how else account for the fine breath of this calm) and every last part which detested me was collected now in the face she showed for her death – if something endured beyond her dying, something not in me, it was vengeance. That delicate anxiety which pulses up to flutter in the nose was on me now. For Deborah would be there to meet me in the hour of my death.

The verdict now came clear. I was not going to call the police, not now, not yet – some other solution was finding its way up through myself, a messenger from that magician who solved all riddles was on his way, ascending those endless stairs from the buried gaming rooms of the unconscious to the tower of the brain. He was on his way and I was doomed if I thought to do my work in jail. For her curse would be on me.

I had an intimation then of Deborah's presence. Did one lift after death like a feather, rising slowly? I went to open the window as though to hope some breeze might seduce her forth, and dropped my hand. For I had the sense I had been touched on the shoulder, there at the precise point where her fingers begged me to let go her throat. Something touched me and now pushed me without touch toward the door. Once again I could have been in a magnetic field where some force without sensation other than its own presence was coaxing me firmly to step away from Deborah, cross the room, and out the door. And I went with this force; it had a promise like the smell of bar whiskey when rich young girls are in a bar. There was a good sound somewhere in my head, and expectation came to life in me, two full breasts came to rest their balm upon my eyes, then dropped in soft taps of curve and fall about my throat, rubbed a turn on my chest, tickled a hair at the belly and came to fold like two does at my root. One kiss of flesh, one whiff of sweet was loose, sending life to the charnel house of my balls. Something fierce for pleasure was loose. And I was out that door and strolling down the stairs, still traveling in the field of force which drifted me clean out of Deborah's room. As I stood at the lower landing of this duplex, I could breathe a tropical bouquet from the woven velvet flowers on the wall, I was near a swamp where butterflies and tropical birds went fanning up – and over the spoil of animals who looked for flesh – and floated on the air which rose from vegetation growing in the damp and drowning in the wet. At the door which opened to the elevator I stopped, turned around completely, and following that force which held me now as closely as an embrace I could not bear to quit, I crossed the hall, opened the door to the room where the maid must sleep, and pushed right in.

The lamp by her bed was on. The windows were closed, the air was close, an oven of burgeonings was that room – and, nice shock, there was Ruta, Fräulein Ruta from Berlin, lying on top of the covers with her pajama pants down, a copy of a magazine in one hand (a flash of nude photographs in color) and her other hand fingering, all five fingers fingering like a team of maggots at her open heat. She was off in that bower of the libido where she was

queen, and those five fingers were five separate lords and
ladies hard at work on her.

We did not say a word. Her face, caught in this pose,
was on the edge of dividing into two women: that queen
for certain of her fevers, and a little girl trapped in a dirty
act. I winked like the friendliest peasant neighbor – I recall
how natural was this wink – and then I stripped my coat
and started to take off my clothes. I removed them with
care enough to fold them neat. And the atmosphere in the
room which had quivered for an instant on my entrance
like a whip of air from a bellows, now flared slowly up
and higher. The maid set down the magazine and turned
her free hand palm up toward me, her fingers long and
thin with a hint of the fine curve in a double curved bow.
I remember seeing that the curve of her fingers, her lips,
and her long thin calves were a part of that sly bright
fever she gave off, and in a new whiff of boldness as if to
be bold was her métier, boldness had brought me to her,
she lifted the other hand (those lords and ladies) and moved
it across to me for a kiss to her fingers. Which I did, getting
one full draft of a heated sex which was full of the flower,
full of earth, and with suspicion of one sly mouse slipping
through the garden, a bit of fish in its teeth. My bare foot
came up from the carpet and I put my five toes where her
hand had been, drawing up on the instant out of her a
wet spicy wisdom of all the arts and crafts of getting along
in the world. She made the high nasal sound of a cat
disturbed in its play – I had stolen something from her,
and she was about to draw back, but there was a look in
my face – I was ready to kill her easy as not, there was
an agreeable balance in the thought that I was ready to
kill anyone at this moment – and my look cracked the
glitter in her eye. She shook her head and gave the prize
to my five toes which moved in the wet with all the deliver-
ance of snakes who have crossed a desert. Something took
me on then – the wisdom in my fingertips was sure; I could

feel where her flesh was alive and where the skin was dead, my fingers played at the edge, making little forays, nipping her to life. I felt for the first time in my life like a healthy alley cat, and I stroked at her with a delicate hatred lacquered clean up to a small flame by the anticipation of my body. It must have been five minutes before I chose to give her a kiss, but I took her mouth at last, pinched the corner in my teeth, and our faces came together with the turn of a glove catching a ball. She had a virtuoso's mouth, thin and alive, stingy and lightly fevered, a woodwind which tickled promise into me, yes those lips spoke of where they had traveled and where they could go now, something hot and mean and greedy to take the low road rose from her lean belly and tricky breasts which now popped out from under my thumb before I caught them, and at each corner of her mouth was a plump little mound, a tidbit for the teeth. Yes, she was sweet oil to the throat. She was breathing the pictures of her brain into mine, all the rosy tan and tinted gold of those pinup pictures in the magazine, and her thin lips now fluttered on my mouth, her warmth was rosy, her mouth offered to go down. I lay back like a king lion and let her romp. She had a gift. I was off on the nicest dream of Berlin nightclubs with their telephones and queer shows, of bal musettes and twisterias, she was giving a short lecture with her tongue on the habits of the Germans, the French, the English (one sorry bite indeed), the Italians, the Spanish, she must have had an Arab or two. All the tars and scents were blending into the one full smell which always makes you begin. I was ready to take the roller coaster, but I didn't want it to end, not this one, not yet, her greed was riding through me, I wanted more and more, and so I slipped free of her mouth and put her on her back.

But then, as abruptly as an arrest, a thin high constipated smell (a smell which spoke of rocks and grease and the sewer-damp of wet stones in poor European alleys) came needling its way out of her. She was hungry, like a lean rat she was hungry, and it could have spoiled my pleasure except that there was something intoxicating in the sheer narrow pitch of the smell, so strong, so stubborn, so private, it was a smell which could be mellowed only by the gift of fur and gems, she was money this girl, she cost money, she would make money, something as corrupt as a banquet plate of caviar laid on hundred-dollar bills would be required to enrich that odor all the way up to the smell of foie gras in Deborah's world and Deborah's friends. I had a desire suddenly to skip the sea and mine the earth, a pure prong of desire to bugger, there was canny hard-packed evil in that butt, that I knew. But she resisted, she spoke for the first time, 'Not there! *Verboten!*'

I had, however, gotten an inch of the *verboten*. A virulent intricate hatred, a detailed specification of the hardest world of the poor, the knowledge of a city rat, came out from her into me and deadened the head of my heat. I could go for a while now. And go I did. That other presence (which, I could remind you, leads to the creation) was lying open for me, and I barreled in on a stroke, expecting glory and the hot beat of jungle wings, but she was slack, her box spoke of cold gasses from the womb and a storehouse of disappointments. I quit her there and went back to where I had begun, the fierce pinched struggle to gain an inch and then a crucial quarter of an inch more, my hand was in her red dyed hair, pulling at a swatch with a twisting upward motion, and I could feel the pain in her scalp strain like a crowbar the length of her body and push up the trap, and I was in, that quarter-inch more was gained, the rest was easy. What a subtle smell came from her then, something back of the ambition, the narrow stubbornness, the monomaniacal determination to get along in the world, no, that was replaced by something tender as the flesh but not at all clean, something sneaky, full of fear, but young, a child in soiled pants, 'You're a Nazi,' I said to her out of I knew not what.

'*Ja.*' She shook her head. 'No, no,' she went on. '*Ja*, don't stop, *ja.*'

There was a high private pleasure in plugging a Nazi, there was something clean despite all — I felt as if I were gliding in the clear air above Luther's jakes and she was loose and free, very loose and very free, as if this were finally her natural act: a host of the Devil's best gifts were coming to me, mendacity, guile, a fine-edged cupidity for the stroke which steals, the wit to trick authority. I felt like a thief, a great thief. And like a thief returning to church, I see-sawed up from that bank of pleasures up to her deserted warehouse, that empty tomb. But it was more ready now. Those flaccid walls had come together — back of my closed eyes I could see one poor flower growing in a gallery — what love she still possessed might have been in a flower. Like a thief I was out of church again and dropping down for more of that pirate's gold.

So that was how I finally made love to her, a minute for one, a minute for the other, a raid on the Devil and a trip back to the Lord, I was like a hound who has broken free of the pack and is going to get that fox himself, I was drunk with my choice, she was becoming mine as no woman ever had, she wanted no more than to be a part of my will, her face, that mobile, mocking, know-the-cost-of-every-bargain Berlin face, was loose and independent of her now, swimming through expressions, a greedy mate with the taste of power in her eyes and her mouth, that woman's look that the world is theirs, and then I was traveling up again that crucial few centimeters of distance from the end to the beginning, I was again in the place where the child is made, and a little look of woe was on her face, a puckered fearful little nine-year-old afraid of her punishment, wishing to be good.

'I have nothing in me,' she said. 'Do we go ahead?'

'Who knows,' I said, 'keep quiet.'

And I could feel her beginning to come. The doubt in

me had tipped her off, the adjuration to be quiet had thrown the bolt. She was a minute away, but she was on her way, and just as if one of her wily fingers had thrown some switch in me, I was gone like a bat and shaking hands with the Devil once more. Rare greed shone in her eyes, pleasure in her mouth, she was happy. I was ready to chase, I was gorged to throw the first spill, high on a choice, like some cat caught on two wires I was leaping back and forth, in separate runs for separate strokes, bringing spoils and secrets up to the Lord from the red mills, bearing messages of defeat back from that sad womb, and then I chose – ah, but there was time to change – I chose her cunt. It was no graveyard now, no warehouse, no, more like a chapel now, a modest decent place, but its walls were snug, its odor was green, there was a sweetness in the chapel, a muted reverential sweetness in those walls of stone. 'That is what prison will be like for you,' said a last effort on my inner tongue. 'Stay here!' came a command from inside of me; except that I could feel the Devil's meal beneath, its fires were lifting through the floor, and I waited for the warmth to reach inside, to come up from the cellar below, to bring booze and heat up and licking tongues, I was up above a choice which would take me on one wind or another, and I had to give myself, I could not hold back, there was an explosion, furious, treacherous and hot as the gates of an icy slalom with the speed at my heels overtaking my nose, I had one of those splittings of a second where the senses fly out and there in that instant the itch reached into me and drew me out and I jammed up her ass and came as if I'd been flung across the room. She let out a cry of rage. Her coming must have taken a ferocious twist. And with my eyes closed, I felt low sullen waters wash about a dead tree on a midnight pond. I had come to the Devil a fraction too late, and nothing had been there to receive me. But I had a vision immediately after of a huge city in the desert, in some desert, was it a place on the moon? For the colors had the unreal pastel of a plastic and the main street was flaming with light at five A.M. A million light bulbs lit the scene.

It had been when all was said a bitch of a brawl. She lay for a minute half in sleep, half in stupor, and her tongue licked idly at my ear. Like a mother cat she was teaching a new kitten how to listen. 'Mr Rojack,' she said at last with gutty fleshy Berlin speech, 'I do not know why you have trouble with your wife. You are absolutely a genius, Mr Rojack.'

'A doctor is not better than his patient,' said I.

There was a wicked look of amusement in her face. 'But you are a *vache*,' she said. 'You must not pull my hair. Not even for that.'

'*Der Teufel* asked me to visit.'

'*Der Teufel!*' She laughed. 'What can a rich man like you know about *der Teufel*?'

'Doesn't *der Teufel* like the rich?'

'No,' she said, 'God protects the rich.'

'But at the end I could not have paid my respects to God.'

'Oh, you are dreadful,' she said, and pinched me a good mean German pinch where my belly was soft. Then she started uneasily.

'Do you think your wife heard?' she asked.

'I doubt it.'

'Are the walls so good?' She sat up now, her tricky breasts lolling nicely. 'No, I feel not so easy now,' she said, 'your wife could come in on us.'

'She would never do something like that. It's not her style.'

'I think you know a woman better than that,' said Ruta. She pinched again. 'You know, at the end, you stole something from me.'

'Half.'

'Half.'

We liked each other. That was fine. But again I could feel a stillness from the room above. Rufa was nervous.

'When you walked in on me,' she said, 'you looked pretty.'

'So did you, I fear.'

'No, but I never do something like that. At least,' she added with a malicious grin, 'not unless I lock the door.'

'And tonight you didn't.'

'No, I was asleep. After I let you in, I went to sleep. I was thinking how unhappy you looked. When you came to visit.' She put her head to one side as if to inquire whether I had been already with my wife in the bed above her, and then didn't ask. 'Of course,' she said, 'you and Mrs Rojack had a reconciliation.'

'Of sorts.'

'What a bad man you are. That's what woke me up – making your reconciliation with Mrs Rojack. I was awake, and I was so excited – I can't explain it.' Her bold pointed spiteful nose made everything she said seem merry.

'How old are you?'

'Twenty-three.'

She was probably twenty-eight. 'You're a charming twenty-three,' I said.

'And you are still a *vache*.'

Her fingers were beginning to play with me.

'Let's sleep another minute,' I said.

'Yes.' She started to light a cigarette, then stopped. 'Your wife thinks you've gone home.'

'Probably.'

'I hope the walls are good.'

'Let's try to sleep,' I said. I wanted the light out. I had a rendezvous in the dark. Something was waiting for me. But the moment I turned the switch, it was very bad. The darkness came over like air on a wound when the dressing is removed. My senses were much too alert. Everything which had passed from her body to mine was now alive inside, as if a horde of tourists, pokey and inquisitive, were wandering through my body. I had one of those anxieties which make it an act of balance to breathe: too little air compresses the sensation of being throttled, but too much – one deep breath – and there is the fear of a fall. There was something in the room besides Ruta and myself, something which gathered force. It was approaching now, but there were no eyes, no claws, just a sense of oppression waiting. I felt vile. 'Do you have a drink?' I asked of Ruta.

'No.' She gave a laugh and whispered, 'When I drink I go out to look for men who will beat me.'

'Crazy,' I said, and got up.

She could hear me putting on my clothes in the dark. The oppression had lifted on the moment I was free of her bed and my fingers were quick. They seemed to float on to each piece of clothing as I needed it.

'When will you be back?'

'Before morning.'

'And you will tell your wife you took a walk and came back and woke me up to let you in?'

'No, I will tell her I left the door unlocked.'

'Don't give all the good things to your wife. Save a present for me.'

'Maybe I will bring back a diamond.'

'I love you a little bit.'

And I was thinking of that empty womb, of that graveyard which gambled a flower and lost.

'I like you, Ruta.'

'Come back, and you will see how much you are going to like me.'

I had a thought then of what had been left in her. It was perishing in the kitchens of the Devil. Was its curse on me?

'*Der Teufel* is so happy,' she said, and a perfect spitefulness of attention came to a focus in her eye. Small cheer that she could read my mind.

'Was that the cloud of oppression which had come to

me in the dark? That the seed was expiring in the wrong field?

'Next time,' said Ruta, 'you must take care of little Ruta.'

'Next time will be an event,' I said. I wanted to blow her a kiss but there was nothing in me to send her way. So I closed the door, and went back up the stairs, up the aisle of that padded jungle, and entered Deborah's bedroom again with the expectation that somehow she would be gone. *There* was the body. It struck my sight like a shelf of rock on which a ship is about to smash. What was I going to do with her? I felt a mean rage in my feet. It was as if in killing her, the act had been too gentle, I had not plumbed the hatred where the real injustice was stored. She had spit on the future, my Deborah, she had spoiled my chance, and now her body was here. I had an impulse to go up to her and kick her ribs, grind my heel on her nose, drive the point of my shoe into her temple and kill her again, kill her good this time, kill her right. I stood there shuddering from the power of this desire, and comprehended that this was the first of the gifts I'd plucked from the alley, oh Jesus, and I sat down in a chair as if to master the new desires Ruta had sent my way.

My breath was bad again. What in hell was I to do with Deborah? I had no solution. If the messenger was on his way, he gave no hint of being near. A first rat's panic began to gnaw. 'Keep cool, you swine,' said a contemptuous voice in me, all but an echo from Deborah.

Let me tell you the worst. I had a little fantasy at this moment. It was beyond measure. I had a desire to take Deborah to the bathroom, put her in the tub. Then Ruta and I would sit down to eat. The two of us would sup on Deborah's flesh, we would eat for days: the deepest poisons in us would be released from our cells. I would digest my wife's curse before it could form. And this idea was thrilling to me. I felt like a doctor on the edge of thunderous new medicine. The details fell into place: what we did not choose to devour we could grind away in the electric Disposall beneath the sink, all the impure organs and little bones. For the long bones, for the femur and the tibia, the fibula, the radius and the ulna, the humerus, I had another plan. I would bind them in a package and hurl them out the window, out across the East River Drive and into the water. No, four lanes of traffic and a pedestrian walk to clear, too long a throw, I would have instead to go out in the street and take a taxicab and then another and then another until I ended at last in the marshes of Canarsie or the stench flats near City Island; there I could fling them in a swamp. With luck those long horsewoman's bones might disappear forever, or would I know for sure? Would I have instead to fill a box with plaster of Paris and imbed the bones, and her teeth as well? But no, the teeth must be disposed of separately, and not in any sewer or trash can, no, they must be buried securely, but where? Not Central Park, not by half, one tooth found, and I was dead: as in a movie I could see the police talking to Deborah's dentist — and bones in plaster of Paris dropped at sea, that was not good either, for how was I to rent a boat in March without drawing attention? *Heiress Is Missing!* the tabloids would scream on the following day and people would remember my face, my heavy package, no, this wasn't going to work: worst of all was Ruta in it with me, for she could yet cause trouble. Now the fantasy approached the vanishing point: I saw myself alone beside the tub with Ruta's body in cadaver — there was a tonic humor at the thought which made me smile. No, this was done, this idea was done, and I lay back weakly in my chair as if a spasm of illness which should have discharged itself from my mouth had lifted instead to my brain. What gifts this girl had given me, what German spice!

Then it came simple as that, the simplest solution of all. The messenger had slipped into the tower. And I smiled in terror, for it was also the boldest choice. Was I brave enough? Something in me lingered back – I had a panicked minute of argument in which I tried to find some other way. Perhaps I could take Deborah to the elevator (my poor wife is drunk) or sneak her down the stairs, no, altogether impossible, and then I sighed: if I missed on this one, it was the electric chair for sure, I had a wistful sadness now I had not tried to cast a baby into Ruta – she might be the last woman for me – and then I stood up from my seat, went to look at Deborah, knelt beside her again, and put my hand under her hips. Her bowels had voided. Suddenly I felt like a child. I was ready to weep. There was a stingy fish-like scent in the air, not unreminiscent of Ruta. They were mistress and maid and put their musk in opposite pockets. I hesitated, and then since there was nothing to do but go on, I went to the bathroom, took some paper, and cleaned Deborah. It was a discipline to be thorough. Then I disposed of the waste, listening to the hound's sigh of the closet water, and came back to look out the open window. No. Not yet. First I turned off the brightest lights. Then in a panic of strength, like the desperation to get out of a burning room, I lifted her up, at what a cost I lifted her up, for her body was almost too heavy (or I was that empty with fright) and balanced her feet on the ledge, it was harder than I thought, and with a fever that no-one see me at the open window now, not this instant, no, I took a breath and thrust her out and fell back myself to the carpet as if she had shoved me back, and lying there, I counted to two, to three, how fast I do not know, feeling the weight of her flight like a thrill in my chest, and heard a sound come up from the pavement all ten stories below, a flat, surprisingly loud and hollow thump as car brakes screamed and metal went colliding into metal with that howl of a shape which is suddenly collapsed, and I stood up then and leaned out the window and looked and there was Deborah's body half beneath the front of a car and a pile-up of three or four behind and traffic screaming to a stall on back, all the way half a mile back, and I howled then in a simulation of woe, but the woe was real – for the first time I knew she was gone – and it was an animal howl.

One scalding wash of sorrow, and I felt clean. I went to the telephone, dialed O, asked, 'What is the number of the police?' The operator said, 'Just a minute, I'll get it for you,' and I waited for eight long rings while my nerve teetered like a clown on a tightrope, and a cacophony of voices rose all ten stories up from the ground. I heard my voice giving my name and Deborah's address to the mouthpiece, and that voice of mine then said, 'Get over here right away, will you. I can hardly talk, there's been a frightful accident.' I hung up, went to the door, and shouted down the stairs, 'Ruta, get dressed, get dressed quick. Mrs Rojack has killed herself.'

3

A Messenger from the Maniac

But now it wasn't possible to wait in Deborah's room until the police arrived. An anxiety went off in me like the quiver of electricity when there is a short in the line. My body could have been on a subway, it felt as if it *were* the subway, bleak, grinding at high speed; I was jangled with adrenalin.

I went out the door, down the steps, and came up against Ruta in the hall. She was standing there half-dressed, a black skirt, no stockings yet, no shoes, a white blouse not buttoned. Her breasts were bare, no brassiere yet either, and her dyed hair now uncombed, still mangled by my fingers, stood up like a bush. Dyed, marcelled, lacquered and then worked over by me, her hair gave off the look of a girl just taken in a police raid. But even at this instant, something relaxed in me. For there was a tough slatternly tenderness in her face, and her prize – those bright little breasts – kept peeking at me through the open shirt. There was an instant between us, an echo of some other night (some other life) when we might have met in the corridor of an Italian whorehouse on an evening when the doors were closed, the party was private, and the girls were moving from bed to bed in one sweet stew.

'I was dreaming,' she said, 'and you called down the stairs.' Suddenly she closed the shirt over her breasts.

'No,' and to my surprise, I gave a pure sob. It was an extraordinary sound. 'Deborah killed herself. She jumped through the window.'

Ruta let out a cry, a thin dirty little cry. Something nasty was being surrendered. Two tears flashed down her cheek. 'She was an ingenious woman,' Ruta said, and began to weep. There was pain now in the sound, and such a truth in the grief that I knew she was crying not for Deborah, not even quite for herself, but rather for the unmitigatable fact that women who have discovered the power of sex are never far from suicide. And in that sudden burst of mourning, her face took on beauty. A nourishment came off Ruta's limbs. I was in some far-gone state: no longer a person, a character, a man of habits, rather a ghost, a cloud of loose emotions which scattered on the wind. I felt as if much of me had gathered like a woman to mourn everything I had killed in my lover, that violent brutish tyrant who lived in Deborah. And I groped toward Ruta like a woman seeking another female. We came together, hugged each other. But her breast came out of the open shirt, and slipped into my hand, and that breast was looking for no woman's touch, no, it made its quick pert way toward what was hard and certain in my hand. It was as if I had never felt a breast before (that gift of flesh) for Ruta was still weeping, the sobs were coming now with the fierce rhythm of a child, but her breast was independent of her. That little tit in my hand was nosing like a puppy for its reward, impertinent with its promise of the sly life it could give to me, and so keen to pull in a life for itself that I was taken with a hopeless lust. Hopeless, because I should have been down on the street already, and yet there was no help for it, thirty seconds was all I wanted and thirty seconds I took, one high sniff of the alley coming from her as I took her still weeping right there in the hall, her back against those velvet flowers while I fired one hot fierce streak of fierce bright murder, fierce as the demon in the eyes of a bright golden child.

Something in her leaped to catch that child, I felt some avarice shake its way through; she was beginning as I was done, pinching and squeezing at the back of my neck: she came in ten seconds behind. 'Oh,' she said, 'you are trying to woo me.' By which time I was cold as ice, and kissed her mockingly on the nose.

'Now, listen,' I said, 'take a shower.'

'Why?' She shook her head, pretending a half-bewilderment. But those forty seconds had drawn us to focus with each other. I felt as fine and evil as a razor and just as content with myself. There was something further in her I'd needed, some bitter perfect salt, narrow and mean as the eye of a personnel director.

'Because, my pet, the police will be here in five minutes.'

'You called them?'

'Of course.'

'My God.'

'They'll be here in five minutes, and I've got to pretend to be overcome. Which of course I am.' And I smiled.

She looked at me in wonder. Was I mad, asked her eyes, or deserving of respect.

'But what,' she said like a German, 'do you have to explain to them?'

'That I didn't kill Deborah.'

'Who says you did?' She was trying to keep up with me, but this last had been a racing turn.

'I didn't like Deborah very much. She detested me. You know that.'

'You were not very happy with each other.'

'Not very.'

'A woman doesn't commit suicide for a man she detests.'

'Listen, pet, I have something awful to tell you. She had a sniff of you on me. And then she jumped. Like that. Before my eyes.'

'Mr Rojack, you are hard as nails.'

'Hard as nails.' I pinched her shoulder a little. 'Are you?'

'Yes.'

'Let's get out of this together. Then we have fun.'

'I'm scared,' she said.

'When the police talk to you, tell them the truth. Except for one obvious detail. Obviously, there was nothing between us.'

'Nothing between us.'

'You let me in tonight. A couple of hours ago. You don't know the time exactly, a couple of hours ago. Then you went to sleep. You heard nothing until I woke you up.'

'Yes.'

'Don't trust the police. If they say I said we were having an affair, deny it.'

'Mr Rojack, you never laid a hand on me.'

'Right.' I took her chin between my thumb and forefinger, holding it as if precious. 'Now, the second line of defense. If they bring me down to see you, or bring you up to see me, and you hear me say we went to bed tonight, then agree. But only if you hear me say it.'

'Will you tell them?'

'Not unless there's evidence. In that case I'll tell the police I wanted to protect our mutual reputation. It'll still be all right.'

'Shouldn't we admit it from the start?'

'More natural to conceal the fact.' I smiled. 'Now, wash yourself. Quickly. If there's time, get dressed. And look –'

'Yes.'

'Make yourself plain. Comb out your hair for God's sake.'

With that, I quit the apartment. The elevator would take too long, but I rang anyway, five piercing rings to manifest impatience and then took the stairs. For the second time that night I was on my way down ten flights of stairs, but this time on the run. When I reached the lobby, it was empty, the doorman was doubtless ascending, a bit of good luck or bad luck (I could not keep up with the possibilities any longer) and then I was on the street and running a few steps to the Drive. There was one instant when the open air reached my nose and gave me a perfect fleeting sense of adventure on the wind, of some adventure long gone – a memory: I was eighteen, playing House Football for Harvard; it was a kickoff and the ball was coming to me, I had it, and was running. Off the river came a light breeze with the hint of turf to it. There was a fence lining the East River Drive, but it had no barbed wire on top, I was able to climb up and get over without ripping my pants, and come down the other side. There was now a jump of eight feet further down to a strip of curb, but I dropped – I hated jumping – but I dropped, jarred my ankle, hurt something minor in my groin, some little muscle, and made my way along the southbound traffic whose drivers were crawling by at five miles an hour in the unobstructed lane. Deborah was a hundred feet down the road. I had a glimpse of four or five cars collided into one another, and a gathering of forty or fifty people. A magnesium flare had been lit and it gave off the white intent glare which surrounds working-men doing serious work at night. Two police cars flanked the scene, their red lights revolving like beacons. In the distance, I could hear the siren of an ambulance, and in the center was that numb mute circle of silence which surrounds a coffin in the center of a room. I could hear a woman weeping hysterically in one of the automobiles which had collided. There were the short, rapt, irritable tones of three big men talking to one another, a professional conversation, two police and a detective, I realized, and farther on an elderly man with dirty gray hair, a large nose, an unhealthy skin, and a pair of pink-tinted glasses was sitting in his car, the door open, holding his temple, and groaning in a whining gurgling sound which betrayed the shoddy state of his internal plumbing.

But I had broken through the crowd and was about to kneel at Deborah's body. An arm in a blue serge sleeve held me back.

'Officer, that's my wife.'

The arm went down suddenly. 'You better not look, mister.'

There was nothing agreeable to see. She must first have struck the pavement, and the nearest car had been almost at a halt before it hit her. Perhaps it pushed the body a few feet. Now her limbs had the used-up look of rope washed limp in the sea, and her head was wedged beneath a tire. There was a man taking photographs, his strobe light going off each time with a mean crackling hiss, and as I knelt, he stepped back and turned to someone else, a doctor with a satchel in his hand, and said, 'She's yours.'

'All right, move the car back,' the doctor said. Two policemen near me pushed on the automobile and retired the front wheels a foot before the car bumped gently into the car behind it. I knelt ahead of the medical examiner and looked at her face. It was filthy with the scrape of asphalt and tire marks. Just half of her was recognizable, for the side of her face which caught the tire was swollen. She looked like a fat young girl. But the back of her head, like a fruit gone rotten and lying in its juices, was the center of a pond of coagulated blood near to a foot in diameter. I stayed between the police photographer who was getting ready to take more pictures and the medical examiner who was opening his satchel, and still on my knees, touched my face to hers, being careful to catch some of the blood on my hands, and even (as I nuzzled her hair with my nose) a streak or two more on my cheeks. 'Oh, baby,' I said aloud. It might have been good to weep, but nothing of that sort was even near. No, shock and stupor would be the best I could muster. 'Deborah,' I said, and like an echo from the worst of one's past came a clear sense of doing this before, of making love to some woman who was not attractive to me, of something unpleasant in her scent or dead in her skin, and me saying 'Oh, darling, oh, baby,' in that rape of one's private existence which

manners demand. So, now, the 'Oh, darling' came out full
of timbre, full of loss. 'Oh, Christ, Christ,' I repeated dully.

'Are you the husband?' a voice asked in my ear. Without
turning around, I had an idea of the man who spoke. He
was a detective, and he must be at least six feet tall, big
through the shoulder and with the beginning of a gut. It
was an Irish voice oiled with a sense of its authority, and
in control of a thousand irritations. 'Yes,' I said, and looked
up to meet a man who did not correspond to his voice. He
was about five-eight in height, almost slim, with a hard,
clean face and the sort of cold blue eyes which live for a
contest. So it was like the small shock of meeting somebody
after talking on the telephone.

'Your name?'

I told him.

'Mr Rojack, there's a series of directly unpleasant details
to get through.'

'All right,' I said dumbly, more than careful not to meet
his eye.

'My name is Roberts. We have to take your wife to Four
Hundred East Twenty-ninth, and we may have to call you
down there to identify her again, but for the minute now
– if you'd just wait for us.'

I was debating whether to say, 'My God, right in front
of my eyes, she jumped like that!' but that was one duck
which would never lift from the lake, I had an uneasy
sense of Roberts which was not unlike the uneasy sense I
used to have of Deborah.

I wandered down the line of banged-up cars, and discovered that the unpleasant elderly man with the pink-
tinted glasses was still moaning. There was a young couple
with him, a tall dark good-looking Italian who might have
been the man's nephew – he showed a family resemblance.
He had a sulky face, a perfect pompadour of black straight
hair, and was wearing a dark suit, a white silk shirt, a
silver-white silk tie. He was a type I never liked on sight,

AN AMERICAN DREAM

and I liked him less because of the blonde girl he had with him. I caught no more than a glimpse of her, but she had one of those perfect American faces, a small-town girl's face with the sort of perfect clean features which find their way on to every advertisement and every billboard in the land. Yet there was something better about this girl, she had the subtle touch of a most expensive shop girl, there was a silvery cunning in her features. And a quiet remote little air. Her nose was a classic. It turned up with just the tough tilt of a speedboat planing through the water.

She must have felt me staring at her, for she turned around – she had been ministering with a certain boredom to the weak gutty sounds of the man in the pink-tinted glasses – and her eyes which were an astonishing green-golden-yellow in color (the eyes of an ocelot) now looked at me with an open small-town concern. 'You poor man, your face is covered with blood,' she said. It was a warm, strong, confident, almost masculine voice, a trace of a Southern accent to it, and she took out her handkerchief and dabbed at my cheek.

'It must have been awful,' she said. A subtle hard-headed ever-so-guarded maternity lay under the pressure with which she scrubbed the handkerchief at my face.

'Hey, Cherry,' said her friend, 'go up front, and talk to those cops, and see if we can get Uncle out of here.' Studiously, he was avoiding me.

'Let it be, Tony,' she said. 'Don't look to draw attention.'

And the uncle groaned again, as if to begrudge me *my* attention.

'Thank you,' I said to her, 'you're very kind.'

'I know you,' she said, looking carefully at my face. 'You're on television.'

'Yes.'

'You have a good program.'

'Thank you.'

'Mr Rojack.' The detective was calling me.

'What is your name?' I asked her.

'Don't even think about it, Mr Rojack,' she said with a smile, and turned back to Tony.

And now I realized the detective had seen me chatting with nothing less than a blonde.

'Let's go upstairs and talk,' he said.

We stepped into a squad car, the siren was opened, and we drove up the Drive to an exit, and then turned back to the apartment. We didn't say a word on the way. That was just as well. Sitting next to me Roberts gave off the physical communion one usually receives from a woman. He had an awareness of me; it was as if some instinct in him reached into me and I was all too aware of him.

By the time we arrived, there were two more squad cars in the street. Our silence continued as we rode up in the elevator, and when we got to the apartment, a few more detectives and a few more police were standing about. There was a joyless odor in the air now somewhat reminiscent of liquid soap. Two of the police were talking to Ruta. She had not combed out her hair. Instead she had done her best to restore it, and she looked too attractive. The skirt and blouse had been changed for a pink-orange silk wrapper.

But she made up for it by her greeting. 'Mr Rojack, you poor poor man,' she said. 'Can I make you some coffee?'

I nodded. I wanted a drink as well. Perhaps she would have sense to put something in the cup.

'All right,' said Roberts, 'I'd like to go to the room where this happened.' He gave a nod to one of the other detectives, a big Irishman with white hair, and the two of them followed me. The second detective was very friendly. He gave a wink of commiseration as we sat down.

'All right, to begin with,' said Roberts, 'how long have you and your wife been living here?'

'She's been here for six or eight weeks.'

'But you haven't?'

AN AMERICAN DREAM

'No, we've been separated for a year.'

'How many years were you married?'

'Almost nine.'

'And since you separated, you've been seeing her often?'

'Perhaps once or twice a week. Tonight was the first time I'd been over in two weeks.'

'Now, on the phone you said this was an accident.'

'Yes, I think I said it was a frightful accident. I think those were my words.'

'An accident in fact?'

'No, Detective. I may as well tell you that it was suicide.'

'Why did you say it was an accident?'

'I had some dim hope of protecting my wife's reputation.'

'I'm glad you didn't try to go ahead with that story.'

'It wasn't until I hung up that I realized I had in effect told the next thing to a lie. I think that took me out of my shock a little. When I called down to the maid, I decided to tell her the truth.'

'All right then.' He nodded. 'It was a suicide. Your wife *jumped* through the window.' He was doing his best to make the word inoffensive. 'Now, let me get it clear. Your wife got up from bed. Is that correct?'

'Yes.'

'Went to the window and opened it?'

'No, I'd opened it a few minutes before. She'd been complaining about the heat and asked me to open the window as wide as I could.' I shivered now, for the window was still open, and the room was cold.

'Forgive me for prying,' said Roberts, 'but suicides are nasty unless they're cleared up quickly. I have some difficult questions to ask you.'

'Ask what you wish. I don't think any of this has hit me yet.'

'Well, then, if you don't mind, had you been intimate with your wife this evening?'

'No.'

'Though there had been some drinking?'

'Quite a bit.'

'Was she drunk?'

'She must have had a lot of liquor in her system. However, she wasn't drunk. Deborah could hold her liquor very well.'

'But you had a quarrel, perhaps?'

'Not exactly.'

'Please explain.'

'She was fearfully depressed. She said some ugly things.'

'You didn't get angry?'

'I was used to it.'

'Would you care to say what she said?'

'What does a wife ever accuse a husband of? She tells him one way or another that he's not man enough for her.'

'Some wives,' said Roberts, 'complain that their husband is running around too much.'

'I had my private life. Deborah had hers. People who come from Deborah's background don't feel at ease until their marriage has congealed into a marriage of convenience.'

'This sounds sort of peaceful,' said Roberts.

'Obviously, it wasn't. Deborah suffered from profound depressions. But she kept them to herself. She was a proud woman. I doubt if even her closest friends were aware of the extent of these depressions. When she felt bad, she would go to bed and stay in bed for a day or two at a time. She would keep to herself. I haven't seen a great deal of her this last year, but you can certainly check with the maid.'

'We got a couple of men talking to her right now,' said the older detective with a wide happy smile, as if his only desire in the world was to assist me.

'How about the coffee?' I asked.

'Coming up,' said Roberts. He went to the door, called

down, and came back. 'What did she have to be depressed about?' he asked easily.

'She was religious. A very religious Catholic. And I'm not Catholic. I think she felt that to be married to me kept her in mortal sin.'

'So as a very religious Catholic,' said Roberts, 'she decided to save her immortal soul by committing suicide?'

There was just the hint of a pause between us. 'Deborah had an unusual mind,' I said. 'She talked often of suicide to me, particularly when she was in one of her depressions. Particularly in the last few years. She had a miscarriage, you see, and couldn't have any more children.' But I had done myself a damage. Not with them; rather with some connection I had to an instinct within me. That instinct sickened suddenly with disgust; the miscarriage, after all, had been my loss as well.

There was of course nothing to do but go on. 'I don't think it was the miscarriage so much. Deborah had a sense of something bad inside herself. She felt haunted by demons. Does that mean anything to you?'

'No,' said Roberts, 'I don't know how to put demons on a police report.'

The older detective winked at me again with great joviality.

'Roberts, you don't strike me as the type to commit suicide,' I said.

'It's true. I'm not the type.'

'Well, then, don't you think a little charity might be in order when you try to understand a suicidal mind?'

'You're not on television, Mr Rojack,' Roberts said.

'Look, I know where I am. I'm doing my best to try to explain something to you. Would you be happier if I were under sedation?'

'I might be more convinced,' said Roberts.

'Does that remark indicate suspicion?'

'I didn't hear you.'

'Does that remark indicate suspicion?'

'Now, wait a minute, Mr Rojack, let's get squared away. There must be newspapermen downstairs already. There'll be a mob at the morgue and another mob at the precinct. It can't come as any surprise to you that this will hit the newspapers tomorrow. It may be front page. You can be hurt if there's a hint of irregularity in what is written tomorrow: you can be ruined forever if the coroner's report has any qualifications in it. My duty as a police officer is to find out the facts and communicate them to the proper places.'

'Including the press?'

'I work with them every day of the year. I work with you just tonight and maybe tomorrow, and let's hope not any more than that. I want to clear this up. I want to be able to go down and say to those reporters, "I think she jumped – go easy on that poor bastard in there." You read me? I don't want to have to say, "This character's a creep – he may have given her a shove."'

'All right,' I said, 'fair enough.'

'If you wish,' he said, 'you can answer no questions and just ask for a lawyer.'

'I've no desire to ask for a lawyer.'

'Oh, you can have one,' said Roberts.

'I don't want one. I don't see why I need one'

'Then let's keep talking.'

'If you want,' I said, 'to understand Deborah's suicide – so far as I understand it – you'll have to go along with my comprehension of it.'

'You were speaking of demons,' Roberts said.

'Yes. Deborah believed they possessed her. She saw herself as evil.'

'She was afraid of Hell?'

'Yes.'

'We come back to this. A devout Catholic believes she's going to Hell, so she decides to save herself by commiting suicide.'

'Absolutely,' I said.

'Absolutely,' said Roberts. 'You wouldn't mind repeating this to a priest, would you now?'

'It would be as hard to explain to him as it is to you.'

'Better take your chances with me.'

'It's not easy to go on,' I said. 'Could I have that coffee now?'

The big elderly detective got up and left the room. While he was gone, Roberts was silent. Sometimes he would look at me, and sometimes he would look at a photograph of Deborah which stood in a silver frame on the bureau. I lit a cigarette and offered him the pack. 'I never smoke,' he said.

The other detective was back with the coffee. 'You don't mind if I took a sip of it,' he said. 'The maid put some Irish in.' Then he gave his large smile. A sort of fat sweet corruption emanated from him. I gagged on the first swallow of the coffee. 'Oh, God, she's dead,' I said.

'That's right,' said Roberts, 'she jumped out the window.'

I put out the cigarette and blew my nose, discovering to my misery that a sour stem of vomit had worked its way high up my throat into the base of my nose and had now been flushed through my nostril on to the handkerchief. My nose burned. I took another swallow of coffee and the Irish whiskey sent out a first creamy spill of warmth.

'I don't know if I can explain it to you,' I said. 'Deborah believed there was special mercy for suicides. She thought it was a frightful thing to do, but that God might forgive you if your soul was in danger of being extinguished.'

'Extinguished,' Roberts repeated.

'Yes, not lost, but extinguished. Deborah believed that if you went to Hell, you could still resist the Devil there. You see she thought there's something worse than Hell.'

'And that is?'

'When the soul dies before the body. If the soul is extinguished in life, nothing passes on into Eternity when you die.'

'What does the Church have to say about this?'

'Deborah thought this didn't apply for an ordinary Catholic. But she saw herself as a fallen Catholic. She believed her soul was dying. I think that's why she wanted to commit suicide.'

'That's the only explanation you can offer?'

Now I waited for a minute. 'I don't know if there's any basis to this, but Deborah believed she was riddled with cancer.'

'What do you think?'

'It may have been true.'

'Did she go to doctors?'

'Not to my knowledge. She distrusted doctors.'

'She didn't take pills,' Roberts asked, 'just liquor?'

'No pills.'

'How about marijuana?'

'Hated it. She'd walk out of a room if she thought somebody was smoking it. She said once that marijuana was the Devil's grace.'

'You ever take it?'

'No.' I coughed. 'Oh, once or twice I might have taken a social puff, but I hardly remember.'

'All right,' he said, 'let's get into this cancer. Why do you believe she had it?'

'She talked about it all the time. She felt that as your soul died, cancer began. She would always say it was a death which was not like other deaths.'

The fat detective farted. Abrupt as that. 'What is *your* name?' I asked.

'O'Brien.' He shifted in his seat, half at his ease, and lit a cigar. The smoke blended easily into the odor of the other fumes. Roberts looked disgusted. I had the feeling I was beginning to convince him for the first time. 'My father died of cancer,' he said.

'I'm sorry to hear that. I can only say I wasn't very happy to listen to Deborah's theories because my mother passed away from leukemia.'

He nodded. 'Look, Rojack, I might as well tell you. There'll be an autopsy on your wife. It may not show what you're talking about.'

'It may show nothing. Deborah could have been in a pre-cancerous stage.'

'Sure But it might be better all around if the cancer shows. Cause there is a correlation between cancer and suicide. I'll grant you that.' Then he looked at his watch. 'Some practical questions. Did your wife have a lot of money?'

'I don't know. We never talked about her money.'

'Her old man's pretty rich if she's the woman I'm thinking of.'

'He may have disowned her when we married. I often said to friends that she was ready to give up her share of two hundred million dollars when she married me, but she wasn't ready to cook my breakfast.'

'So far as you know, you're not in her will?'

'If she has any money, I don't believe she would have left it to me. It would go to her daughter.'

'Well, that's simple enough to find out.'

'Yes.'

'All right, Mr Rojack, let's get into tonight. You came to visit her after two weeks. Why?'

'I missed her suddenly. That still happens after you're separated.'

'What time did you get here?'

'Several hours ago. Maybe nine o'clock.'

'She let you in?'

'The maid did.'

'Did you ever give the maid a bang?' asked O'Brien.

'Never.'

'Ever want to?'

'The idea might have crossed my mind.'

'Why didn't you?' O'Brien went on.

'It would have been disagreeable if Deborah found out.'

'That makes sense,' said O'Brien.

'All right,' said Roberts, 'you came into this room, and then what?'

'We talked for hours. We drank and we talked.'

'Less than half the bottle is gone. That's not much for two heavy drinkers over three hours.'

'Deborah had her share. I only took nips.'

'What did you talk about?'

'Everything. We discussed the possibility of getting together again. We agreed it was impossible. Then she cried, which is very rare for Deborah. She told me that she had spent an hour standing by the open window before I came, and that she had been tempted to jump. She felt as if God were asking her. She said she felt a woe afterward as if she'd refused Him. And then she said, "I didn't have cancer before. But in that hour I stood by the window, it began in me. I didn't jump and so my cells jumped. I know that." Those were her words. Then she fell asleep for a while.'

'What did you do?'

'I just sat in this chair by her bed. I felt pretty low, I can tell you. Then she woke up. She asked me to open the window. When she started to talk, she told me . . . do I really have to go into this?'

'Better if you would.'

'She told me my mother had had cancer and I had had it too, and that I gave it to her. She said all the years we were lying in bed as husband and wife I was giving it to her.'

'What did you say?'

'Something equally ugly.'

'Please go into it,' said Roberts.

'I said that was just as well, because she was a parasite and I had work to do. I even said: if her soul were dying, it deserved to, it was vicious.'

'What did she do then?'

'She got out of bed and went over to the window, and said, "If you don't retract that, I'll jump." I was confident she didn't mean it. Her very use of a word like "retract." I simply told her, "Well, then jump. Rid the world of your poison." I thought I was doing the right thing, that I might be breaking into her madness, into that tyrannical will which had wrecked our marriage. I thought I might win something decisive with her. Instead, she took a step on the ledge, and out she went. And I felt as if something blew back from her as she fell and brushed against my face.' I began to shudder; the picture I had given was real to me. 'Then I don't know what happened. I think I was half ready to follow her. Obviously I didn't. Instead I called the police, and called down to the maid, and then I must have passed out for a moment because I came to lying on the floor, and thought, "You're guilty of her death." So go slow for a while, will you, Roberts. This has not been easy.'

'Yeah,' said Roberts. 'I think I believe you.'

'Excuse me,' said O'Brien. He got up just a bit heavily and went out.

'There's a few formalities,' said Roberts. 'If you can take it, I'd like you to come down to Four Hundred East Twenty-ninth for the identification, and then we'll go over to the precinct and check out a few forms.'

'I hope I don't have to tell this story too many times.'

'Just once more to a police stenographer. You can skip all the details. No hell, heaven, cancer, nothing like that. None of the dialogue. Just that you saw her go.'

O'Brien came back with another detective who was introduced as Lieutenant Leznicki. He was Polish. He was about

Roberts' height, even thinner than Roberts, and looked to have an angry ulcer, for he moved with short irritable gestures. His eyes were a dull yellow-gray in color, and about the tint of a stale clam. His hair was an iron-gray and his skin was gray. He must have been fifty years old. Just as we were introduced, he sniffed the air with a boxer's quick snort. Then he smiled irritably.

'Why'd you kill her, Rojack?' he asked.

'What's up?' said Roberts.

'Her hyoid bone is broken.' Leznicki looked at me. 'Why didn't you say you strangled her before you threw her out?'

'I didn't.'

'The doctor's evidence shows you strangled her.'

'I don't believe it. My wife fell ten stories and then was struck by a car.'

Roberts sat back. I looked to him as if he were the first ally and last best friend I had in the world, and he leaned forward and said, 'Mr Rojack, we handle a lot of suicides in a year. They take pills, they cut their wrists, they stick a pistol in their mouth. Sometimes they jump. But in all the years I've been on the Force, I never heard of a woman jumping from an open window while her husband was watching.'

'Never,' said O'Brien.

'You better get yourself a lawyer, buddy,' said Leznicki.

'I don't need one.'

'Come on,' said Roberts, 'let's go over to the precinct.'

As they stood up, I was aware of a mood which came from them. It was the smell of hunters sitting in an overheated hut at dawn waiting for the sun to come out, drunk from drinking through the night. I was game to them at this moment. As I stood up, I felt a weakness go through me. No adrenalin followed. I had been taking more punishment than I thought and had the same sense of surprise a fighter knows in the middle of a fight when his legs go mellow and there is nothing left in his arms.

When they took me through the hall, Ruta was nowhere in sight. I could hear voices however in her room.

'The specialist get here yet?' asked Leznicki of the police-man on guard at the door.

'That's them in there,' said the cop.

'Tell them I said to give one hundred per cent to this job, and one hundred per cent to the job upstairs.'

Then he rang for the elevator.

'Why don't we take him though the back door,' said Roberts.

'No,' said Leznicki, 'let him meet The Press.'

They were downstairs on the street, about eight or ten of them, and they did an odd dance about us, their flashbulbs going off, their questions flying, their faces overcheerful and greedy. They could have been a pack of twelve-year-old beggars in some Italian town, hysterical, almost wild, delighted with the money they might be thrown, and in a whinny of fear they would get nothing. I made no attempt to cover my face — at the moment there seemed no harm worse than to have to look at myself tomorrow in a tabloid with my head humped behind a hat.

'Hey, Leznicki, he do it?' one cried.

Another darted up to me, his face full of welcome, as if to give surety he was the one man on the street I could trust. 'Would you care to make a statement, Mr Rojack?' he asked with concern.

'No, nothing,' I said.

Roberts was guiding me into the back seat.

'Hey, Roberts,' another cried, 'what's the word?'

'Suicide or what?' asked another.

'Routine,' said Roberts, 'routine.'

There was a low undertone of bickering, not unlike the sound an audience gives off when it is announced the understudy will play the part tonight. 'Let's get going,' said Roberts.

But he sat in front beside the driver, while I was plumped into the back cushions between Leznicki and O'Brien. We are driving now in an unmarked battered sedan, a detective's car, and as we took off from the curb, more flashbulbs went off through the window at me, and I could hear them scrambling for their cars.

'Why'd you do it?' asked Leznicki in my ear.

I didn't answer. I did my best to stare back, as if I were in fact a husband who had watched his wife go out a window and he was no more than some animal barking at me, but my silence must have been livid, because an odor of violence came off him, a kind of clammy odor of rut, and O'Brien, on my other side, who had shown a pronounced smell already, oversweet and very stale, was throwing a new odor, something like the funk a bully emits when he heads for a face-to-face meeting. Their hands twitched in their laps. They wanted to have a go at me. I had a feeling I wouldn't last thirty seconds between them.

'Did you use a stocking to strangle her?' asked Leznicki.

'He used his arm,' said O'Brien in a big hollow gloomy voice.

It had started to rain. A light fall, almost a mist, settled in a delicate wash of light over the streets. I could feel my heart beating now like a canary held in my hand. It throbbed with a tender almost exhilarated fatigue; I could have been no more than a drum with a bird's heart trapped inside, and the reverberations seemed to sound outside my body, as if everyone in the car could hear me. There were cars following behind, the photographers and the reporters no doubt, and their headlights gave an odd comfort. Like a bird indeed in a cage in a darkened room, the passing flare of light from outside gave some memory of the forest, and I felt myself soaring out on the beating of my heart as if a climax of fear had begun which might race me through swells of excitement until everything burst, the heart burst, and I flew out to meet my death.

The men in the car looked red to me, then green, then red again. I wondered if I were close to fainting. It was suffocating to sit between those men — it was like being a fox in a bog while hounds crooned on either bank. I knew at last the sweet panic of an animal who is being tracked, for if danger were close, if danger came in on the breeze, and one's nostrils had an awareness of the air as close as that first touch of a tongue on your flesh, there was still such a tenderness for the hope one could stay alive. Something came out of the city like the whispering of a forest, and on the March night's message through the open window I had at that instant the first smell of spring, that quiet instant, so like the first moment of love one feels in a woman who has until then given no love.

'Going to marry the maid after you grab your wife's dough?' asked Leznicki.

'You strangled her,' O'Brien said in his hollow voice. 'Why'd you strangle her?'

'Roberts,' I asked, 'can you call off these hoodlums?'

There was one instant in which both came so close to hitting me that I felt a wave of frustration fly out from Leznicki's hand and move across my face with the small impact of a flashlight in the eye. They sat there, their hands on their thighs, shaking, Leznicki with the muscular beat of a piston and O'Brien quivering like a sea-jelly disturbed in its ooze.

'You say that again,' said Leznicki, 'and I'll give you a pistol-whipping. You've been put on warning now.'

'Don't threaten me, friend.'

'Let it go,' said Roberts to all of us. 'Knock it off.'

I sat back, feeling the damage I had done. Now the adrenalin was going through their body like a mob in a riot.

We went the rest of the way in silence. Their bodies were so heated with anger that my skin felt the kind of burn one knows from staying too long beside an ultra-violet-ray lamp.

We were at the morgue for only a few minutes. There was a walk down a corridor with an attendant unlocking the doors for us, and then the room with sheets over two cadavers lying on stainless steel tables and a bank of refrigerated bins where the bodies were kept. The light had a color like the underbelly of a whale, that denuded white of fluorescent tubes, and there was now new silence, a dead silence, some stretch of the void with no sense of events beneath, just a silence of the waste. My nostrils hurt from the antiseptic and deodorant and the other smell (that vile pale scent of embalming fluid and fecal waters) insinuated its way through the stricken air. I did not want to look at Deborah this time. I took no more than a glimpse when the sheet was laid back, and caught for that act a clear view of one green eye staring open, hard as marble, dead as the dead eye of a fish, and her poor face swollen, her beauty gone obese.

'Can we get out of here?' I asked.

The attendant put the sheet back with a professional turn of his wrists, casual but slow, not without ceremony. He had the cheerful formal gloom of a men's room attendant. 'The doctor'll be here in five minutes. You going to wait?' he asked.

'Tell him to call us at the precinct,' said Leznicki.

In a corner, on a desk, at the end of this long room, I could see a very small television set about the size of a table radio. It was turned down low and had gone out of synchronization, for the picture was flaring bright, then dark, then flaring up again, and I had the insane clarity to recognize that it was speaking to the neon tubes and they were answering back. I was close to nausea. When we quit the corridors and left the hospital, I turned to one side and tried to throw up but produced no more than a taste of some bile and the intimate lighting of a photographer taking a picture.

On the way to the precinct, we were silent again.

Whatever Deborah would deserve, that morgue was not the place for her. I had a reverie of my own death then, and my soul (some time in the future) was trying to lift and loose itself of the body which had died. It was a long process, as if a membrane trapped in mud were seeking to catch a breeze which would trip it free. In that morgue (for that was where I pictured my own death) the delicate filaments of my soul were also expiring in a paralysis of deodorant while hope withered in the dialogue between the neon tube and the television set. I felt guilty for the first time. It was a crime to have pushed Deborah into the morgue.

There were more photographers and reporters at the entrance to the precinct, and again they were all shouting and talking out at once. 'Did he do it?' I heard one yell. 'You holding him?' cried another. 'What's the pitch, Roberts, what's the pitch?' They came in behind us and then were left as we passed through the Desk Sergeant's room where a cop was sitting high up on that square raised desk which had always reminded me of a tribunal (but it was only in movies I had ever seen this desk before) and then we passed into a larger room, a very large room, perhaps sixty feet by forty feet, the walls painted a dark institutional green up to the height of one's eyes and then a dirty worn-down institutional tan all the way up to the dirty-white tin plates of the ceiling, those eighteen-inch-square cheap tin plates, each decorated with some nine-teenth-century manufacturer's impression of a fleur-de-lis. I saw nothing but desks, twenty desks perhaps, and beyond, two small rooms. Roberts stopped by the door between the Desk Sergeant's room and this large room, and made a short speech to the reporters. 'We're not holding Mr Rojack for anything. He's just accommodating us by coming here to answer questions.' Then he shut the door.

Roberts led me to a desk. We sat down. He took out a folder and wrote in it for a few minutes. Then he looked up. We were alone again. Leznicki and O'Brien had disappeared somewhere. 'You're aware,' said Roberts, 'that I did you a favor out there.'

'Yes,' I said.

'Well, it was against my better judgment. I don't like the feel of this one. Neither does Leznicki or O'Brien. I'm going to tell you: Leznicki is an animal when it comes to this sort of stuff. He's convinced you killed her. He thinks you broke her hyoid bone with a silk stocking wrapped around her neck. He's hoping you did it a couple of hours before you pushed her out.'

'Why?'

'Because, friend, if she was gone for a couple of hours, it could show up in the autopsy.'

'If it does, you have a case.'

'Oh, we have the beginnings of a case. I have a nose for one thing. I know you were making out with that German maid.' His hard blue eyes looked into me. I held the stare until my eyes began to water. Then he looked away. 'Rojack, you're lucky nobody got hurt too much in that five-car crack-up. If they had, and we could stick your wife's fall on you, the papers would handle you as Bluebeard, Jr. I mean think if a kid had been killed.'

Indeed, I had never considered this until now. It had not been part of my intent after all to telescope five cars on the East River Drive.

'So, look,' he went on, 'you're not in the worst of spots. But you are at the point where you have to make a decision. If you confess this – forgive your feelings – but if you have any infidelities on your wife's part to bring in as evidence, a smart lawyer could get you off with twenty years. Which as a practical matter is usually about twelve years and can be as little as eight. We'll cooperate to the extent that we'll say your confession was given us of your own free will. I'll have to mark down the time of it which will mean you didn't confess for the first few hours, but I'll say you were in shock up to then. I won't mention the kind of bullshit you've given us. And I'll stand up for you in court. Whereas if you wait till all the evidence accumulates, and then confess, you'll get life. Then, even at best, you won't be out for twenty years. And if you fight it all the way, and we get a lock on the case, you could face the chair, buddy. They'll shave your head and give your soul a charge of voltage. So sit on this, and think. Think of that electric chair. I'm getting some coffee.'

'It's way after midnight,' I said. 'Aren't you supposed to be home by now?'

'I'll bring you a cup.'

But I was sorry he was gone. It had been easier somehow when he had been there. Now there was nothing to do but think of what he had said. I was trying to calculate how much time had gone by from that moment I recognized Deborah was dead until she struck the ground on the East River Drive. It could not be less than half an hour. It could be as much as an hour, conceivably an hour and a half. I had had a knowledge of anatomy once, but now I had no idea how long the cells might remain intact, nor how soon they might begin to decompose. While I was sitting here, it was likely they were doing an autopsy on Deborah. A leaden anxiety settled in my stomach; just that sort of bottomless pit I used to feel when I had been away from Deborah for a week or two and was suddenly powerless not to call her. It was difficult to sit still and wait for Roberts to come back, much as if that merciless lack of charity which I had come to depend on in Deborah (as a keel to ballast the empty dread of my stomach) was now provided by the detective. I knew they were probably watching me, and that I should not move too much; I was aware that once I began to walk about, my anxiety would show in every step I took, and yet I did not know if I could expend much more of my will in remaining motionless: I had been firing guns for hours – the armory was near to empty.

Still I forced myself to study the room. There were detectives talking to people at four or five of the desks. An old woman in a shabby coat was busy weeping at the nearest table, and a very bored detective kept tapping his pencil and waiting for her to cease. Further down a big Negro with a badly beaten face was shaking his head in the negative to every question asked him. In the far corner behind a half partition I thought I could hear Ruta's voice.

And then across the room I saw a head with long blonde hair. It was Cherry. She was with Uncle and Tony, and her friends were arguing with Lieutenant Leznicki and two detectives I had not seen before. I had been in this room for a quarter of an hour, and had been looking at nothing but the expression in Roberts' face. Now I was suddenly aware that there was as much sound as one might find in the dark night ward of a hospital, there was all but a chorus of protests and imprecations, and the leathery pistol-shot insistence of the policemen's voices, I could almost have allowed myself to slip into the anteroom of a dream where we were all swimming about in a sea of mud, calling to each other under the crack of rifles and a dark moon. Voices picked up from one another, the old woman wept louder as our Uncle across the room began to talk in his whining stammering voice, and then Ruta, still out of sight behind the partition, picked up something shrill in tone from the old woman's weeping and the Negro with the smashed-in face was talking faster, nodding his head in rhythm to some beat he had extracted from the sounds. I wondered if I were in fever, for I had the impression now that I was letting go of some grip on my memory of the past, that now I was giving up my loyalty to every good moment I had had with Deborah and surrendering the hard compacted anger of every hour when she had spoiled my need, I felt as if I were even saying goodbye to that night on the hill in Italy with my four Germans under the moon, yes, I felt just as some creature locked by fear to the border between earth and water (its grip the accumulated experience of a thousand generations) might feel on that second when its claw took hold, its body climbed up from the sea, and its impulse took a leap over the edge of mutation so that now and at last it was something new, something better or worse, but never again what it had been on the other side of the instant. I felt as if I had crossed a chasm of time and was some new breed of man. What a fever I must have been in.

A face was looking at me.

'Why'd you kill her?' asked Leznicki.

'I didn't.'

But Leznicki seemed happier now. His narrow face was relaxed and the stale clam color of his eyes had a hint of life. 'Hey, buddy,' he said with an open grin, 'you're giving us a hard time.'

'All I want is a cup of coffee.'

'You think you're kidding. Listen,' and he turned a wooden chair around, sitting with its back against his chest, and leaned his face toward me so that I caught the iron fatigue of his breath and his bad teeth, he doing this with no embarrassment the way a race track tout will feed you the good news about the horse with the bad news which rides on the smell of his breath, 'listen, do you remember Henry Steels?'

'I think I do.'

'Sure you do. We cracked the case right in this precinct, right at that desk over there,' and he pointed to a desk which looked to me exactly like all the others. 'That poor guy, Steels. Twenty-three years in Dannemora, and when they let him out, he shacks up with a fat broad in Queens. Six weeks later he kills her with a poker. You remember now? By the time we pick him up two weeks later, he's knocked off three queers and two more fat ladies. But we don't know. We just got him for the first job. A patrolman sees him in a hallway in a tenement on Third Avenue, rolls him over, recognizes him, brings him here, and we're just giving him a little cursory questioning to wake him up prior to turning him over to Queens, when he says, "Give me a pack of Camels, and a pint of sherry, and I'll tell you all about it." We give him the sherry and he knocks us on our ass. He produces six murders. Fills in half the Unsolveds we had in New York for that two-week period. Phenomenal. I'll never get over it. Just an old con, neat in his habits.' Leznicki sucked on a tooth. 'So, if you want to talk, I'll give you a bottle of champagne. Maybe you'll give us six murders, too.'

We laughed together. I had come to the conclusion a long time ago that all women were killers, but now I was deciding that all men were out of their mind. I liked Leznicki enormously – it was part of the fever.

'Why didn't you tell us,' he went on, 'that you had a Distinguished Service Cross?'

'I was afraid you'd take it away.'

'Believe me, Rojack, I never would have given you that kind of hosing if I'd known. I thought you were just another playboy.'

'No hard feelings,' I said.

'Good.' He looked around the room. 'You're on television, right.' I nodded. 'Well,' he went on, 'you ought to get us on a program some night. Assuming the department would approve, I could tell a story or two. Crime has got a logic. You understand me?'

'No.'

He coughed with the long phlegmy hacking sound of a gambler who has lost every part of his body but the wire in his brain which tells him when to bet. 'A police station, so help me, is a piece of the action. We're like Las Vegas. I know when we're going to have a hot night.' He coughed again. 'Sometimes I think there's a buried maniac who runs the mind of this city. And he sets up the coincidences. Your wife goes out of a window, for instance.

Because of cancer, you say, and five cars smack up on the East River Drive because of her. Who's in one of the cars but little Uncle Ganooch, Eddie Ganucci, you've heard of him.'

'In the Mob, isn't he?'

'He's a prince. One of the biggest in the country. And he falls into our lap. We've had a Grand Jury subpoena on him for two years, but he's out in Las Vegas, in Miami, only once or twice a year does he sneak into town. And tonight we got him. Know why? Cause he's superstitious. His nephew told him to take a walk, get lost in the crowd. No. He's not leaving the car. There's a dead woman on the road, and she'll curse him if he walks away. He must have had twenty guys killed in his time, he must be worth a hundred million bucks, but he's afraid of a dead dame's curse. It's bad for his cancer, he tells his nephew. Now just look at the connection you could make. Your wife you say had cancer, Uncle Ganooch is swimming in it. There it is.' Leznicki laughed as if in apology for the too-rapid workings of his mind. 'See why I leaned on you so hard? You can appreciate that the minute I got word Ganucci was our baby tonight, I didn't want to waste time with you.'

'What about the girl? Who's she?' I asked.

'A broad. The nephew's got an after-hours spot, and she sings there. A very sick broad. She makes it with spades.' He named a Negro singer whose records I had listened to for years. 'Yeah, Shago Martin, that's who she makes it with,' said Leznicki. 'When a dame dyes her straw, she's looking for a big black boogie.'

'Beautiful girl,' I said. Her hair hardly seemed dyed to me. Perhaps it was tinted a bit.

'I'm getting to like you more and more, Mr Rojack. I just wish you hadn't killed your wife.'

'Well,' I said, 'here we go again.'

'No, look,' he said, 'do you think I like to exercise my

83

function on a man who's won a Distinguished Service Cross? I just wish I didn't know you did it.'

'What if I tried to tell you I didn't.'

'If they brought the Good Lord Himself to this room . . .' He stopped. 'Nobody ever tells the truth here. It's impossible. Even the molecules in the air are full of lies.'

We were silent. The Negro with the beat-up face was the only one talking in the room. 'Now, what do I want with that liquor store,' he said, 'that liquor store is boss, I mean that store is *territory*, man. I don't go near territory.'

'The arresting officer,' said the detective next to him, 'had to subdue you right in that store. You cracked the owner in the face, you emptied the register, and then the patrolman caught you from behind.'

'Shee-it. You got me mixed up with some other black man. No cop can tell one nigger from another. You got me mixed up with some other nigger you been beating up on.'

'Let's go in the back room.'

'I want some coffee.'

'You'll get some coffee when you sign.'

'Let me think.' And they both were silent.

Leznicki put a hand on my arm. 'It's beginning to go bad for you,' he said. 'That German girl is cracking.'

'What has she to confess? That I tried to kiss her once in the hall?'

'Rojack, we got her worried. Right now she's thinking about herself. She don't know if you killed your wife, but she admits you could have, that she admitted after we had a matron strip her down. A medical examiner took a smear. That German girl has been in the sack tonight. We can take you out and give you an examination too, and see if you've been working on her tonight. Do you want that?'

'I don't see what the maid had to do with this,' I said.

'There's male body hair in her bed. We can check to see if it's yours or not. That is, if you're willing to cooperate. All we have to do is pull a few out with a tweezer. Do you want that?'

'No.'

'Then admit you gave the maid a bang this evening.'

'I don't see what the maid had to do with this,' I said. 'An affair with the maid woudn't give me cause to murder my wife.'

'Forget these petty details,' said Leznicki. 'I want to propose something. Get one of the best lawyers in town, and you can be on the street in six months.' At this moment he looked more like an old thief than a Lieutenant of Detectives. Twenty-five years of muggers and dips, safe men and junkies and bookies and cons had passed before him, and each must have charmed some fine little cell. 'Rojack, I know a man, an ex-Marine, whose wife told him she went down on all his friends. He beat in her head with a hammer. They kept him under observation until his trial. His lawyer got him off. Temporary Insanity. He's on the street. And he's in better shape today than you are with your suicide story. Because even if you get out of this, which you won't, nobody will believe you didn't push your wife.'

'Why don't you be my lawyer?' I said.

'Think!' said Leznicki. 'I'm going over to visit Little Uncle.'

I watched him cross the room. The old man stood up to meet him, and they shook hands. Then they put their heads together. One of them must have told a quick joke for they both started to laugh. I saw Cherry look over at me, and on an impulse I waved. She waved back merrily. We could have been Freshmen at a state university catching glimpses of one another at different registration desks.

A policeman came out with a pot of coffee and poured me a cup. Then the Negro shouted to him, 'I want a cup, too.'

'Keep your voice down,' said the cop. But the detective

who was sitting with the Negro gave a signal to come over. 'This boogie is dead drunk,' said the detective, 'give him a cup.'

'I don't want any coffee now,' said the Negro.

'Sure you do.'

'No, I don't. It gives me butterflies.'

'Take some coffee. Sober up.'

'I don't want coffee. I want some tea.'

The detective groaned. 'Come in the back room,' he said.

'I want to stay here.'

'Come in the back room and take some coffee.'

'I don't need none.'

The detective whispered in his ear.

'All right,' said the Negro, 'I'll go in the back room.'

The woman who had been weeping must have signed some paper for she was gone. There was no-one near me now. And I was watching a film of a courtroom. The defense counsel with a dedicated emollient in his voice: 'Then, Mr Rojack, what did your wife say?' 'Well, sir, she spoke of her lovers and she said they had made a favorable comparison of her actions in the sexual act with the sexual actions of a plumber – as it is called – in a Mexican brothel.' 'And would you, Mr Rojack, tell the court what a "plumber" is?' 'Well, sir, a "plumber" is the lowest prostitute in a house of prostitution and will commit those acts which other prostitutes for reasons of relative delicacy refuse to perform.' 'I see, Mr Rojack. What did you do then?' 'I don't know. I don't remember. I had warned my wife of my terrible temper. I have been suffering blackouts ever since the War. I had a blackout then.'

A faint nausea, kin to the depression with which one could wake up every morning for years, drifted through my lungs. If one pleaded Temporary Insanity, Leznicki and I would be brothers, we would be present in spirit at each other's funeral, we would march in lock-step through Eternity. Yet, I was tempted. For that emptiness in my chest, that sense of void in my stomach were back again. I did not have any certainty at all that I would go on. No, they would question me and they would question me; they would tell truths and they would tell lies; they would be friendly, they would be unfriendly; and all the while I would keep breathing the air of this room with its cigarettes and cigars, its coffee which tasted of dirty urns, its distant hint of lavatories and laundries, of junk yards and morgues, I would see dark green walls and dirty white ceilings, I would listen to subterranean mutterings, I would open my eyes and close them under the blistering light of the electric bulbs, I would live in a subway, I would live for ten or twenty years in a subway, I would lie in a cell at night with nothing to do but walk a stone square floor. I would die through endless stupors and expired plans.

Or I would spend a year of appeals, spend a last year of my life in an iron cage and walk one morning into a room where ready for nothing, where nothing done, failed, miserable, frightened of what migrations were ready for me, I would go out smashing, jolting, screaming inside, out into the long vertigo of a death which fell down endless stone walls.

It was then I came very close. I think I would have called Leznicki over and asked him for the name of a lawyer, and stuck my tongue out in some burlesque of him and me and our new contract, and rolled my eyes, and said, 'You see, Leznicki, I'm raving mad.' I think I really would have done it then, but I did not feel the strength to call across the room. I had a horror of appearing feeble before that young blonde girl, and so I sat back and waited for Leznicki to return, experiencing for still one more time tonight what it was like to know the exhaustion and the apathy of those who are very old and very ill. I had never understood before why certain old people, sniffing displeasure in the breath of everyone who stared at them, still held with ferocity to the mediocre tasteless continuation of their days, their compact made with some lesser devil of medicine – 'Keep me away from God a little longer.' But I understood it now. Because there was a vast cowardice in me which was ready to make any peace at all, ready to pillage in public the memory of that wife I had had for near to nine years, ready to mock the future of my brain by preparing to cry out that I too was insane and my best ideas were poor, warped, distorted, and injurious to others. No, I wanted out, I wanted to get away from this trap I had created for myself, I would have given up if my cowardice had the simple strength to throw my voice across the room. But it didn't, it could only rivet the cheeks of my buttocks to the chair and order me to wait, as if some power had cast a paralysis upon me.

Then the Negro started up in the other room. I could not see him but now I could certainly hear him. 'I don't want the coffee,' he cried out, 'I want some Seagram's Seven. That's what you told me I could have, and that's what I want.'

'Drink your coffee, Goddamn you,' shouted the detective, and through the open door was a glimpse of him walking that big Negro back and forth, and there was a patrolman on the other arm, a hard-faced dull young cop with straight black hair and eyes you see in tabloids on the face of young killers who never miss a Mass until the morning after the night they go berserk, and they were both walking the Negro, they were out of sight now, there was the liquid splattering sound of coffee falling in a large splash and the thump of the mug on the floor, and then there was another splattering sound, the sound of a fist on a face, and the dull thump of a knee in the back, and the Negro groaned, but almost agreeably, as if the beating were his predictable sanity. 'Now give me the Seagram's Seven,' he cried out, 'and I'll sign that paper.'

'Drink coffee,' shouted the detective. 'You can't even see right now.'

'Shee-it on that coffee,' muttered the Negro, and then came the sound of new beating on him, and all three, all with a stumbling grappling hold on each other went out of view, came into view again, went out again, and more sounds of splattering.

'Goddamn you,' cried the detective, 'you Goddamn stubborn boogie.'

And a new detective had taken the seat beside me, a younger man, thirty-five perhaps, with an anonymous face and a somewhat gloomy mouth. 'Mr Rojack,' he said, 'I just want to tell you that I enjoy your television program very much, and I'm sorry we have to meet under these circumstances.'

'Unnh,' grunted the Negro, 'unnh, unnh, unnh,' as the punches went into him, 'that's the way, daddy, unnh, unnh, keep moving, you're improving all the time.'

'Now, why don't you drink some coffee,' shouted the detective who was beating him.

I have to confess that at this instant I put my head down and whispered to myself, 'Oh, God, give me a sign,' crying it into the deeps of myself as if I possessed all the priorities of a saint, and looked up with conviction and desperation sufficient to command a rainbow, but there was nothing which caught my eye in the room but the long blonde hair of Cherry standing across the floor. She, too, was looking at the room where the beating went on, and there was a clean girl's look on her face as if she had been watching a horse who had broken his leg and was now simply miserable before the proportions of things. I stood up then and started out with some idea of going to the back room, but the dread lifted even as I stood up and once again I felt a force in my body steering away from that back room, and a voice inside me said, 'Go to the girl.'

So instead I walked across the big room and approached Leznicki and Ganooch and Tony and Cherry and Roberts and O'Brien and even a few others, detectives and lawyers, and stopped near Cherry. I had a good look at her now and she was older than I had expected, she was not eighteen or twenty-one as I had thought on the street but twenty-seven perhaps or twenty-eight, and there were pale green circles of chronic exhaustion beneath her eyes. But I still thought her very nice. She had an elusive silvery air as if once there had been a huge disappointment and now a delicate gaiety had formed to cover the pain. She looked a little like a child who has been anointed by the wing of a magical bird. And she also looked wretched just now.

'Tony, can't you do something about that beating?' she asked.

He shook his head. 'Stay out of it, huh?'

Roberts spoke to her. 'The boy they got in there tried to beat an old man to death tonight.'

'Yes,' she said, 'but that's not why *they're* beating on him.'

'What do *you* want?' said Roberts, looking at me.

'Roberts, I think she's right. I think you ought to call off that detective.'

'Planning to talk about it on your program?' asked Leznicki.

'May I invite you when I do?'

'It's better to stop these things,' said Uncle Ganooch. 'There's too much friction in the world today.'

'Hey, Red,' Leznicki shouted to the back room, 'he's drunk. Stick him in a cell for the night.'

'He tried to bite me,' Red yelled back.

'Stick him in a cell.'

'Now,' said Uncle Ganooch, 'can we finish our business? I'm a very sick man.'

'It's simple,' smiled Leznicki, 'we just need some assurance you'll show up to honor your subpoena.'

'We're going over the ground,' said Ganooch's lawyer, 'I will stand manifest for him.'

'And what the hell does that mean?' asked Leznicki.

'Let's go back,' said Roberts, looking at me. 'I want to talk to you.'

I nodded. And then moved next to the girl. Her friend Tony was standing on her other side and he gave me a look which had power to quiver in my skin. It was a look which said, 'Don't talk to this girl or somebody will break your arm.'

But I was thinking that I might as well take that girl for a sign – she was the only one in sight. So I said to her, and my voice was easy, 'I'd like to come and hear you sing.'

'Well, I'd like you to,' she said.

'Where is your place?'

'Down in the Village. Just a little place. Just opened up.' She looked at Tony, and hesitated, and then gave me the address in a clear voice. Out of the side of my eye I could see the Negro being led out of the big room.

'Let's go, Rojack,' said Roberts. 'We have something new to talk about.'

It must have been three in the morning, but he still looked neat. Once we sat down, he smiled. 'There's no use in asking you for a confession, is there?'

'No.'

'All right, then. We're going to let you go.'

'You are?'

'Yes.'

'Is it all over?'

'Oh, no. No. It's not over for you till the coroner brings in a report of suicide.'

'When is that?'

He shrugged. 'A day, a week. Don't leave town till the coroner is heard from.'

'I'm still under suspicion?'

'Oh, come on. We know you did it.'

'But you can't hold me?'

'Yeah, we could hold you as a material witness. And we

could work on you for seventy-two hours, and you would crack. But you're in luck, you're in great luck. We have to stick with Ganucci this week. We don't have time for you.'

'You also have no evidence.'

'The girl talked. We know you've been with her.'

'Means nothing.'

'We have some other evidence, but I don't want to get into it now. We'll see you in a day or two. Stay away from your wife's apartment. And stay away from the maid. You wouldn't want to tamper with a potential witness.'

'No, I wouldn't.'

'By the way, no hard feelings.'

'Oh, none.'

'I mean it. You hold up all right. You're not bad.'

'Thank you.'

'This may interest you. We got the autopsy report. There's evidence your wife did have cancer. They're going to make some slides to verify it, but it does look good for you.'

'I see.'

'That's why we're letting you go.'

'I see.'

'Don't relax too much. The autopsy also showed that your wife's large intestine was in an interesting state.'

'What do you mean by that?'

'You'll get your chance to worry later this week.' He stood up. 'Good night, pal.' Then he stopped. 'Oh, yes. Forgot to ask you to sign the autopsy papers. Would you sign them now?'

'Your autopsy was illegal?'

'I'd say it was irregular.'

'I don't know if I want to sign the papers.'

'Suit yourself, pal. If you don't, we can put you in a cell until the coroner brings back his report.'

'Beautiful,' I said.

'Not that good,' said Roberts. 'Just a goof. Here, sign here.'

Which I did.

'Well,' said Roberts, 'I'm going home. Can I drop you off?'

'I'll walk,' I said.

I did walk. I walked for miles through the long drizzle of the early morning, and close to dawn I found myself in the village outside the after-hours club where Cherry was singing. I had lived through a night, I had come into a morning. It was morning outside on the street; I could think of the sun coming up. But it would rise into a wintry smog, a wet wan morning gray with mist.

The entrance to the joint was a battered metal door which opened at my knock. 'I'm a friend of Tony's,' I said to the man in the hall. He shrugged, and let me by. I walked down a corridor and went through another door. The room had once been the rear of a large basement loft but now it was decorated like a bar in Miami, an after-hours box of leatherette, flame-orange stuffing for the booths, the stools, the face of the bar, some dark burnished midnight of black carpet and purple wine ceiling. There was a man playing the piano, and Cherry was singing. She saw me come in and she smiled on the breath she took and made a little sign to indicate that yes she would have a drink with me as soon as her set was done. Well, if Deborah's dying had given me a new life, I must be all of eight hours old by now.

4

Green Circles of Exhaustion

In fact, I was so far into the fevers of fatigue that the bourbon revolved a majestic route down through my chest, the congestions of my lungs, the maze of my belly, those peppered links in my gut. The police were gone and would be back again tomorrow; the newspapers were already being dropped at the early morning stands; in a few hours the details of my daily life would erupt like a house gone mad with the electric dishwasher screaming at the delivery boy, the television studio would be on the phone, and I might have to be on the phone to the university, Deborah's friends would call, there would be the funeral, God, the funeral, the funeral, and the first in a new thousand to twenty-two thousand lies. But I was like a wrecked mariner in the lull between two storms. Rather I was close to a strong old man dying now of his overwork, passing into death by way of going deeper to himself. Rich mahoganies of color move in to support his heart and there are tired angels to meet him after work, a tender heaven to approve of how he spent those hard bleak years. I think that shot of bourbon may have been the best single drink I ever had – relaxation came to me on the gift of wings and I swam through some happy mood deeper than air, more perfumed than water. As Cherry sang, I drank her in – my ear for a singer had never been so fine. Which is not to say that she was a great singer: she was not. But I enjoyed her, I was resting on a point of balance kin to one of those little dots of light which used to dance above the printed words on a movie screen when the adults and children were invited to sing on Saturday. She had what was near to a conventional voice – she accepted teachings from others; styles had been borrowed and not quite made her own, but she had a lithe riding beat and odd details were striking. She was singing *Love for sale, love that's fresh and still unspoiled, love that's only slightly* . . . Then she did something tasty with *soiled*, something rueful as though to show that what had been lost was worse than the dirt. Yes, the voice was only a lift above ordinary, but the experience in the voice was not, and so it brought the people in this room a shift in mood together, and that was an achievement, for they were not near to lovers, not this crowd: an Italian judge with two tarts, a pair of detectives, one light-skinned plump young Negro with a mandarin's goatee, some old woman with a set of diamond rings whose glow was stolen from the aurora borealis; those north lights were her motto; they moaned: I'm twice a widow and believe in God for that is what young men are – the young man with her was undeniably queer. Finally, at the bar, a party of five, two girls with three men who looked like friends of Tony, for the men were all wearing platinum-white silk ties, white silk shirts and dark blue suits. One of them was a former prizefighter, a very good retired welterweight I recognized on the instant, he had a very bad reputation in the ring. Add a few more and you had the size of the crowd, nothing very big for a wet dawn, but that little voice of hers was giving me pleasure (the singing voice being considerably smaller than the voice with which she spoke to me on the street), that little voice had something of a clean nerve.

If you want the thrill of love, I've been through the mill
    of love,
Old love, new love, every love but true love,

Love for sale. Appetizing young love for sale.
If you want to buy my wares, follow me and climb the
stairs —
Lu, uh, ove, love for sale.

The spotlight was good for her, a pink pearly violet for hue, a good light on a pale blonde since it gave one edge of silver to the shadows in her face and deepened those pale green circles beneath her eyes to hollows of glamor. She did not look in the least like Marlene Dietrich, but the glamor was there, that curious hint of no-man's-land where one cannot distinguish exhaustion from the shade of espionage. Then the demon, good or ill, of the telepathic powers vaulted with a leap onto her stage, and she began to sing 'The Lady Is a Tramp,' but in a harsh groaning strained and curious flat version as if indeed Dietrich had touched a finger to her larynx. 'Stop,' I thought to myself, 'better to stop,' and Cherry burst into laughter, that false laughter of a singer who is a suspicion too drunk, and then she slapped her thigh, giving a new beat to the pianist (a vigorous muscular beat) while she closed her eyes and laughed merrily.

'Oil it, honey,' cried the prizefighter. And she came back with another voice, belting the same song now, swaying her hips, tough and agreeable and very American as if she were an airline hostess or the television wife of a professional football star. There was another spot on her, an orange spot, Florida beaches, the red-orange tan of an athlete. Now the powder showed on her face and light reflected from it, little lights of perspiration bright as the sun on a wet snow. She was hard now, nightclub hard, an embodiment now of greed, green-eyed, brown-skinned flaming golden blonde — that was orange spotlight. *Life without care. I'm broke. It's oke. Hate California, it's cold and it's damp, that's why the lady is a tramp*, but grinding the words as if they were part of some rich sausage her voice was ready to stuff.

Well, the set went on. There was a champagne light which made her look like Grace Kelly, and a pale green which gave her a little of Monroe. She looked at different instants like a dozen lovely blondes, and now and again a little like the little boy next door. A clean tough decent little American boy in her look: that gave charm to the base of her up-turned nose tip-tilted (I was reminded again) at the racy angle of a speedboat skipping a wave, yes that nose gave character to the little muscle in her jaw and the touch of stubbornness of her mouth. She was attractive, yes. She had studied blondes, this Cherry, she was all of them, some blonde devil had escorted her through the styles. It was a marvel – sipping my bourbon – to watch such mercury at work. She could have been a nest of separate personalities if it had not been for the character of her bottom, that fine Southern piece. Occasionally she would turn, she would sing over her shoulder, and show that of course her butt had nothing to do with her face, no she drove it on its own rhythms, pleased with itself and her, practical, the heart of every Southern girl's pie, marvelous, just a little too big and round for the waist, a money-counter, Southern-girl ass. 'This bee-hind is for sale, boy,' said it to me, 'but *you* ain't got the price, *you!*' Her face, having nothing to do with all of that, smiled demurely at me for the first time.

I was floating on a zephyr of drunkenness, a magic riser. My brain had developed into a small manufactory of psychic particles, pellets, rockets the length of a pin, planets the size of your eye's pupil when the iris closes down. I had even some artillery, a battery of bombs smaller than seeds of caviar but ready to be shot across the room.

Exhibit for some future court: The prizefighter said, 'Oil it' once again to Cherry, and I fired a battery of guns at him. His laughter stopped in the middle; he scowled as if four very bad eggs had been crushed on his head. His nostrils screwed down to the turn of disgust I expected would be in the smell. He looked about. He, in his turn, calculated (he was no stranger to such attacks), located me as the probable source, and proceeded to kick an imaginary foot deep into my crotch. My shield went down to block it. Blocked! 'Your foot hurts,' said my mind to him, and he looked depressed. After a while he started to rub the toe of that shoe against his calf.

Exhibit: The first tart with the judge giggled hysterically each time Cherry tried to hit the G below high C. Cherry's voice was not particularly ready. One strand of her sound curled up to the pitch. The rest of her fell away. But the attempt was brave. So I called on one of those magic bullets I maintained in orbit swinging through the room above the solar center of my head. I instructed it, 'Next time she giggles, take a fling through her head, ear to ear, score her good.' Which the pellet promptly did. Like a bullet going through a ten-inch plank, my pellet sizzled a new streak of emptiness through the core of that tart's thoughts; her dear head quivered as the bullet went through; when she giggled again, the sound was hollow, the empty dopey giggle of a sweet-faced tart.

Exhibit: The judge turned his head as the planet chirruped by his ear. Then he looked about. He could not find me. I shot a mental flare to tickle the tip of his nose. 'Come here, baby,' said my mind to the judge, 'this is your radar.' He found me then. Anathema began in his chest, rolled off his shoulders, ground clouds of legal gas. I had not been prepared for that. The gas went up my nose, dullness, sanity, the immeasurable continuum of cigar smoke, boredom; I was deadened, but not so down that I could not blow a flame from my mouth to ignite his cloud and send it retreating back in counter-anathema upon his table. Now the judge slumped and stared ahead, his eyes open and blank. Like a flower gone to pollen, out of spice, the ear curls on the other tart drooped suddenly to her neck, singed little bloom.

Exhibit: One of the detectives had a case of hiccups.

Exhibit: One of the Irish politicians wept.

Exhibit: The room had a field of silence. A bomb had gone off. Into this silence, Cherry was singing: *When the deep purple falls over sleepy garden walls. On sleepy garden walls* she struck five perfect notes, five, like the five bells of an angel come to the wake of a bomb, clear, a cluster of the loveliest consecutive sounds I ever heard. A rare moment of balm in this battered room to hear the song of a lovely woman's body.

She did not like the moment. She tossed her head, beat her foot, and went off into *Here is the story of a most unfortunate Memphis man who got stranded down in old Hong Kong*.

'Another bourbon, waiter,' I cried out.

I was watching her foot beat the rhythm. She was wearing sandals which exposed her toes, and she had painted her nails. I was taken with this vanity, I was absorbed with it, for like most attractive women, her toes were the ugliest part of her body. Not ugly exactly, not deformed, but certainly too large. Her big toe was round, round as a half dollar, and larger than a quarter – it was one round greedy self-satisfied digit, and the four little toes were not so little either, each of them round balls, each of them much larger in their pads than the size of the nail might justify, so that one had to peek at five sensuous, even piggish, but most complacent little melons of flesh surrounding five relatively tiny toenails, each broader than they were long, which depressed me. She had the short broad foot of that very practical kind of woman who has time to buy the groceries and time to jazz the neighbor next door, and I looked from there up to the delicate silvery cut of her face, that delicate boy-girl face beneath the toned blonde hair, and was struck with a vision of how drunk I was, as if drunkenness were a train which rocketed through the dark and I was sitting in a seat which gave out backward on the view and so receded further and further from some fire on the horizon: thus came each instant nearer to the murmur one hears in the tunnel which leads to death. Women must murder us unless we possess them altogether (so said the luminous logic of this liquor in my hand) and I had a fear now of the singer on the stand, for her face, yes, perhaps I could possess that altogether, perhaps that face could love me. But her behind! of course I could not possess that ass, no-one ever had, maybe no-one would, and so all the difficulty had gone down to her feet, yes the five painted toes talked of how bad this girl could be. So I saw her, that was the way I saw her: in a magic spite, feeling as wicked as a titled child, I shot an arrow into her big toe, into the fat bullying certainty of that toe, and saw it twitch on the beat. I shot three more arrows into the same spot and saw the foot retreat beneath her long skirt. Then, as if a curse were on me (and so I must do the opposite of what I might intend) whatever, from a motive I did not know (I wished only to call back the move) I shot one needle of an arrow into the center of Cherry's womb, I felt it got in. I felt some damage lodge itself there. She almost lost her song. One note broke, the tempo shuddered, and she went on, turned to look at me then, a sickness came off her, something broken and dead from the liver, stale, used-up, it drifted in a pestilence of mood toward my table, sickened me as it settled in. And there was a touch of regret in that exhalation from her, as if she had been saving such illness in the hope she might inflict it on no-one, that her pride would be to keep her own ills to herself, rather than pass them on. I had shot that arrow and pierced her shield. Nausea was collecting in all my pipes.

I went in a rush from the table to the men's room, and in the stall, locked the door, knelt, and retched again for the second time that night, feeling as humble as a saint, I knew now that a saint would set his head near a throne

expecting the cleanest air to lay like a halo on the edge of
the fumes. Perhaps I caught a hint of that air, for my
burned-up lungs went clear – once again this night I was
taking one of those fine new breaths I had not known in
twenty years, so it seemed, and then I vomited with all
the gusto of a horse on a gallop, cruds, violations, the rot
and gas of compromise, the stink of old fears, mildew of
discipline, all the biles of habit and the horrors of pretense
– ah, here was the heart of the puke! – came thundering
out with the fluid intent downrushing sounds of a stream
tearing through the wood to recover its river, I felt
like some gathering wind which drew sickness from the
lungs and livers of others and passed them through me
and up and out into the water. I was draining the poison
from the wound I had inflicted in Cherry's belly, and yes
in confirmation her voice came rowdy-dah, rooty-toot,
ringing through the men's-room walls, loud and laughing
and triumphant, *When the saints come marching in*, soaring
like a golden bird free at last from the cage of her throat,
laughing happily at the antique of the song, and I held
to the bowl and shook with sickness, and thought that
if the murderer were now loose in me, well, so too was
a saint of sorts, a minor saint no doubt, but free at last
to absorb the ills of others and regurgitate them forth,
ah yes, this was communion and shuddering rings of
nausea and Leznicki, oh here came Leznicki, up from
the belly, up, up, and the presence of Roberts up and
splat! Pea beans and shreddings of puke came up from the
basement of my belly, the police were saying good-bye to
my body.

Peace. And peace. Nausea faded like the echo of a locomotive in the gloom of that toilet stall, and I was lighting
matches to search for specks and the hint of spatterings
on my jacket, as if a more simple search in the light by
the sink outside would be less devoted and so less effective.
I washed my face in cold water, but carefully, once again

carefully, as if I were washing a new face. And in the mirror my eyes were bright, bright and merry as the eyes of a yachtsman catching the sun off the water – was the mirror my sanity or helping to drive me mad? Still I used it to comb my hair and reset my tie. The collar of my shirt was surprisingly fresh – I remembered the devotion with which I had put it on just after washing (the corpse of Deborah lying of course flat on the floor in the other room) and I wondered if the freshness it still maintained could be a small gift of life from the devotion I had given to the material then. Hierarchies of soul and spirit turned in my brain – drink, or a visitation from Deborah, had me insane as the Celts: I was trying to calculate how a shirt might have a spirit which laundries smashed and tender fingers restored. Still, there was the evidence of the shirt. Ripped off to make love to Ruta, whipped on again, subjected to a grilling from the drilled eye of the police, and a walk in the rain, a psychic artillery battle in the bar, a round of heaves here, and still keeping its front! – my shirt must be as fortified as a superior ego. I had one wistful passing sadness that my mind would have the liberty to adventure no longer for would I be dead in three days? – I seemed somehow to think this quite likely – or incarcerated? or just deadened with the anxiety that questions and more intolerable questions were to be answered. And at this moment far from mourning Deborah, I hated her guts. 'Yes,' I thought, 'you're bitching me still.'

But Cherry was finishing her set. Or that was the way the music felt as it came through the walls. Looking in the mirror I tipped my left hand to my left eye in a mock salute and the lights dimmed for an instant again as they had in the other bathroom, dimming now either in fact or in the center of my imagination, and I said to myself, 'Yes, you certainly will be dead in three days.' Then I walked out and sat down at my table, just as she was finishing the last few bars of 'I've Got You Under My Skin.'

Which was just a little too late, for as she walked past me to the bar, a professional half smile on her face, her eye chose almost not to see me.

'Let's have a drink,' I said to her.

'I'm having a drink with some friends,' she said, 'but come over and join us.' And she gave a smile which was somewhat better, and walked over to the three men and two women I had decided earlier were Tony's friends. She did not know the women, she went through some measured greeting with them, radar to radar, shaking hands finally with each of those two girls, and then she kissed two of the three men in a big wet friendly fashion like a smacking handshake and being introduced to the third man, the former prizefighter, Ike Romalozzo, Ike 'Romeo' Romalozzo was his name I remembered now, she hesitated, then said, 'What the hell,' in a very loud very broad Southern accent and kissed Romeo for greeting to him as well.

'You could charge five bucks for those kisses,' Romeo said.

'Honey, it feels better to give them away.'

'This girl's a swinger, Sam,' said Romeo to one of the two other men, a short man, perhaps fifty-five, with gray hair, a leathery gray skin, and a wide thin mouth. This man now touched the head of the stone in the stickpin of his white tie as if to give warning. 'She's the friend of a friend,' said Sam.

'Give us another kiss, sweetheart,' said Romeo.

'I'm still,' said Cherry, 'recovering from the last one.'

'Gary, where does her friend hide?' Romeo asked.

'Don't ask,' said Gary. He was a tall heavy man about thirty-eight with a long nose, a puffy face, and nostrils which cut the air with such an edge that his intelligence seemed to be concentrated there.

Sam whispered in Romeo's ear. Romeo was silent. Now they all were silent. Sitting where I was, not fifteen feet from the bar, I had come to the conclusion that if I were to be dead in three days, Romeo was the man who was likely to do the job. I had no idea if this thought came from what was most true in my instinct, or if my mind was simply sodden with idiocies. Nonetheless, something now decided I must go up to Romeo in the next few minutes.

'You'll never get past the police,' said my mind to me, 'unless you take the girl home from this bar.' And on the echo of this thought, I noticed the detectives were gone. I felt the anxiety of a man hearing he must undergo a dangerous operation.

'They're going to make a movie of my life,' Romeo said to Cherry.

'What are they going to call it?' asked Gary, 'Punch-drunk and Paunchy?'

'They're going to call it the story of an American boy,' said Romeo.

'Lover!' said Sam.

'The people I'm with got a ghost writer working now. Story of a kid who goes bad, turns straight, goes bad again.' Romeo blinked his eyes. 'It's the fault of the company he keeps. Bad influences. Cheap whiskey. Broads. He don't make champion. That's the price he pays.'

Romeo was not bad-looking. He had curly black hair which he wore long and thick on the sides and he had had his nose bobbed once he retired from the ring. His eyes were dark and flat in expression, flat as Chinese eyes. He had put on weight. He would have looked like a young prosperous executive in Miami real estate if it had not been for the thick pads of cartilage on the sides of his temples which gave him a look of still wearing his headgear.

'Who puts up the money for this movie?' Cherry asked.

'Couple of guys,' said Romeo.

'Mutt and Jeff,' said Sam.

'You don't believe me?' Romeo asked.

'They ain't going to make a movie of you,' Gary said.

'If they get a good enough actor to play my part they are going to make a very good movie,' said Romeo.

'Say, Romeo,' I called out, 'I got an idea.' I said this from my seat fifteen feet away, but the words were out. I stood up and walked towards them. My idea was unfortunate, but it was the best I could muster. I kept hoping something better might reach my mind.

'You,' said Romeo, 'got an idea.'

'Yes,' I said, 'when they make your movie, I'll play your part.'

'You can't,' Romeo lisped, 'you're not sufficiently queer.'

Romalozzo had been famous for his tricky left hook. I had just walked into it. A snicker began with Gary, passed on to Sam, reached Cherry and the two girls. They stood at the bar laughing at me.

'I owe everybody a drink,' I said.

'Bartender,' shouted Romeo, 'five Bromo-Seltzers.'

Gary slapped Sam on the back. 'Our boy gets better and better.'

'Talent is in its infancy,' said Romeo. 'When they get done with this movie, the class, the fanciest broads in town will say, "We had Romalozzo for dinner last night." '

'Yeah,' said Sam, 'and that Guinea ate all the pizza.'

'Caviar foie. Hey, Frankie,' Romeo yelled to the bartender, 'bring some caviar foie with the Bromo-Seltzer.'

Cherry laughed again. She had an unusually large laugh. It would have been perfect and merry and a gain to anticipate if it had not been for a suspicion of something mulish and bragging, a bit of small-town Southern jackass in the sound. I realized what a tension had begun in me that she be perfect.

'Romeo,' Cherry said, 'you're the funniest man I've met today.'

'It ain't me,' said Romeo, 'it's my friend. My new friend.' He looked at me with his flat eyes. 'Sam, isn't this my new friend?' he asked.

Sam looked at me with even eyes. 'Well, Romeo, he's not my friend,' Sam said after a little pause.

'Maybe he's your friend, Gary?'

'Never saw the gentleman before,' Gary said

'Sweetie,' said Romeo to one of the girls, 'is he yours?'

'No, but he's cute,' said Sweetie.

'Then, Honey, he must belong to you,' Romeo said to the other girl.

'Not unless we met in Las Vegas five years ago. I think,' said Honey, trying to be helpful, 'that we may have met at the Tropicana sometime like five or six years ago, do I care to count, ha ha.'

'Shut up,' said Gary.

The mulatto with the plump mandarin face and the goatee was staring at me from his table. He looked like one of those jungle crows who sit high on a tree and watch the lions and the lion cubs take blood, foam and flesh from the entrails of a wounded zebra.

'I guess,' said Romeo, 'he's nobody's friend.'

'He's yours,' said Sam.

'Yes,' said Romeo. 'He's mine.' He looked at me. 'What do *you* say, pal?'

'You didn't ask the lady,' I said.

'You mean the lady who was entertaining us? The lady who was singing?'

I didn't answer.

'Since you're my friend,' said Romeo, 'I'll fill you in. This lady is my escort for the evening.'

'I'm surprised,' I said.

'It's a fact.'

'I'm really surprised,' I said.

'Buddy, you played out your string,' said Romeo. 'Now beat it.'

'You couldn't think of a more agreeable way to ask me to leave?'

'Move on.'

I was ready to go. There was very little keeping me. But there was something. It was the glitter of light in Cherry's eyes, bright and prideful. That fed the anger to stare back into Romeo's eyes. For she had been using me – so I understood it now. And felt an icy rage against all women who would use me. It was still another relative of insanity – I who had visited so many members of the clan tonight – but now I said, 'I'll move on when the lady asks me to move, and not before.'

'The condemned man ate a hearty meal,' said Gary.

I did not take my eyes from Romeo's eyes. We locked one stare into the other.

'You're going to get hurt,' said his eyes. 'I have something going for me,' said my eyes back. His expression turned dubious. The odds were not established for him. He had no ideas in his eyes, only pressure. Maybe he thought I had a gun.

'You invite this guy over?' asked Romeo.

'Of course I did,' said Cherry, 'and you gave him one bitch of a greeting.'

Romeo laughed. He laughed with a big flat dead sound at the center of his amusement, a professional laugh, the professional laugh of a fighter who has won a hundred fights and lost forty, and of those forty, twelve were on bad decisions, and six were fixed, and for four he went in the tank. So it was the laugh of a man who has learned how to laugh through all sorts of losses.

'Say,' said Cherry, 'this gentleman's a celebrity. He's Mr Stephen Richards Rojack whose televison program you are all familiar with, *click*?'

'Yeah,' said Sam. 'Click,' said Gary. 'Sure I know it,' said one of the girls, Sweetie, with the happiness of a dull pupil answering a quick question in class. 'I'm impressed to meet you, Mr Rojack,' said Sweetie. She *was* sweet. Sam looked sick at being there with her.

'And now since Mr Rojack is very special to me,' said

Cherry, putting one perfumed run of four fingertips on the back of my neck, 'we're going to go in the corner and have a few drinks.'

'You're on again in fifteen minutes,' said the bartender.

'I didn't hear you,' said Cherry. She gave a silvery smile as if the terrors of men were about as admirable as the droppings of hippopotami.

We took a little table with a lamp shaped like a candle about ten feet from the isolated stand with its deserted piano and empty microphone. Sitting next to her, I seemed to feel not one presence in her, but two, an ash-blonde young lady of lavender shadows and curious ghosts, some private music, a woman with a body one might never be allowed to see in the sun; and then the other girl, healthy as a farmer, born to be photographed in a bathing suit, brisk, practical, clean, the kind who looked to sex for exercise.

'You're still angry,' she said to me.

'Yes.'

'You didn't have to get mad,' she said. 'They were just putting you on.'

'So were you. If I had walked away, you'd be here with Romeo.'

'I might be.'

'And feeling no different.'

'That's evil to say,' she said in a little Southern girl voice.

'Evil says what evil sees.' I didn't know exactly what I was saying, but it pleased her immensely. We could have been adolescents. She flickered the backs of her fingers under my chin, her green eyes working full of pepper in the glow of the candle, glints of brown and gold and yellow. In this light she was a pure cat, cat's eyes, cat's nostrils, cat's knowing mouth. 'Mr Rojack, can you tell funny jokes?'

'Yes.'

'Tell me one now.'

'I'll tell you later.'

'When?'

'When we're about to leave.'

'You're rude. In fact . . .'

'Yes?'

'*Ass*,' she said with a Southern bray, and we beamed at each other like two jewelers finding a gem for a partner. Then we leaned forward and gave a kiss. With all that booze I came near to passing out. For a draft of something sweet and strong came off her mouth and spoke of what she knew, of small Southern towns and the back seats of cars, of expensive hotel suites and years of listening to good jazz, of simple honest muscle in her heart and the taste of good wines, jukeboxes and crap tables, stubborn will, something compromised, inert, and full of gas, something powerful and dull as her friends, the smell of bourbon, too, the raw red promise, so much I closed my eyes and fell back into a swoon for an instant or two, she was too much for me — it is the truth — it was exactly as if I'd been sparring with a bigger man and got hit with a full right hand, not a bare fist but a hand in a boxing glove, and went out of consciousness for a second and took another slow second to come back because punishment was ahead. It was not the nicest kiss I ever had, but it was certainly the most powerful, there was something in it of the iron motor in the hearts of a good many men she must have kissed.

'You're such a sweet kisser,' she said.

Yes, we could have been adolescents. I had not felt this peculiar mixture of promise and respect, a little awe (as if I were walking blindfolded and might at any moment fall down a flight of stairs: but there were cushions at the bottom — part of the game), the expectation that life had something to offer which few people knew anything about, the happiness that there was a body next to me which was feeling just about the sweet way I felt, sweetness itself. I was afraid to make a move.

'Ass,' she said now, 'you came over like you had a cricket in each pocket.'

'I was scared.'

'Of what?'

'Voodoo.'

'You voodoo. You bongo nutty. I didn't introduce you because you weren't my friend no more. You were King Creep.'

'I guess I was.'

'Awful!'

The bartender came over. 'It's time for you to go on.'

'Not singing any more tonight.'

'I'll have to call Tony,' he said.

She had the expression on her face of a soldier who has found a fresh peach on an autumn tree and has stopped to eat it. In a minute he will begin to march again. 'Call Tony,' she said, 'and bring us two doubles.'

'I don't want to make a call to him.'

'Frank, I wish you would call Tony. I don't care about that. I really don't. But don't make me feel bad that I'm making you feel bad.'

Frank merely looked at her.

'Besides, Mr Rojack doesn't like my singing. It makes him want to puke.'

We all laughed.

'He likes it,' said Frankie. 'He gave me the evil eye every time I rattled a glass.'

'Mr Rojack is indiscriminate in his use of the evil eye,' said Cherry, 'whoops!' And the glass on which she was sipping flew out of her hand.

'You're really not going to sing, are you?' asked Frank, looking at the broken glass on the floor. When she shook her head, he walked away.

'Thanks a lot, Cherry,' he said.

'Well,' said Cherry, 'that breaks one beautiful mood.' She struck a match and blew it out. Then looked in the ashtray for a divination. 'Bad turns ahead.'

'You think I'm crazy?'

'Oh, no.' She laughed happily. 'You're just spoiled.' We kissed again. It was within easy distance of the first kiss. Something might actually be waiting for us.

'*I* think I'm crazy. My wife is dead. I've drawn a blank.'

'Something wrong behind you and you don't want to look?'

'Exactly.'

'I've been feeling that way for a week.'

The accompanist, a Negro, went to the piano. As he went by Cherry, he shrugged. Then he picked out a moody chord, dropped on to two or three other moody chords, and went off into something fast and sulky.

'Maybe you were in love with her,' said Cherry, 'and that's why you don't get anything back. It's the women who can hardly wait to be widows that scream at the funeral.'

The phone was ringing. 'Mr Rojack, for you.' Frank called out, and nodded at a booth off the bar. As I passed, I noticed that Romeo, Sam, Gary, the girls, all were gone.

'Rojack?'

'Yes.'

'Roberts.'

'You still up?'

'Yes, buddy, I'm still up.'

'Where are you?'

'In Queens. I was just going to bed.' He paused with that righteous arrest of time which is common to authority.

'Who'd you get a call from?'

'Higher up.'

'And what did they say?'

'Rojack, don't give me any more of that upper-class zazz. I know where you were born.'

'You do? I don't know where you were born.'

'You son of a bitch,' said Roberts, 'you're loaded.'

'Well, so are you,' I said. 'You're boozing.'

'Yes.'

'I thought you never drank.'

'Once a year,' said Roberts.

'I'm honored to be your occasion.'

'You upper-class finks,' said Roberts.

'We're very bad,' I said.

'Listen, get out of the place you're in,' said Roberts. 'You're not one hundred per cent safe.'

'I may not be safe, but I'm certainly not suffering.'

'That girl you're with.'

'Yes.'

'Know who she is?'

'Poison. Pure poison.'

'Better believe it, buddy.'

'Roberts, it takes all kinds to make a world.'

'Ever hear of Bugsy Siegel?'

'Of course I've heard of Bugsy Siegel. How can you be a self-respecting drinker if you haven't heard of Bugsy Siegel?'

'Well, Rojack, the little girl you're with now could have opened a school for Bugsy Siegel.'

'Then, why,' I asked, 'is she singing in an after-hours joint and making one hundred fifty a week?'

'I can't say more,' said Roberts.

Now I was angry. 'I thought you had to give your attention to Eddie Ganucci.'

'Your case is taking some turns.'

'What do you mean?'

'You didn't tell us everything about your wife.'

'Everything?'

'Either you know what I'm talking about or you don't.'

'Obviously I don't.'

'Let it go.'

'This new information – is it good or bad?'

'Come to the precinct at five-thirty this afternoon.'

'That's all you care to tell me?'

'I hear your father-in-law is flying into town this morning.'

'Where did you hear that?'

'On the radio.' Roberts laughed. It was his first joke of the morning. 'I heard it on the radio. Now, Rojack, give me the bartender. I want to talk to *him*.'

When I got back to the table, Tony was there. He looked worried. He had the look of a man who has conflicting worries and is worrying over which one to worry first. He gave me a limp hand to shake and a flick of his eye. Hatred came off him like scent, dull and powerful, an essence of that taint I felt in Cherry the moment I came near to passing out. Standing near Tony, the full face of that hatred brought me close again to nausea; there was menace and such little precision in the menace (as if one were expiring inside a plastic sack) that I felt a quick panic to quit them both, and held on where I was out of some instinct that the worst moment of suffocation must always be the first. To Cherry I said with a smile, 'Can you believe it? The police think I ought to leave.'

'Some police are intelligent people,' Tony said.

'Still, they're taking the best care of me. They were sufficiently worried to talk to your bartender after they spoke to me.'

'We never have trouble in here,' Tony said. 'Trouble comes in packages. Out on the street.' But he had another worried look on his face, as if he had five errands now and only three delivery boys.

'It's hard to trust anyone nowadays,' I said.

'Friends,' he said.

'Friends get tired.' This remark cost nothing.

'All right, get up and do your set,' Tony said to Cherry.

'I'm not in the mood.'

'I'm not in the mood either. Don't pull this on me.'

She looked at my expression. 'Do you have a funny story, Mr Rojack?'

'I have a poem,' I said.

'Tell me.'

'Witches have no wit, said the magician who was weak.'

'Is that the first line of your poem?' asked Cherry.

'Yes. Want to hear the second?'

'Yes.'

'It's the last line.'

'Yes?'

'Hula, hula, said the witches.'

She pealed with mirth as if a silver witch and a black witch were beating their wings at one another. 'Repeat it,' she said.

'Witches have no wit, said the magician who was weak. Hula, hula, said the witches.'

She made me say it again while she memorized it. At the expression on Tony's face, she gave a creamy smile.

'You going to sing a set?' he asked.

'I'll sing one song.'

'What do you mean – one song?'

'Mr Rojack's poem put me in the mood,' she said. 'I'll sing one song or I won't sing anything.'

'Go up,' he said.

When she was on the stand, he turned and said to me, 'She'll do a whole set.'

But Cherry was in consultation with the pianist. I could see him shake his head, and give the weak grin of a weak man. While they parleyed, his fingers were nervously tapping out a riff on the keys, *What's that hear my baby say? Funky-butt, funky-butt, take it away.*

Cherry smiled at the microphone. '*Funky-butt, funky-butt, take it away,*' she murmured, and seemed to catch some electronic thread in the microphone for her sound came out breathy and then the microphone squealed. She put her hand to it, smiled at the dozen customers still left in the bar. 'Time for breakfast,' she said.

A patter of applause.

'I know we're all afraid to go out and look at that sun.'

'It's raining,' the judge with the two tarts called out. A few people guffawed.

'Yes, your Honory, but the sun is shining in court,' said Cherry, which brought a slow ripple. 'Yes, we're all scared of breakfast,' said Cherry, 'but I'm going to sing one song. Then we all go home. Crash.'

'She's only kidding,' said Tony. His voice was carefully wrapped, but it had the suppressed clangor of a sewer cover being lifted from its hole and dropped to the asphalt. 'She's only kidding,' Tony repeated.

'Yes,' said Cherry. 'A round of applause?'

She clapped her palm to give substance to the small bored skittering of palms which answered her. Then the pianist hit a few chords. Cherry was going to sing a hymn.

Every day with Jesus, sang Cherry.
Is sweeter than the day before.
Every day with Jesus.
I love him more and more

She stopped for her pause, looked at the audience and brought her hands together in devotion. She looked like she was ready to burst into a belly laugh.

Jesus saves and keeps me.
He's the one I'm waiting for.
Every day with Jesus
Is sweeter than the day before.

It was the best song she had sung all night, it had the most of her in it. A Southern Baptist congregation of small-town women came trooping into my mind, the light on the drinking glasses like the light off their eyeglasses, white lined faces with vertical wrinkles on the upper lip, passion scarred by righteousness, madness in the eye, that insane lust which whips over empty graves, devotion locked in arthritic joints.

Every day with Jesus, I love him more and more, sang Cherry, running up and down the pianist's chords with a body's joy in her throat, balm to the nettles these ladies must have left in her, and yet there was art in the song for she did not hate them altogether, they were witches too, hateful little old witches now, but they had had love for somebody, for a nephew or a brother or a young uncle long dead, they had kept somebody's old letters tied about with ribbon, or helped one pregnant girl; in the icelocks of their rheumatism flowed a nerve of Christian vein, romance to remind them of one soft lover dead and life in the breath of their loss. *'Every day with Jesus is sweeter than the day before*. Everybody sing,' said Cherry, and as if I were a middle-aged prep-school type come to reunion after all those years of waiting, I got to my feet and sang the lines with her, moving my highball glass in great sweeps of my arm like a beer stein used as a pendulum. *Sweeter than the day before.*

We were alone. The humors of this intoxication flowed from her to me and then flowed back again, while the pianist came into it now and then like an animated movie mouse prancing in time at a wedding of two great cats. But that was next to all of it. A drunk who had just come in bellowed the last word of every line, and the judge's tarts started to sing in tender little falsettos only to be decapitated by a look from the judge. Others were silent. Tony was livid. As Cherry came off the stand, she said, 'Okay, that's it.'

'You're not quitting,' Tony said, 'you're fired. You're crazy.'

'I have an American flag, Tony, and I'm going to send it to you for Christmas. As a tablecloth.'

'Sing in the bathtub, baby, that's where you're singing

now. I'm going to bum-rep you at every joint in town.'

'I'm going to change my clothes,' Cherry said to me.

'I'll wait for you,' I said.

Tony and I were now alone. We avoided each other's eyes and stood there side by side in a contest: his presence against my presence, two sea creatures buried deep in the ocean silt of a grotto, exuding the repellent communications of sea creatures. Tony's oppression was muddy, a stench of wet concrete. I could feel him burying me beneath it. So I called on Deborah. How many times talking to Deborah had my hand gone to my throat — doubtless she had been drawing an imaginary razor down one ear and up the other. Small wonder she believed in miracles. Now I in turn put my hand in my pocket to feel my pocketknife and took it on a small mental trip into my palm where figuratively I opened it, reached across, and made a slash into Tony's neck deep across the apple. 'That's the way,' said Deborah in my ear, 'at last you're learning. Put some salt in the wound.'

'Where do I find salt?' I asked of her.

'From the tears of anyone this man has been able to oppress. There's your salt. Rub it in.'

So I called for some distillate of sorrow, and so powerful was the impression returned that my fingertips felt a grit of white crystal with which they could travel to Tony's neck, and there some part of my mind must have rubbed it in.

I could feel his discomfort. He shifted his feet. Then he spoke. 'It's hot in here.'

'Yes,' I said.

'Too bad about your wife.'

'Dreadful,' I said.

It did not put him off. 'I used to know her,' he said.

'For fact?'

'I had another joint uptown. She used to drop in with friends.'

Cherry had come out of a back room. She was carrying a suitcase and wearing a street dress and cloth overcoat. 'Let's get out of here,' she said to me, and without a backward look at Tony went for the door. I started to follow her, but the center of my back told me Tony was going to loose a knife and loose it good. 'Yes,' said Tony, 'your wife, Mr Rojack, was a real swinger.' 'You know,' I said to Tony, 'it's a pity about your uncle's disease.'

'He takes it well,' said Tony.

On that echo, I left with her.

We had breakfast in a coffee shop, eating a little pinched meal of English muffins and tea, each of us silent for much of the time. Once, as I brought the cup to my lips, I noticed my hand was trembling. So did she.

'You've had a night,' she said.

'It isn't the night,' I said, 'it's the morning ahead.'

'You're afraid of the next few hours?'

'I'm always afraid,' I said.

She didn't laugh, she nodded. 'I went to a shrink,' she said.

'Any good reason?'

'I was feeling suicidal.'

'Beautiful women do.'

'Spookier than that.'

'Yes.'

'Don't you think there's a moment when it's right to commit suicide?'

'Perhaps.'

'Like it's your last chance?'

'Explain that to me.'

'You ever live with the dead?' She said this with her practical American face.

'No,' I said. 'I don't really know.'

'Well, I lived with my mommy and daddy all the while I was growing up, and they were dead. They died when I was four years and five months old. They smashed up in an automobile. So I lived with an older brother and older sis.'

'Were they nice?'

'Shit, no,' said Cherry, 'they were half crazy.'

She lit a cigarette. The circles beneath her eyes looked black with fatigue, the green going to purple at the edges of her lids and fading out along her cheek to a bruise-colored yellow. 'When you live with the dead you come to see,' she said, 'that there is a particular day in a particular year when they're ready to welcome you. You have to take that day. Because if you don't, you can die on a day when nobody is waiting for you and you just wander. That's why, when it comes, the impulse pulls so hard. I know. There was a day for me. I didn't take it. I went running to a shrink.'

'Well,' I said, 'maybe you have to take a chance on dying that particular day. But if you take the chance and get through it, maybe you're not as close to suicide the next time. Maybe, whatever it is, can't draw on you as hard.'

'You're an optimist.' She touched my hand. 'Still feeling scared?' she asked.

'Not as much.' But I was lying. The dread had settled in on my last brave speech. To be not afraid of death, to be ready to engage it – sometimes I thought I had more of a horror of dying than anyone I knew. I was so unfit for that moment. 'It's going to be full moon for how many days?' I asked.

'Three days more,' she said.

'Yes.'

'You say you're afraid,' she said, 'do you mean of women?'

'There comes a moment when I don't believe I belong in them.'

'You don't?'

I was close to telling her something I had not told anyone

else. 'I wouldn't want to make too much of it,' I said.

I did not go on to say that when I was in bed with a woman, I rarely felt as if I were making life, but rather as if I were a pirate sharpening up a raid on life, and so somewhere inside myself – yes, *there* was a large part of the fear – I had dread of the judgment which must rest behind the womb of a woman. A small perspiration came out along my back.

'How about a drink?' I asked. 'You serving drinks?'

'We can't go to my place,' Cherry said. 'Tony will telephone every fifteen minutes. Then he'll send somebody around to knock on the door.'

'Well, we can't go to my place. There'll be nothing but reporters, friends, business associates, and – family.' Barney Oswald Kelly was coming to town. Or at least he was coming to town if Roberts was telling the truth, and why should he not? The thought of my father-in-law, whom I had not seen eight times in my married life, but knew well enough to fear profoundly, was a subject so vast, however, I put it away from me altogether, the way one can separate one's mind from a contemplation of the land mass of Asia. 'Yes,' I said, 'let's stay far away from my apartment.'

'I don't want to go to a hotel,' she said.

'No.'

She sighed. 'I have a place. It's a special place.'

'I'll treat it with respect.'

'It's too soon to go there,' she said.

'We have no choice, princess.'

'Oh, Stephen,' said Cherry, 'Hula, hula.'

5

A Catenary of Manners

We took a cab to the Lower East Side and there on this cold misty March morning with a gray in the sky to equal the breath of those wet city streets, we climbed the five flights of a tenement, up past the sweet bruised rotting wood odors of a warehouse cellar for cheap wine, on up the stairs, the dirty light bulbs at each landing covered by a wire cage with threaders of dust as thick and intricate as moss. The garbage was out on the landings, the high peppery smell of Puerto Rican cooking, that odor of garlic, pig's viscera and incompatible condiments, a teeming misery. At the top of each flight, the door to the latrine was open, moisture seeped off the floor. The stench of slum plumbing gave a terror of old age – how ill is illness, how vile the suggestion of villainous old bowels. Going up those stairs I was no more a lover than a soldier crossing enemy land. 'Fail here at love,' said the odor, 'and you get closer to subsisting like me.' Some mambos were playing, a child was screaming in mortal terror, she sounded like she was being whacked to death, and at every landing the doors opened a split and brown eyes looked forth, five feet high, three feet high, eyes a foot from the floor – one-year-olds who had not yet learned to stand.

Cherry had her keys out and opened the door after turning the tumbler in two separate locks, but the bolts flew up with a clanking sound, surprisingly sepulchral for two cylinders so small, and I could feel the ears which connected to all those eyes bright as marmosets watching us.

'I run that gauntlet every time,' she said. 'I've come here at three in the morning and one in the afternoon, and they're always looking out the door.' She took off her coat, lit a cigarette, put it out, lit the gas heater, and went to a cupboard where she got two glasses and a bottle to pour us each a drink. The refrigerator was an old beat-up double-door box and the dirty smell of river ice came off the lead-gray cubes she chiseled free from the tray. I had been about to help but she did the job with one quick thump from the heel of her hand on an ice pick, and went on talking easily as she washed the rocks in the water from the sink, the pipes growling like some old dogs chased in their sleep.

'My sister used to live here,' Cherry said. 'She wanted to study painting. So I staked her a little bit. Just a bit. It's her furniture.'

'And she moved out?'

After a pause, 'Yes, it's my place now. Sometimes I feel guilty,' she said, 'that I keep it and hardly use it when all these families are here jammed into one another. But it was my younger sister's place. I don't want to give it up.'

There was only the one room in which we stood, a living-room dining-room kitchen and bedroom twelve feet by twenty-five. The plaster walls were white and very cracked and the colors of the furniture were innocent – tomato orange, reds, green, the sort of colors full of appetite a young girl who knew nothing of fashion might pick for her first year in New York. There was a double bed on legs with no headboard, a couch with one broken leg, a bridge table, two metal folding chairs, a movie director's canvas seat and an easel. On the wall were a number of paintings hung unframed but for a quarter-inch width of pine stripping, and at the far end of the apartment two windows had the luck to present a long view. There, beyond the back of the tenement, was a cemetery, one of the few left on Manhattan Island.

'Are these your sister's paintings?' I asked. I did not wish to ask the question but I could feel her waiting.

'Yes.'

'Let me look.'

But I was irritable suddenly, a sign of fatigue, the only sign of fatigue I could feel: my adrenalin had lit a new fire for the new drink. Sometime in the next hours or the next day would come a moment when I would lie down, when I would sleep – when I would try to – and then the memories of this night gone through would rise like the mutilated corpses of a battlefield. Now the liquor still enclosed me, a golden carriage lined with red velvet: installed inside I could drive over the battlefield, stare back at the battered face of Deborah which rose from each corpse.

I did not want to look at the paintings. I could see much too much, and there was much which was dull in Cherry's sister, much which was mess, wads and drippings, a red maniacal edge altogether unstable.

The paintings made a sad contrast to the tomato-orange and bright green of the furniture. She must have seemed an exuberant girl. I hesitated to go on. There was a tension in me like the taste of the bit in the jaws of a horse who wanted to gallop. Put it simply, I was the equal of a cigarette smoker who has been three days without a butt – underneath everything I wanted sex now, not for pleasure, not for love, but to work this tension: ignore the leaden, almost sensuous fatigue I felt in my heart as I climbed the stairs, I needed sex, I wanted it very much. I could not lie, however, I had some sense her sister's paintings were more than a fence to be gone over as nicely as possible – no, they were the door to some private estate. If I went on, I could spoil it all. Yet the paintings made me irritable; they were piggish.

But we could not begin with a lie between us. It was as if I had some desperate knowledge now, as if some message had come to me from the end of the world that I was close to the end of the world. If I was to make one last play, well, no carfare home, the money had to be put up now. I made a curious speech. 'I can't lie to you,' I said, 'I'm not going to until I lie the first time.'

'All right,' said Cherry.

'Something happened to your sister, didn't it?'

'Yes.'

'She crack up?'

'She cracked up and then she died.' There was no emotion in her voice. Something flat and little had settled on the event.

'How did she die?'

'She got hurt by a man she was going with. He was nothing but a pimp. He beat her up one night and she didn't recover from that. She just crawled back here. She asked me to take care of her.' Cherry revolved her glass in a small circle, rattling the cubes, exorcising a curse. 'Then a couple of days later,' Cherry said in a bright voice, 'she waited till I went out and took thirty sleeping pills and cut her wrist. After which she got up from bed, and died at the window there. I think she was trying to jump. She wanted to be in the cemetery, I suppose.'

'What happened to the pimp?' I asked at last.

Cherry's face took on the look of a rock-hard little jockey recollecting an ugly race. Something cruel and dedicated went by her mouth. 'I had him taken care of,' she said.

'Did you know the pimp?'

'I don't want to talk about it any more.'

I had the clean eye of a district attorney who has missed a career in surgery. 'You knew the pimp?'

'I didn't know him. She was only going with that pimp because she was half-crazy. She had been in love with somebody else. And she lost him. To me. I took her boy friend away.' Cherry shivered. 'I never thought I'd do something like that, but I did.'

'Was it Tony?'

'Oh, Jesus, of course it wasn't Tony. It was Shago Martin.'

'The singer?'

'No, honey, Shago Martin the explorer.'

Now Cherry finished her drink and poured another. 'You see, baby,' she said, 'dig: my sister was just one of six girls Shago had waiting for him every time he passed through New York. And I decided she was too dedicated to him; she was just a kid. So I got together with her and Shago to shame him out of it, and crash! I became one of the six girls he had waiting for him in New York. I mean Shago's a *stud*, Mr Rojack.'

The word went in like a blow to the soft part of my belly. There was something final in the verdict as if there were a sexual round robin where the big people played. All the big Negroes and the big Whites.

'Bless me for taking your time,' I said.

She laughed suddenly. 'I don't want to chase you clean out of your pants. It wasn't so bad as that. I was in love with Shago. Then after a while he was in love with me. He couldn't help it. A nice White Southern Girl like me. I suppose when a man's in love, he's no more of a stud than any other man who's in love.' She smiled. She gave me a wry smile.

'Well, I happen to feel like a stud right now,' I said. It was true. I was reacting from that blow to the belly and a mean edge was up again in me. I could see Deborah's face staring in the morgue, the one green eye, but I felt no fear this time, I felt instead as if I owned the hatred in her eye.

'I'm feeling pretty mean myself,' Cherry said.

It was in that glow that we made ready to go to bed. She opened a screen about the kitchen sink and walked behind it to undress, while I picked off my clothes and got shivering between the sheets of her small double bed, the sheets expensive (she, not her sister, must have brought them in) and lay there shuddering with cold, for the iron ice of a tenement's winter had settled on the cloth. I thought of graveyards and the cemetery outside and the Romanesque stone arch of Sever Hall at Harvard — I had not thought of Sever Hall in twenty years, perhaps it was twenty years since I felt such cold — but I knew at this instant I could have stood at the North Pole and pulled off my clothes, it was as if all the iron in me had gotten itself together for one good show against the winds.

She slipped out from behind the sink. Wearing a wheat-colored wrapper, and the pained professional smile of a modesty which had been disregarded a hundred times, she slipped modestly into bed beside me.

Her ass was indeed a prize — with my hands on her, life came back to me again across all the glaciers of my fatigue. But we did not meet as lovers, more like animals in a quiet mood, come across a track of the jungle to join in a clearing, we were equals. So we made love without preliminary — not thirty seconds had gone by before I slipped quietly into her. The separate cheats of her body and her life collected on one scale of justice to match the weight I could put on mine — her life up to this moment was the equal of my own, good to good, bad to bad, the submerged vision of my sex moved with a freedom from vanity or the haste to give pleasure. It was cool in mood, as if we were two professional dancers in a long slow study alone at night on a moonlit floor. I felt I could go on forever. Exhaustion had freed me. I was alive in some deep water below sex, some tunnel of the dream where effort was divorced at last from price. She was exquisite. She was exquisitely sensitive. Again, I had expected no less. Some cool blonde sense of violet shadow lived in the turn of her flesh. I had never moved so well. It was impossible to make a mistake.

Yet only the act was tender. Nothing was loving in her; no love in me; we paid our devotions in some church no larger than ourselves, we met in some depth beneath the lights and salts of one's eyes and mind. Fatigue had left me all but dead — I had no brain left, no wit, no pride, no itch, no smart, it was as if the membrane of my past had collected like a dead skin to be skimmed away. From some great distance, as if I were an observer on the moon, I had some distant awareness that my breath could hardly be good and her lungs breathed back an air of ashes and the tomb, but this rot of liquor and nicotine we now passed back and forth had nothing to do with the part of me now alive. I traveled (eyes sealed) through some midnight of inner space, aware of nothing but my will, that casing of iron about my heart, and of her will anchored like a girdle of steel about her womb. We reached into some middle ground of a race; we were like bicycle riders caught in the move of lap after lap around a track, soon we would be nothing but a rhythm which was nothing but a rhythm which would pump on to a climax I knew now would never come, and in the center of this vortex she flattened her fingers on the back of my neck with a hard little gesture, as if to ask, 'Do you want to now?' but from an instinct I did not question, I said, 'No, I don't want to . . . I can't so long as you have that thing in you,' which I never said before, and she shifted, I was out, the shock comparable to banging one's head on a low beam, and then I searched for that corporate rubbery obstruction I detested so much, found it with a finger, pulled it forth, flipped it away from the bed. Like diving on a cold winter day back to a warm pool, I was back in her, our wills now met, locked in a contest like an exchange of stares which goes on and on, wills which begin at last in the force of equality to water and to loose tears, to soften into some light which is shut away again by the will to force tears back, steel to steel, until steel shimmers in a mist of dew, is wiped, is wet again. I was passing through a grotto of curious lights, dark lights, like colored lanterns beneath the sea, a glimpse of that quiver of jeweled arrows, that heavenly city which had appeared as Deborah was expiring in the lock of my arm, and a voice like a child's whisper on the breeze came up so faint I could hardly hear, 'Do you want her?' it asked. 'Do you really want her, do you want to know something about love at last?' and I desired something I had never known before, and answered; it was as if my voice had reached to its roots; and, 'Yes,' I said, 'of course I do, I want love,' but like an urbane old gentleman, a dry tart portion of my mind added, 'Indeed, and what has one to lose?' and then the voice in a small terror, 'Oh, you have more to lose than you have lost already, fail at love and you lose more than you can know.' 'And if I do not fail?' I asked back. 'Do not ask,' said the voice, 'choose now!' and some continent of dread speared wide in me, rising like a dragon, as if I knew the choice were real, and in a lift of terror I opened my eyes and her face was beautiful beneath me in that rainy morning, her eyes were golden with light, and she said, 'Ah, honey, sure,' and I said sure to the voice in me, and felt love fly in like some great winged bird, some beating of wings at my back, and felt her will dissolve into tears, and some great deep sorrow like roses drowned in the salt of the sea came flooding from her womb and washed into me like a sweet honey of balm for all the bitter sores of my soul and for the first time in my life without passing through fire or straining the stones of my will, I came up from my body rather than down from my mind, I could not stop, some shield broke in me, bliss, and the honey she had given me I could only give back, all sweets to her womb, all come in her cunt.

'Son of a bitch,' I said, 'so that's what it's all about.' And my mouth like a worn-out soldier fell on the heart of her breast.

That was the way I fell asleep. And I fell asleep. I went sliding down a run, a bounce and tumble buffeted with pillows. Then my flesh gave out from the center of itself a sweet sigh of fatigue — I slipped into sleep like a boat garnering its dock on the last swell of momentum, motors stopped: there was a delicious instant when I knew that nothing would blow, no break would call me back from rest.

Once years ago, in those years when our marriage first was fortified with the taste of cruelty more gamy than pleasure, I said to Deborah, on an evening when all went bad, 'If we were in love, we would sleep with our arms around each other, and never want to move.'

'Darling, I'm withering from fever,' Deborah answered.

I went to sleep with my arms around Cherry. Hours went by, four hours, five hours — I came up like a diver, resting at each level, my body waking as I emerged. When I finally opened my eyes (I must have been ready ten minutes before the desire arrived) I knew everything was all right inside the room. Outside everything was wrong. Knowledge arrived from outside — the way a Negro child might understand on one particular morning that he is black. There was no desire to take my pulse. I was a murderer. I was: murderer. No rush to do more than study her. She had a different set of features for each station of her dream. She was so sound asleep. Masks of greed and cruelty came into focus in her face, became intense, broke apart from their own force. A soft child's face unfolded beneath. One was watching a film which gathered into a minute that metamorphosis of the weeks when the hard envelope of a bud cracks away, and the flower opens. Then, abruptly, the flower wilted. A new bud, hard, all horn at the point, came through the dying leaves, a vulgar ego-mania passed through the hardness of its spike, sensual features thrusting at me through sleep, pitiless calculation of a female with velvet to sell, she drew cupidity out of her limbs, whore's lore, her expression steeped into a cream of past thieveries, swallowed on the edge of curdling, turned sour, a sour mask now of disappointments, bitcheries, mean self-pity, yes, the mask was harsh again, it came to its crust, cracked, and in her sleep a sweet blonde girl of seventeen smiled back at me, skin almost luminous, a golden child, pure Georgia peach, a cheer leader, sweet fruit, national creation. I touched the tip of her nose. Dumb little nose, the nostrils were all visible in the tilt of its tip, confident nostrils ready to breathe the air directly in front of them.

I wanted to wake her up then. I had a need to talk a little, and I concentrated on the wish she awaken, concentrated so powerfully she began to stir, but then, as if the fatigues she must clear had flashed some panic at being unhonored, her face turned old, she looked middle-aged, a pinched concern drew worried lines about her nose, crimped her mouth, she groaned like an invalid crying out, 'I sicken if I awake, my separate lives must come together while I sleep,' and I thought, 'All right, then, sleep your sleep.' She relaxed, a smile, a little curl of amusement gave the scent of flesh to the open curl of her lip.

There was a clock above my head. It was half-past three in the afternoon. I was due to see Roberts at half-past five. So I got up then, separating myself like an artist, feeling no desire to fleece her rest, and put on my clothes in the dry warm air. Her gas heater had been going, and the air was close but the exhaust was vented into the fireplace so there was no smell – I had a passing fancy that the way I felt was kin to a pie in a warming oven, yes that was how my skin felt. I got dressed and did not bother to look for a razor. I would shave at home. Before I left I stopped to write a note.

Hey, you sleep deep. But what a sight!
See you soon, beautiful, I hope.

And then I wondered where she would be when I was ready to come back. Once again I came close to waking her. 'Going to try to be here by tonight,' I put in parentheses at the foot of the page. 'If you have to be out, leave a note where, when,' and came close to an instant of pure anguish. Would I ever get back to this place? The thought of Leznicki opened a grave in my stomach.

Well, I closed her door behind me, gently, so the spring lock would not snap too loud, and went down the stairs, sensing the eyes of Puerto Ricans upon me, and on the street fresh air came into my lungs like an intricate message of alarm. I was back, the world, an auto horn struck my ear like a screamer on an unhappy New Year's Eve, there was ambush everywhere. I was still drunk, I suppose. My head felt clear, too clear, I had a deep headache back of my eyes. But it was not painful so much as open to the promise it would last for more than a day. My body was drunk. Its nerves were alive, my flesh felt new – fact, it was almost a pleasure to walk, for I could feel the links which went into a step. And the air came into my nose with the history of its circuits – all the compromised souls of the dead up from the river and cobblestones permeated with the horse wagons of the last steep century, dogs around the corner, hot-dog grease from a griddle like the stale savory of the poor in rut, the blast of gas from a bus (that Egyptian mummy which lives beneath the rot) a moment of stiflings and suffocations like some childhood fight in which one is being extinguished by a bully (Deborah must have died with such smell in her lungs) and then I heard from clear across the city, over the Hudson in the Jersey yards, one fierce whistle of a locomotive which took me to a train late at night hurling through the middle of the West, its iron shriek blighting the darkness. One hundred years before, some first trains had torn through the prairie and their warning had congealed the nerve. 'Beware,' said the sound. 'Freeze in your route. Behind this machine comes a century of maniacs and a heat which looks to consume the earth.' What a rustling those first animals must have known.

I got a taxi. The driver was smoking a cigar and talked about Harlem all the way up, his absolute refusal to enter it. Finally I shut his sound out and sat there grappling with a ravening desire for drink. I don't know if I ever wanted one so much – I cried within like a just-cracked vase might shriek for cement (that second when I thought of Leznicki had separated me one half from the other) I sat up straight in the rear of the cab with a weak sick perspiration oozing my clothes – that much was I reduced by the effort not to tell the driver to stop each fifty yards we passed a bar. I remember pressing my jaws molar to molar, hanging on, knowing I was at a turn, knowing if I took a drink now – I, who loved to drink, I who could use whiskey for blood – that the corner would be turned, I'd be hooked, whiskey my opium. No, I had to get through the day, hold out, I had to hold out, not take a drink, not till I was back with Cherry – that was the first demand from my new contract, that moment in the morning when I had made a pact. And I thought of Ruta then, and the desire for drink added her to everything. Sick, wet, shivering with panic, I had nonetheless a quick thought of her up against these flowers of red-velvet flock, red pepper to the itch, Satan's heaven at the thought of diving into a bar, and calling her.

'Ruta, do you remember your friend the doctor, the crazy doctor who was no better than his patient?'

A moment. 'Ah. Yes. The Genius.'

'The Genius sees you sitting in the lap of blue uniforms.'

'The New York *gendarmerie* are handsome when the case is good.'

'Could you consider leaving them?'

'Only for the most thorough examination, *geliebter Doktor*.'

'See me for a consultation.'

'But you have moved your office.'

'Merely to the Irish bar on First Avenue . . .'

We would drink for hours, then disappear into some Germanic fleabag of a hotel, a bed fortified with the crazy molecules of a thousand fornications, one hundred sodomies, and the Devil's tale of the tongues. We would tie one good one on, two days, three days, five empty bottles at the foot of the bed.

My heart was racing up like a trapped bird once more. I was on the run. Like a petty criminal I had sold my jewels last night to the Devil, and promised them again this morning to some child's whisper. I had a literal sense of seed out on separate voyages, into the sea of Cherry's womb, into the rich extinctions of Ruta's kitchen. That second time I made love to Ruta – where had I left it then? I could not remember, and this fact: yes to the Devil, yes to the Lord, now seemed rabid with importance, more important than Leznicki, Deborah, Deborah's father – my heart bolted like a horse – more important even than my desire for a drink.

Do you know psychosis? Have you explored its cave? I had gone out to the end of my string. It was stretching behind me – I could feel it ready to snap.

'He hails me and I don't even want to look at him. But there's a cop at the intersection . . .'

My mind was going off to chase the million fish of its expired seed, my brain was lifting behind it, my brain had decided to float away.

'And he gives me a hard time. The cops are chicken about niggers in this town.'

'Stop here,' I said.

'Well, to make a long story short . . .'

'Take your fare.'

The fresh air was keeping me alive. I passed a bar. Walked on. My feet led me past.

The sweat no longer oozed – it had collected into rivers. I was weak but I was coming back to my separate parts: college professor, television performer, marginal socialite, author, police suspect, lecher, newly minted lover of a thrush named Cherry. I had roots, weed's roots: Jewish father, immigrant stock; Protestant mother, New England banking family, second-drawer. Yes, now I was back with the living. I could pass the bars. They went by like milestones, satisfying my sense of distance traveled on away from a crossroads where an ambush had been waiting. Now I felt small as a business man with a load of worries equal near to bankruptcy.

I bought several newspapers, took another cab, and went back to my apartment. On the ride I did my reading. There was no need to go too thoroughly through the news stories. They splashed the front page, spoke of the death as suicide, gave details about Deborah and details about me, half of them correct, half incorrect, gave promise in their excitement that the story was good for two days more and probably a feature for the weekend round-up, they hinted – but very lightly – that police were in the scene, they announced me as unavailable for comment, Barney Oswald Kelly as unavailable for comment, and the television studio and the university as willing to give no comment. An unidentified colleague at the university was quoted as saying, 'They were a splendid couple.' Two of the papers had used the same picture of Deborah. It was a terrible picture and years old. 'Beautiful Young Society Matron Takes Life in Plunge,' said the little headline over the photograph, and beneath was Deborah looking fat and ugly and somewhat idiotic for she was getting out of a limousine at a wedding and was caught with a frozen supercilious smile as if her mind had said to the news photographer, 'Shall I look like this for the masses?'

I turned to the society page. There was a column I always read: 'The Social Reins' – Francis 'Buck' Buchanan. He was a friend of Deborah's, for all I knew he was a beau, and for the year of our separation I had sometimes been able to follow the turns of her feeling toward me since Buchanan printed what she desired to have put in print, and a nice remark meant I was in her favor once more; my exclusion from a party list of twenty names signified she was displeased still again.

'Deborah Is No Longer With Us,' went Buchanan's headline, and it ran from left to right across the top of the page.

> Polite Society and Night Society were reeling in the wee hours this morning from the shock of Deborah Kelly Rojack's unforgettable and tragic demise. None of us could believe that the charming Deborah, oldest daughter of internationally respected king-maker Barney Oswald Kelly and Newport queen-mother Leonora Caughlin Mangaravidi Kelly, was no longer with us. The beautiful Deborah is dead. Never again will we hear the patrician tones of her merry laugh or see the wicked wit in her eye. 'I want to dance till the last note is played,' was Deborah's motto. 'The salad years are not over, they're just a little weary, poor glorious salad,' was Deborah's private confession to friends. Too proud ever to tell a soul, she must last night have heard the last note. Those of us who knew her well know she brooded in secret over the failure of her marriage to former Congressman Stephen Richards Rojack, and it is even reported as we go to press that Steve was in the room when Deborah took the step. Perhaps she wished him to hear the last note. Perhaps . . . Deborah's end is shrouded in mystery. We cannot believe her dead. She was so alive. Poor Tootsie Haenniger. Tootsie loaned Deborah her *bijou* East Side duplex for the month she was in Europe. Now Tootsie must come back to echoes.

It went on. On for a double column the length of the page and inches of overflow into a new column, a quick haul of anecdotes, it listed fifty people – her dearest friends –

and then like a trumpet blowing taps to the mournful grandeur of a violent death, as if one virtue of violent death might be to open at last some secret gates for conscientious readers, Buchanan finished with a laid-out table of everything to which Deborah had at one time or another belonged: charities, leagues, cotillions, balls, foundations, sisters, societies, and such odd-name congeries as The Caveat Napoleon, the Lasters, the Bahama Rifles, the Clambs, the Quainger, the Croyden Heart, the Spring Oak Subscription, the Philadelphia Riding, the Kerrybombos.

What a secret life had Deborah. I had not known a third of everything to which she enlisted. That endless stream of intimate woman's lunches into which she disappeared every perfumed noon over the years — what princes must have been elected, what pretenders guillotined, what marriages turned in their course. With the insight of an ice pick the precise thought came to me that I had lost my own marriage without ever a chance to fight for it on an open field. What a garroting must have been given my neck by the ladies of those lunches, those same ladies or their mothers who worked so neatly to make me a political career all eighteen years ago. It didn't matter. At this instant the past was like a burned-out field after the blaze has gone through.

I had a bad moment turning the key to the apartment. I was like a gambler who lives in fear of a card. It is the Queen of Spades, and each time it appears disaster has come up another step. So each time I felt the presence of Deborah, it was as if the card turned high. And she was everywhere in my apartment, there in the echo of all those nights I slept without her, fighting those early-morning wars when every one of my cells insisted I was losing her into still another depth of separation, and my pride swore I would not pick up the phone. Now in the apartment something had died — all memories of Deborah living. An odor of death in a trash pit rose from the wastebaskets with their stale cigarettes, the garbage can in the kitchen, the musk of stale memories in stale furniture, death lived like a beast in this air. Would one go scraping over the crusted lip of the incinerator into the sour end of sour ashes? Like a fever the desire for one stiff drink came over me again. I passed through the living room, that hateful living room of champagne-colored settees and champagne paper on the walls, another of Deborah's flings with a decorator, silver-gray, pale green, cream, all the colors of face powder, the arbitrary palette of elegance: I had always felt like Deborah's footman sitting in that room. My fist was clenched.

The phone was ringing. It went four times, five times, the answer service picked it up, and I kept hearing an after-ring – the phone sounded like some spoiled child screaming in the attic of a house. There must be a hundred messages by now but I could not think of them. I did not know how long I could bear this apartment – dread worked up through my middle like the gray water in the machines of a midnight laundry. In the bathroom, I could have been buried to the waist in this grease water of dread: only the touch of the razor was alive – it drew something clean across my cheek like the smell of the ocean on a summer morning. My cheek felt like a window looking out on such a light while I remained prisoner in the closet. The phone was ringing still again. I rinsed my face, made a debate whether to dress first or first take care of messages, but the answer was simple: I had to be dressed so I could get out in a minute. I picked a summer gray suit with a quiet superimposed gray plaid, black shoes, a blue-gray shirt, a black knit tie, a handkerchief for the breast pocket, and dressed all the way, even brushed my shoes, breathing all the while with the anxiety of an asthmatic on the edge of an attack.

Once again the phone was ringing. This time I answered. It was the producer of my television show. 'Steve, oh boy, oh friend. How do you feel?'

'Cold as ice, Arthur.'

The answer service was also on the line. 'Mr Rojack, will you call us soon as you finish this call. We have to give you several messages.'

'Yes, Gloria, thank you.'

'Oh, Christ, boy, you've laid this studio in a panic. Will you take our commiserations?'

'Yes. Thanks, Arthur.'

'No, I mean, Steve, *anxiety* is loose here today. It hasn't been so bad since Kennedy stood up to Khrushchev with the missiles. Poor Deborah. I only met her once, but she's a great woman.'

'Yes. *Was*.'

'Steve, you must be in a state of shock.'

'I'm a little rocky, kid.'

'I'll bet. I'll bet. These dependencies we feel on women. When they go, it's like losing mother.'

If Deborah were not dead, but had merely run off to Europe with another man, Arthur would have said, 'It's like losing mother's tit.'

'Have you seen your analyst this morning?' I asked.

'You bet on that, Steve. I was there at eight A.M. I caught the news on the midnight news last night.'

'Yes.'

His voice shifted for a moment, as if, suddenly, he was aware again of the fact. 'Steve, are you really all right? Can you talk?'

'Yes, I'm really all right.'

'My analyst said I have to level with you. One of the great hang-ups on the program is that I've never been able to enter a relation with you. My anxieties tend to submit to social patterns rather than drive into personal focus. I guess I've been defeating myself before your sense of social superiority.'

'Arthur, stop this slop, will you. I'm going to scream.'

'I've tried to reach you six times today. I got myself up

for it six times, and each time, Steve, I caught your fright-
wig answer service. I'm raddled now, Steve, I'm hysterical.
The pressure here this morning has been pressure cooker.
The newspapers want a statement on the future of the
show.'

'I can't think about that now.'

'Baby, you got to. Look, I know I've always been
deficient in the amenities, and think too much in terms of
social response, status, public reaction . . .'

'Check.'

'. . . rather than trying to manifest some sort of false
gentry's grace for hideous moments like this.'

'You damned beggar!' I shouted at him. 'You shitface.'

'You're bereaved.'

I took the phone away from my ear. I could hear expli-
cations running into qualifications, then the considered
tone of self-examination, the scar tissue at the top of his
nose where the adenoids had been removed vibrating now
with the complacency of an oboe reed. Then I heard him
pause and shift – we had come to another body of the
conversation.

'It's cancer gulch down here, admittedly, but a local
station suffers from tensions the networks are not subject
to. You know we've been embattled more with your program than anything else, and now you see we've got a
couple of cathexis-loaded projects besides yours, a real
collision load. You know we're beginning the Shago Martin
show next month, it's our integration bit, the first time
we're going to have a Negro singer doing lowdown funky
intime duets with a white canary.'

'What's her name,' I asked, 'the canary.'

'Rosalie . . . I think.'

'Not Cherry?'

'No, Cherry Melanie was up for it but got axed.'

'How do you spell Melanie?'

'M-e-l-a-n-i-e. Are you drunk?'

'Why didn't she get it?'

'Because Rosalie does her libidinal bit with Numero Uno.'

'Dodds Mercer Merrill?'

'Dodds, our boss Dodds, that roaring faggot, believe it or not. He makes the chick scene from time to time.' Arthur giggled. 'You know what he said to me once, "It's all friction." '

'And he's putting his girl Rosalie in with Shago Martin?'

'Dodds is gone on black men, boy. Don't you dig these things?' He paused. 'Stephen,' he went on in a level voice, 'my analyst gave me a formal verbal directive not to get sloughed in talking to you. The point of this conversation has still not been engaged. We're in difficulties, boy.'

'Why don't you just say the show will not be on the air for a short period.'

'Steve?'

'Yes.'

'Remember you once said Marx said, "Quantity changes quality"?'

'I remember there were fifty letters complaining I quoted Marx favorably.'

'This is one of those times. The quantity of publicity, and the contingent innuendo . . .'

'That's good, boy. That's corporation lawyer.'

'Steve, it's not that anybody thinks you gave Deborah a shove. Christ, I don't. I stood up to Dodds for five minutes today telling him you were essentially a sweet guy with a brilliant mind, a latent genius, and if you had a personal problem or two, well you weren't the only man on television who was known to tipple a bit and chase hump. But that didn't crack ice. I've never seen ice like the ice here this morning. A morgue. A polar morgue.'

'A polar morgue.'

'Dodds said the critical factor is this: no audience is going to trust a man whose wife takes a leap.'

'Check.'

'See what I mean? No audience in the world.'

'I see.'

'I could cry, Steve.'

'Check.'

'It was a great program, Steve.'

'Nice to be associated with you, Arthur.'

'Bless you, baby, for saying that. I dig, now I dig the anxiety this conversation gave me in advance. It was a cancerous demand that was made on me to have to do this to you.'

'Bless, Arthur, bless.'

'Yeah.'

'So long.'

'*Ciao*.'

The phone rang. It was the answer service. The messages were not as numerous as I had expected. There was a request from the head of the Psychology Department to call him, there were indeed five calls from Arthur, three calls from three different newspapers, several from good friends I wanted to talk to and did not care to talk to, and a request from Barney Oswald Kelly's secretary to telephone Mr Kelly at his suite in the Waldorf Towers. There were no calls from any of Deborah's friends, nor were there any from the friends I had supposed we might have in common. I had never had much illusion that Deborah's friends were ever the least divided in their loyalty, but the absolute silence of this moment seemed to deepen their silence in my apartment. 'Gloria,' I said to the operator when she finished, 'do me a favor. Call the Waldorf Towers and make an appointment with Mr Kelly. Tell his secretary I'd like to see him at seven-thirty tonight. If the time isn't good, call me back.'

'All right, I will, Mr Rojack, of course I will . . . and listen, Mr Rojack . . .'

'Yes.'

'The girls here all want to say that they feel with you in your tragic loss.'

'Oh, thank you, Gloria, it's good of you to say that.'

Was this how the French had felt when the Nazis invaded the Maginot Line from the rear, that they must lift their guns from their concrete emplacement and turn them around? I had a knowledge I must not stop making telephone calls until I was ready to leave.

I dialed the head of my Department. 'Dr Tharchman,' I began.

'Stephen,' he said, 'I'm awfully glad to hear from you. I've been so worried. I can't imagine a more heinous occasion for any of us, poor man.'

'It's been difficult, Frederick. As you know, Deborah and I have not been very close for a while, but it's been an earthquake, yes.'

'Just Godawful, I'm sure.'

There was a silence between us.

'I suppose the university has been bombarded by the newspapers.'

'They're termites,' Frederick said. 'I really believe they're termites eating at the very substance of Western civilization.'

The second silence was definitely lame.

'It's good of you to call, Stephen. I appreciate your consideration.'

'Actually, I wanted to. I don't mind being on the phone.'

'Stephen, as you know, I'm not a very religious man, but I went to chapel this morning. I wanted to say a prayer for Deborah.'

I could see his thin gray Presbyterian conscience taking him through the morning rain. He had met Deborah just once at a faculty dinner, but she had charmed him utterly as a demonstration of what she could do for me.

'Well, Deborah was religious, as you know,' I said now, 'and perhaps she heard the prayer.'

Now we were both embarrassed. I could feel him smarting to reply, 'Good God, I hope not.'

'Dr Tharchman, I know we have to talk about practical matters, and I think under the circumstances, I'm the one who must bring it up.'

'Thank you, Stephen, we do have to talk. You see, it would help if the university could give just one simple statement to those damnable termites. What I'm afraid of is they'll start to talk to the professors and, God help us, the worst of the graduate students. You know how reporters are. They look for the married men with the beards.' He searched his throat for clearance. 'I won't pretend, Stephen, that I've been enraptured with the pure tenor of your ideas, but what you quite properly have not been aware of is the particular protection I've tried to set up about you. I hate to think of the way you could be presented. One professor called this morning, I won't tell you his name, he insisted that one of his doctoral candidates who had taken the Voodoo seminar with you had the idea – I'm afraid I have to tell you this – that you had been administering voodoo rites to Deborah. For some time.'

'Good God.'

'It's enough to depress one about the nature of a faculty. High scholarship, innocence, and an absolute fever.'

'I never knew I was talked about that way.'

'Stephen, you're a living legend.' The dry little voice stuck an instant over the last two words – discipline, envy, and decency were the separate protagonists of his character. I was liking Frederick for the first time. He had come in some years ago from the outside (from the Midwest) to be made head of the Department, and he was considered pedestrian, good for keeping the Ph.D. mill a Ph.D. mill. Nonetheless, it must not have been easy for him to grind out his decent portions of salt and meal for each of us. Good old Protestant center of a mad nation. I could hear his fingers drumming on his desk.

'Well, Fred, what do you suggest?'

'The first question is whether you feel up to taking your

classes immediately. I should think you don't.' His voice closed that gate all but perfectly.

'I'm not sure,' I said. 'I need a week to think.'

'Right there is the difficulty. We must say one thing or another to the papers right away. Mass communication breeds in a vacuum.'

'But, Frederick, I can't decide today.'

'Well, I don't see how you can.'

'But I think work may be what I want.'

'That's what I don't know. I've thought about it all morning. If you were teaching organic chemistry or statistics, I'd say, "Plunge in. Work to the exclusion of all else." But your courses are personal. You have to use yourself.'

'Nonsense, Fred, I've been teaching for years.'

'Nonsense – no. Magic, dread, and death as the center of motivation – it's not the sort of subject to give you peace. I should think there'd be an awful strain in the classroom. You might break under it.'

'You mean some angel of the Corporation is afraid I might bring a bottle to school?'

'Don't you agree we take as good a stand toward the trustees as any university you could name. But we can't despise them *altogether*, can we?'

'Fred, do you realize what a conversation this is?'

'I don't know if I've had one like it before.'

'Really,' I said, 'what could you lose?'

'It's not measurable. A university can absorb scandal upon scandal. Then, one too many, and it's incalculable what could happen.' He coughed. 'Steve, this is academic. I can't believe you want to go back to work right away.'

'But if I do? Fred, what if I insist? What will you do?'

'Oh, if you insist, I'll be forced to go to the president, and tell him it's your right to work.'

'And what will he do?'

'He will overrule me.' Church humor. I heard a delicate little flutter in Frederick's throat.

'Since I have tenure, I suppose I might be forced to go so far as to sue the university.'

'Oh, you wouldn't do that,' Frederick said. 'The case would be disagreeable in the extreme.'

'What are you getting at?'

'I don't want to talk about it any further. Your wife's death is sufficiently tragic without beginning to mention the unhappy ... the dreadful ... the *ambiguous* aspects of it all.'

'Oh, no!'

'Steve, this is the most unendurable conversation I've had with anyone in years. We'll never forgive each other for this one.'

'We won't.'

'I've managed it abominably. Accept the reality, accept the reality. See it from the university's point of view. Perhaps we feel we've done our honorable best to pay the indefinable price and, yes, perhaps gain the even more indefinable benefit of having a creative intelligence in the Department who inspires most respectable people with a deep-seated sense of uneasiness. Consider that not every university would have put up with that television program of yours. Steve, can't we just leave it that this is a bastard of a day for everybody?'

Silence.

'All right, Fred. What do you want?'

'Take a leave till the beginning of the fall semester. We'll announce your bereavement and retirement from active teaching duties for an indefinite period. Then we'll see.'

'Fred, somehow you've won this one.'

'I haven't, believe me.' Then he said quickly, 'Steve?'

He was in a hurry to move on. His voice faltered for the first time. 'Steve, I can't imagine anything more inappropriate, but I must ask you this. Perhaps you don't know it, but my wife is a religious cultist.'

'I didn't know.' But I should have guessed. I could see

Gladys Tharchman up in Vermont for the summer, a purple dress, silver-rimmed eyeglasses, white hair, and her dowager's hump over a thin body.

'She subscribes to some of your ideas.'

'What?'

'Oh, with sex extracted, of course.' He gave a chuckle; we were coming back on course. 'You see, she believes that the last meal a person eats before they die determines the migration of their soul.'

'You mean if you die with a belly full of cereal you migrate to the wheat fields!'

'In her mind, it's somewhat more complicated than that. Has to do with omens and lots and portents and whether one's a meat soul or fish soul, and of course it's not divorced from the phases of the moon and the horoscope.'

'Demeter and Persephone. You poor bastard, Tharchman.'

'She's a marvelous woman, my wife, and this may be a small cross to bear. But I can tell you she'll give me no quarter if I don't ask. Because, you see, in all good intention, she wishes to reach Deborah – Deborah made a vast impression on her – and for that she needs to know –'

'What Deborah ate?'

'Dear God yes, Steve. Hecate has to know.' Now a skinny little sense of hilarity, as if he were a skinny boy in the blissful discomfort of asking an athlete the last line of a dirty joke, came into his voice. 'Yes. Steve, what was in her tummy at the end?' I could not resist. 'Why, Fred, I'll tell you,' I said.

'Yes.'

'It was rum. A bottle of rum, just about.' And hung up.

In ten seconds the phone rang again. It was Tharchman. He was angry now. 'You shouldn't have disconnected, Stephen,' he said, 'because there was one thing more.'

'Yes?'

His voice had a Midwestern twang, a sort of 'Don't kid

with me, *boy.*' He clicked his tongue once. 'I think you ought to know,' he said. 'I've been formally questioned about you today.'

'By police?'

'No. Somebody much more hush-hush. What in Hell have you and Deborah been up to?' And then *he* hung up.

Next moment the phone rang again. My perspiration flowed.

'Hello, Stephen?' came a breathless voice.

'Speaking.'

'Stephen, I have to whisper.'

'Who is it?'

'Chookey-bah.'

'*Who?*'

'Chookey-bah lamb. Gigot!'

'*Gigot*, how *are* you?'

'Chookey-bah, I'm just chookey-bah.'

'Well, crash!'

It was idiotic to have said this, but I was in a kind of exhilaration by now. There was a curious exhilaration as if we were all the subjects of a nation which had just declared war. So I said, 'Crash,' said it again.

'Well, no,' said Gigot, 'I'm not chookey-bah really. I have to whisper. Blake's in the next room, and doesn't want to speak to you. But I must.'

'Speak to me.' She was one of Deborah's ten best friends, which is to say she was Deborah's best friend for one month in every ten. She was also huge. She was five feet eleven and must have weighed one hundred and eighty pounds. She had a fortune of blonde hair which hung down to her waist or piled like a palisade six inches above her brow. She had the voice of a tiny little blonde five years old.

'Blake thinks I'm bound for the crazy house again. I told him I would ask Minot to shoot him if he committed me, and he said, "Your brother Minot can't even shoot a hole in his own pants." Blake was *obscene.* I think he's crazy.

147

He never talks like that. Besides he knows Minot is sexy. I told him so.'

'That brought peace.'

'Blake thinks I'm cockaloo over Deborah. I'm not. I told her to jump last year. I said, "Honey, you better go jump and squash yourself. You're getting fat." And Deborah just gave that little pig laugh of hers, oink, oink, you know, and she said, "Bettina, your advice is exquisite, but if you don't stop, I'm going to call Blake and tell him it's time to have you *cooped* again," and she'd do it. She did it to me once. I told her I knew she'd been up to something with her Daddy-O, and she called my family, and had me in the hatch six hours later, in *Paris*, just the two of us, she was my *roommate*.'

'When, Gigot?'

'Oh, years ago, I don't know, some *fearful* time past. I never forgave her. French mental hospitals are unspeakable. I almost didn't get out. I had to threaten my family that I would marry the *resident* there, a funny little old dark French Jewish doctor who smelled like the *Encyclopaedia Britannica*, I swear he did, and my family sprung me. They weren't going to have some ratty little French Jew slurping up their soup and telling them how to go on a wild boar hunt, you know the French, they tell you everything whether they know it or not. God, I hate the French.'

'Honey, I wonder if you don't have a tidbit for me.'

'I do. But I can't tell you now. My scalp is itching and that means Blake is going to come right back in this room.'

'Well, before he does.'

'Oh. I can't remember. Yes, now I do. Listen, when I said to Deborah that she ought to jump, she gave that bitchy smile of hers and poured me a glass of sherry, no, it was hundred-and-fifty-year-old Maderia, I remember, she said, "Let's finish off Steve's Madeira, it gets him so frantic if there is none," and then she said, "Pet, I'm not going to jump, I'm going to be murdered."'

'What?'

'Yes. She said that. She said it was in her horoscope. She said it was going to be terrifically catastrophic because Venus was together with Saturn and Uranus was in Aquarius. It was even worse than that. Every single planet was bad for her kind of Scorpio.'

'You mean she said she was going to be killed last night?'

'I think she did.'

'She killed herself. Gigot, you forget.'

She sighed audibly. 'Steve, you didn't do it, did you?'

'I didn't,' I said softly.

'Steve, I'm glad I called you. I thought I ought to call the police. Blake said he'd break my nose if I called them and got my picture in the papers. And he would break my nose, too. He hates my gift of smell — I once caught the teeniest whiff of perfume on him even though he'd gone to a sauna bath afterward and tried to come back smelling like birch twigs. But I could smell the perfume and I could even smell the hands of the coon who'd been giving him a massage. How do you like that?'

'Phenomenal.'

'Steve, you *are* telling me the truth. I know you like me.'

'Well, Gigot, if I had done it, could I tell you the truth, could I?'

'But you didn't?'

'Well, maybe I did. You seem to think so.'

'Oh, I guess she could have committed suicide. She was very upset about Deirdre, you know. She didn't know what to tell her about her father.'

'Pamphli?'

'How do we know Pamphli was the father? We don't do we, sheik?' said Gigot.

'I never had any reason to doubt it,' I said.

'Well, a man never has anything but empty space between his certainties,' Gigot said. 'Oh, darling Steve, I know it wasn't suicide. Deborah *knew* she was going to be murdered. She was *never* wrong about that sort of thing. Steve, maybe somebody gave her poison that sent a message to her brain to make her jump. You know, some new hallucinatory drug or something. All the doctors are flippo now. They spend their time cooking up things like that. I mean maybe the maid slipped it into her rum.'

'Come on, love bucket.'

'No, the maid was in cahoots.'

'Angel Bettina . . .'

'I know something you don't know. Deborah never told you anything. You know why I was her best friend? Because no matter what she told me, nobody ever believed it. And besides, I know something about that maid.'

'What?'

'Promise to believe me?'

'Promise.'

'That maid is Barney Kelly's mistress. You know the kind a man his age has. They always have those thin lips which can go anywhere.'

'Now why would Barney Kelly be so interested in what Deborah was doing that he would give up such a mistress?'

'All I know is the maid came as a condition of Deborah's allowance.'

'She didn't have one.'

'Kelly gave Deborah five hundred dollars a week. Did you think you were supporting her by yourself, Horatio Alger?'

'I don't know what to think.'

'Somebody killed her.'

'I really doubt it, Gigot.'

'She was done in.'

'I don't think so.'

'I *know*.'

'Then go to the police.'

'I'm afraid to.'

'Why?'

'Because I think there are *repercussions* to this.' Bettina spoke in a whisper which was quite inside her normal whisper. 'Deborah was a spy.'

'Bettina, you *are* mad.'

'Better believe me, handsome.'

'Why in the name of heaven would Deborah be a spy?'

'Steve, she was bored. She was always bored. She'd do anything to avoid being bored.'

'Who was she a spy for?'

'Well, I don't know. She was capable of *anything*. I once accused her of being CIA and she laughed. "Those *idiots*," she said. "They're all college professors or gorillas wearing paratroop boots." Anyway, I know she used to be MI6.'

'When?'

'When we were in the convent in London. That's how she would get a pass to get out. She had a boy friend who was MI6, *anyway*.'

'Gigot, you're really a very silly little girl.'

'And you're a fathead. Blake's a fathead and you're a fathead.'

'Chookey-bah, I do adore you.'

'You better.'

'I always thought Deborah was a Communist,' I said.

'Divine lamb, that's what I was going to tell you. I'm willing to bet she was some kind of double agent, you know, a spy within a spy. I have something I want to tell you about that.'

I groaned. There was an awful possibility that some blighted hair of truth was still alive in all of this. I could feel mysteries revolving into mysteries like galaxies forming themselves, and knew with some sort of defeated woe that I would never learn a tenth of what had really happened, not ever.

'Cheese it, the cops,' whispered Bettina. 'Why, Blake,' she said loudly, 'you angel ape of a stud, who do you think I'm talking to? It's Marguerite Ames. She's calling me from a phone booth. Hang on, Marguerite, Blake wants to talk to you. Oh, darling, get a nickel up fast, or call me back . . . Damn, we lost her.'

I hung up even as I could feel him reaching for the phone. My shirt was wet. I was like a man in a burning house who has three minutes to get the valuables together. I had just those three minutes to hold myself in line, and then the desire for a drink would sear the walls. I stripped off that wet shirt I had chosen with such care, scrubbed my back and under my arms with a dry towel, put on something else quick as I could find it, and stepped out the door. I didn't realize until I reached the street that I had been holding my breath. My uneasiness was almost tangible now; I could feel some sullen air of calm, exactly that torporous calm which comes before a hurricane. It was nearly dark outside. I would be late, but I had to walk to the precinct, I had the conviction that if I entered a taxi there would be an accident. I turned abruptly and felt a flicker in the mood. There was some sense of a dull but intent intelligence nearby. Then I knew I was being followed. My eye picked out a man half a block back on the other side of the street who went on strolling. A detective, no doubt. That was almost pleasing. Had they been following me since I left the precinct last night?

For this interview Roberts' office was in the basement, a box of a room ten feet by twelve with a desk, a few wooden chairs, two file cabinets and a wall calendar. There was also an enlarged map of the precinct with red pins in it. I had been led here by a policeman on duty near the desk sergeant's tribunal, and we had gone down a flight of iron stairs and down a long corridor which gave a view through one window of the cellblock, a row of steel doors and walls of yellow institutional tile. As we went by, I could hear somebody yelling – one of the drunks.

Roberts did not get up to shake hands. 'You're late,' he said.

'I needed a walk.'

'Sweating out some booze?'

'You look hung yourself.'

He nodded. 'I'm not used to living with the poison.' His blue eyes, alert last night and precise as a micrometer, now seemed larger and red-rimmed and somewhat boiled – the blue had gone pale. As he leaned forward, a waft of exertion came off him, sour with use, and also too sweet, as if he had borrowed some of O'Brien's smell. Then he opened a file. 'We have the autopsy now. Yes, we got it all here,' he said, and tapped the file slowly. 'It doesn't look so good for you.'

'Care to give detail?'

'I have enough here to lock you up.'

'Why don't you?'

'Probably I will.'

'Maybe the time has come for me to get a lawyer.' I put no emphasis on this. I still could not be certain whether he was serious or merely beginning a serious game.

'I'd rather talk a while first.'

'Why?'

'You're an intelligent man. I think you're entitled to know how bad your situation is. I want your confession, this evening, right here.'

The desire for a drink had passed. It was as if I'd been laboring these last few hours to get myself ready to meet him.

'You know, of course,' he said, 'that when a body has been dead for six hours, rigor mortis sets in.'

'Yes. I know that.'

'Well, there was no evidence of rigor mortis on your wife when we found her on the street.'

'How could there be?'

'There wasn't. However, we know another way to measure the time of death. I don't imagine you're familiar with that.'

Something in his posture told me not to answer.

'Ever hear,' Roberts asked, 'of dependent lividity?'

'I'm not positive.'

'Well, Rojack, when a death occurs, the body blood begins to coagulate at exactly those parts of the body which are touching the floor or leaning against a wall. That's dependent lividity. Within an hour and a half you can begin to see black and blue areas with the naked eye. Now by the time the autopsy was made on your wife, her body was covered with dependent lividity front and back.'

She had been lying on her face and then I had turned her over.

'Your wife was lying on her back in the street. That could possibly account for the dependent lividity there, but it doesn't explain why she had it on her cheek, her breasts, her ribs, her belly, her thighs, her kneecaps and the ends of her toes. Care to comment?'

'Not yet.'

'This evidence by itself is enough to get you the chair' – his eyes looked at me bleakly as if they saw nothing but stone – 'but it is merely the first of three clearly defined pieces of evidence we have.'

'I'm not guilty. So I assume there's something wrong with your evidence.'

'Point two: your wife's hyoid bone was broken. That's a direct sign of strangulation especially when it's accompanied, as the autopsy shows, by massive hemorrhaging.'

'There must be another reason.'

'Care to offer it, Rojack?'

'You're convinced I did it. Why go on?'

'Let me give you the alternatives: A: You talk your way out of here no worse than you came in. B: You give me a confession. C: You don't say a thing, and I lock you up right in that cellblock over there. Tomorrow we'll have you arraigned.'

I had gone through this day on the hope I would be

able to get back to Cherry tonight. If at this exact instant Roberts had offered me twenty-four hours of freedom I think I would have signed his confession, for I had to see her again, simple as that. Some dim caution tried to argue not to say more without a lawyer, yet I could not stop here. 'Roberts,' I said, 'admit that if I were guilty I'd make a phone call right now to the best criminal lawyer in town.'

'I recommend that you do.'

'You want me to discuss it with you,' I said, 'and yet you won't agree I give away some advantage by disclosing a possible line of defense.'

'What do you give away? You think we can't think for ourselves.' He smashed his fist down on the desk. 'You want to talk,' he said, 'because you're the kind of degenerate who chases every hundred-to-one shot. You want to be back on the Lower East Side with your new broad tonight. Don't piss on me, buster. Just sit down and dictate a little confession and I'll give you a night with her in a midtown hotel with a police guard outside the door.'

And the guard would have their ear to the door. How much he wanted this confession. There was something wrong. He wanted my confession too quickly. I knew I should be silent, but I also knew that whatever strength I had, I certainly did not have the simple strength to sit in a cell. Talking to him, I could keep my strength; alone, something would begin to unravel in me, I would come apart, yes, I would come apart.

'I'm waiting,' he said.

'Roberts, you can always find one expert to contradict another. Deborah jumped out that window, that's all I know. Your expert says she had to be dead before the fall. I could find an expert to explain that her dependent lividity was a direct result of the impact of striking the ground from ten stories up, and then being buffeted by the car which hit her, broke the hyoid bone in her neck, and caused a massive hemorrhaging.'

'Dependent lividity doesn't come from a body rolling over and over. It comes from resting in one place. When was she resting on her stomach?'

'When they put her on the stretcher.'

'What?'

'Yes, I remember thinking how unusual that was, and then realized why. The back of her head was crushed, and you know . . . You remember it was bad . . . They didn't want her head to lie on the stretcher.'

'Well,' Roberts grinned, 'you missed a promising legal career.' He sat back in his chair. 'I have to admit your account could take care of a few details. Conceivably. One chance in ten. I won't go into the technical evidence any further, but I suppose it's possible you could find one unqualified expert to get up on your side for every ten professionals we could find. But skip that. The way we stand, as I follow you, is that you're prepared to sign a statement she was alive when she jumped through the window.'

'Yes, I'll sign such a statement.'

'Well, we could take the time to get a police stenographer down here and type it up, but that would just use the next half hour, and I don't need it, I don't require that kind of leverage on you. The fact of the matter, Rojack, is that you still haven't heard Point Three.'

'Point Three?'

'Why should *I* disclose a piece of evidence *we* can use at the trial? I mean why should I offer it to you for nothing?'

'For the same reason I'm ready to talk openly to you.'

'Stop horsing around. You give me your confession and I'll give you room to put in anything and everything on the line of Temporary Insanity. I'll even give you a tip or two on the kind of material to include. But if you don't throw in your hand, if you insist on trying to get away with this, so help me, Rojack, I'm going to make it a personal crusade to get you and get you right, get you so bad even the governor will hesitate to commute the electric chair to life.' He was breathing heavily.

'That's quite a speech,' I said.

'Sit back and listen to Point Three. Your wife was alive when she went through the window. That you are ready to claim. Correct?'

'Correct.'

'Well, you ignored her large intestine.'

'What are you talking about?'

'Believe it or not, these details are no more agreeable to me than to anyone else, but the autopsy does show a complete evacuation of her bowels before she jumped.'

'I don't see the significance,' I said.

'Strangulation results in a total relaxation of the anal sphincter. Get it?'

'While we were talking, Deborah went to the bathroom.'

He gave me a look of disgust, as if I were a hired athlete trying to cheat the business office. 'I assume,' he said, 'that when she engaged in such activities she was not in the habit of leaving traces on her negligée.'

'Those traces could have come from the fall, or been deposited afterward. Some actions continue after death.' We could have been talking about a stranger. I had a distant moment of woe as if some exorbitant price were eventually to be paid for disposing of Deborah's privacy this way.

Roberts gave a broad happy grin. 'We gave a thorough examination to the apartment. Particularly to her bedroom. Rojack, the carpet was soiled sufficiently for us to establish a certain fact beyond dispute. The carpet provided a laboratory sample of the same precise foreign material we're talking about. When you explain that to my satisfaction you can walk out of this room.'

I knew which story had to be told next, but I did not know if I could tell it. 'Roberts, I'd like to keep something private about my wife.'

'Try convincing a court with that sentiment.'

'Deborah was unbalanced at the end.'

'You hinting what I think you're hinting at?'

'I can't go into it.' But of course I could. Some chamber of the brain had prepared this story, and I was now equipped to give it, detail upon detail, Deborah's precise if imaginary speech, 'Now that you've seen this, there's not much left to see,' and her body quick to the window and out in three steps; yes, this imaginary account now had the vividness of the real. I knew if I ever stepped over into psychosis the story would accompany me in exchange. Roberts had a look of half-convinced attention, the expression he had had for a little while in Deborah's room last night. But I could not go on. Let this story stick to Deborah, and the past would sink in like disease.

'No,' I said, 'you may as well lock me up.' His phone buzzed once.

'Why not sign a confession?' he asked.

'No.'

Roberts picked up the phone. 'No . . . no. He won't give it. He needs seventy-two hours . . . What? Son of a bitch, no.' He swore for the next twenty seconds, his eyes so full of blood I thought he was going to beat on the side of my head with the receiver. Then he put his hand to his jaw and held his chin in a grip which must have been equal to pressing a button in the machinery of himself for it served to return his control. 'Wait here,' he said. 'I'll be back in a couple of minutes.' He was not a big man, but he padded out like an overstuffed cat at the end of a chain.

Roberts had left his file on the desk. I took a quick look. He did not have a report of the autopsy, he had notes on the autopsy, and while I did not understand much of the terminology, I could see he had not been telling me the truth: the medical report was qualified – so far as I could understand his notes, the suicide was in doubt, but so was any certainty that Deborah had been dead before the fall. Only traces on the carpet stood out — someone had used red ink to underline.

And there were tear sheets from an article by me which he had taken from a professional journal, the text of a Prize Lecture I had given at the university my first year there, the first year I had been married to Deborah. Now like an old maid's faded flower in a Bible were the faded words of this lecture. Reading them in this room with the radiator hissing irritably at my back, looking at the walls, that dirty weathered color of a bleached cigar, I had a quick grasp of the secret to sanity — it had become the ability to hold the maximum of impossible combinations in one's mind, Roberts' red pins on the precinct map and a paragraph from the middle of the Clark Reed Powell Prize Lecture: *On the Primitive View of Mystery.*

> In contrast to the civilized view which elevates man above the animals, the primitive had an instinctive belief that he was subservient to the primal pact between the beasts of the jungle and the beast of mystery.
>
> To the savage, dread was the natural result of any invasion of the supernatural: if man wished to steal the secrets of the gods, it was only to be supposed that the gods would defend themselves and destroy whichever man came too close. By this logic, civilization is the successful if imperfect theft of some cluster of these secrets, and the price we have paid is to accelerate our private sense of some enormous if not quite definable disaster which awaits us.

It was a lecture which proved agreeable and had been reprinted in a monthly magazine — revised, enlarged, and in two parts — there had been I suppose something pleasantly meretricious in the sonority of the style. Now, reading it back to myself, it revolved into my ear with the force of a real idea and I had a sudden anxiety for Roberts to be back as if some determination to resist him might be lost if I remained alone too long in the stale air of this room. So, forcing myself to concentrate on the file, I saw it was almost by chance this lecture had been deposited here, for the portfolio held a scattering of a few of the things I had written, plus gossip columns in which my name appeared, even a criticism or two of the television show, a loose collection which Roberts must have looked over with half an eye. Then I could hear his step in the hall, and got back to my seat.

He came in whistling. It was the cool controlled whistling of a man who has a boil on his neck. 'Well, Rojack,' he said, showing his upper teeth in a smile, 'you're free of suspicion. Let's go out and have a beer.' His eyes were a void. 'I knew,' he said, 'I knew there was something wrong with this one from the beginning.'

'What are you telling me?'

'The official medical report came in. Suicide. Yes.' He nodded. 'You have a big brother somewhere.'

I felt as if I had to begin asking questions, or I would give myself away. 'Is that why you wanted my confession in such a hurry?' I asked.

'I could just as soon have waited. It was Leznicki's idea to put the screws to you.' With each breath Roberts was becoming more genial. It was as if we'd been wrestlers and Roberts had proceeded on the assumption it was his night to win. Then the referee had whispered in his ear – his turn to lose. So he bulled around the ring. Now we were back in the dressing room exchanging anecdotes, trading apologies.

'But you got word last night to let me go?'

'Let's say we took a hint. I was for letting you go anyway – I figured you'd be interesting to watch.'

'And you were expecting pressure today?'

'I'd give a lot, Rojack, to know how much you really know.'

'I don't know very much.'

'Dad, you drive me to drink.'

'Did you think if you got a confession from me you could stand up to the pressure?'

He had never looked more like a cop. The dedication of his short straight nose hung above the confirmed grin of corruption at the corner of his mouth. Rectitude, cynicism, and greed threw off separate glints from his eyes. 'Well, we didn't know,' he said. 'Maybe we could take the pressure, maybe we would have had to swap you off for something else. But a confession would have been interesting.' He gave the leathery smile of a baseball manager who has lost a rookie he might have developed or sent back to the minors on a trade. 'Don't worry about police politics,' he said. 'We could talk about it all night and you wouldn't know any more.'

'I'd like to listen.'

'What do you want, a winning ticket on a lottery? Settle for a beer.'

I smiled. 'I'm on the wagon for another hour.' I stood up. 'It's been a pleasure knowing you, Roberts.'

He grinned again, 'If you weren't such a big man, I'd say, "Keep your nose clean." '

'I'm not a big man.'

He looked worried, as if it might be a mistake to ask the next question. 'Listen,' he said finally when I was at the door, 'if you answer something for me, I think I could offer you something in return.'

'Let's hear your question.'

'Rojack, are you CIA?'

'I can't tell you something like that.'

'All right, take this for nothing. Maybe you know it already. We had Eddie Ganucci on a technicality. We weren't sure we could hold him more than a couple of hours in any case. But there was a very funny pressure to let him go. And my feeling is it came from the same place yours did.'

'Do you know for certain?'

'I don't. Pressure never has a name on it.'

'You're not stupid, are you, Roberts?'

'I was a good FBI man once upon a time.' He rapped me on the back. 'Keep your end up.'

It had turned cold outside. I passed a bar and then another bar. I had no idea whether to celebrate or run for cover. At a corner telephone booth I stopped and made a call to my answer service. They had reached Mr Kelly's secretary and now had a message: Mr Kelly would see me at midnight.

'Call back, Gloria, and tell them I'll try to be there,' I said.

'I don't know if we're supposed to give this service as a regular thing, Mr Rojack.'

'Gloria, just for today,' I asked.

In the cab, on the way downtown, it all came over me, wave after wave, dangerous waves as though pilings were riding through the water, and smashing the shore. The wind was up. Each time I closed the cab window the air from the heater was foul, a bad exhaust had seeped in. But with the glass rolled down, I could hear the wind too well, and it had the long ripping sound of a voracious wind at sea which tears off the water and snatches at the roots of the grass. There was some break in the heavens tonight: a siren was blowing, an attention was present, I could all but sniff the sour rot of clotting blood in the pits of this wind. And I lay back on my seat and felt something close to nausea because mystery revolved about me now, and I did not know if it was hard precise mystery with a detailed solution, or a mystery fathered by the collision of larger mysteries, something so hopeless to determine as the edge of a cloud, or could it be, was it a mystery even worse, something between the two, some hopeless no-man's-land from which nothing could return but exhaustion? And I had a sudden hatred of mystery, a moment when I wanted to be in a cell, my life burned down to the bare lines of a legal defense. I did not want to see Barney Oswald Kelly later tonight, and yet I knew I must for that was part of the contract I had made on the morning air. I would not be permitted to flee the mystery. I was close to prayer then, I was very close, for what was prayer but a beseechment *not* to pursue the mystery, 'God,' I wanted to pray, 'let me love that girl, and become a father, and try to be a good man, and do some decent work. Yes, God,' I was close to begging, 'do not make me go back and back again to the charnel house of the moon.' But like a soldier on six-hour leave to a canteen, I knew I would have to return. I had not escaped a whiff of the trenches, I could hear Deborah in rut, burning rubber and a wild boar, some voice almost slipped into me on the wind, that high wind – from whose summit did it derive? – and then the cab pulled up at Cherry's street, and with a beating heart, I walked up all those sordid defeat-infested stairs, and knocked on her door, and knew in the instant I heard no sound of stirring that stronger than my fear was the other fear she might not be there. Then I heard her move, the door opened, we embraced.

'Oh, honey,' she said, 'Something is bad tonight.'

We embraced again, and I led her to the bed. We sat down beside each other and touched fingertips. That made me feel good for the first time since I went out the door this afternoon. Relief came over me like a winner's victorious sleep.

'Do you want a drink?' she asked.

'In a while.'

'I love you,' Cherry said.

'Yes. I love you.'

She had rested. The exhaustion was out of her face and she looked like a seventeen year old.

'Were you ever a cheer leader?' I asked.

'I think I was kind of funny-looking in high school.'

'Even by your senior year?'

'No, I was getting there then. The captain of the football team spent a whole year trying to take my dear name away from me.'

'But you managed to keep it?'

'I didn't.'

Suddenly we laughed at each other. 'How come no one ever ate you alive?' I said.

'Oh, they tried, mister, they sure did try.' And she gave me a kiss like the kiss last night in the bar, but the iron was out of it, some of the iron, and I smelled the honeysuckle which had lived on the air one hot June night long ago in the back seat of a car. 'Let's go,' I said, 'let's go back to this morning.'

We did. Somewhere in the middle, born out of fatigue and tension and the exhaustion of every lie I had told today, like a gift I did not deserve, that new life began again in me, sweet and perilous and so hard to follow, and I went up with it and leaped and flew over, vaulting down the fall to those washed-out roses washed by the tears of the sea, they washed out to me as my life went in, and I met one cornucopia of flesh and sorrow, scalding sorrow, those wings were in the room, clear and delicate as a noble intent, that sweet presence spoke of the meaning of love for those who had betrayed it, yes I understood the meaning and said, for I knew it now, 'I think we have to be good,' by which I meant we would have to be brave.

'I know,' she said. Then we were silent for a while. 'I know,' she said again.

'You sure?' I asked. I put my foot on to hers, 'you really sure?'

'Yes, I'm sure.'

'Don't you know what Broadway says?'

'What does Broadway say?'

'Why, "Shit, señorita," says Broadway.'

'Oh, Lordy. Oh, Lordy! You're such fucking sugar,' she said, and bent over and kissed my toe.

6

A Vision in the Desert

I lay there, content to touch the tip of a finger to the tip of a breast, and had that knowledge which falls like rain, for now I understood that love was not a gift but a vow. Only the brave could live with it for more than a little while. So then I thought of Deborah and those nights years ago when I lay beside her with a love somewhat different, but I had had a hint of this before, had it with Deborah, had it with others, girls I had known for a night and never knew again – the trains were going in opposite directions. Sometimes with women I had seen for many a month I might have found it on one particular night at the bottom of a barrel of booze. It had always been the same, love was love, one could find it with anyone, one could find it anywhere. It was just that you could never keep it. Not unless you were ready to die for it, dear friend.

Well, I went back to that embrace with Cherry. We were done, and yet we were not done, for we had a moment when we touched and met the way a bird might light on an evening sea, and we floated off with the tide, deep in each other as the long wash of memory late at night. I could not keep from holding her – had flesh ever promised to forgive me so? I put my hand on her waist: some offer rose from her breast and took my hand. I sat up in bed, bent forward to touch her foot. It was there for me to examine now, those toes I dislike so much, the short broad shape of the instep, the calluses, the sole. Her foot gave promise of traveling in its own direction, and yet I embraced it. I gripped her foot as if to say, 'You're coming with me.' That foot had a mind to hear my thought, it warmed my hand like a small dog with a stout heart. Then I looked up from those toes, across all the shades of her body up to the subtle hints of lavender and silver in the shadows of her face and smiled happily and said, 'Do you think we're allowed a drink?'

She brought out the bottle, and we drank slowly, I do not suppose I had taken my liquor sip by sip since I could remember. It seemed enough to drop some ice into a tumbler, pour a quarter-inch of alcohol down a cube and watch the current as the whiskey gave up its gold to the water. Indeed, the objects in the room – the worn-out movie director's chair, the brass handle at the top of the faucet on the kitchen sink, the chewed tassels of the lampshade – seemed to stand about us like sentinels possessing some primitive property of radio, as if they would be the first to inform us of a visitor on the stair. I was telling her about my television show – it was now somehow a part of what we talked about when we met on the street, and so I went on about it, but in fact it was agreeable to hold off the moment when we came to talk about ourselves; therefore it was almost agreeable to think about the show. We had begun by being an avant-garde circus: interviews with bearded studs who had been smoking marijuana for twenty-two years, confessions by ex-criminals about homosexuality in the prisons, a lecture by myself on 'Picasso and His Pistol' (a homemade study of Picasso as Master of Ceremonies to the cannibalistic urge of modern Europe – the most difficult lecture in the history of television), a chat with a call girl, with the leader of a motorcycle gang, with the leader of a gang in Harlem, with a housewife who lost one hundred and eighty pounds in a year, with an unfrocked priest, with a failed suicide (a girl, three scars on the wrist). I had had an idea in the beginning, I assured her, I wanted to clear a path through psychoanalysis and social welfare.

'You're just bright,' she said. And took a nip of skin from my ear in a bite so neat and small a toothpick could have pricked me. 'Remember,' she said, putting a pearl of saliva on my ear for balm, 'that review Mac N. Ryan wrote: "This is a carnival of bad taste which violates the canons of dignity television has achieved."' She laughed at the sounds. 'You know I went out on a date with Mac N. Ryan once.'

'He violate any canons?'

'Oh, he hated to leave me unloved, but did I have a disease? So I said to him, "Well, you know, honey, syphilis is on the up and up." That did his little thing in. I had to put him in a cab.'

I laughed. Something dull in the bruise was gone. Poor Mac N. Ryan. With his honorable exception, the television critics had ignored the show. We were always losing sponsors and finding worse ones, the FCC was daily on the phone, the producer (you have met him) was on tranquilizers, and I was just not good enough. The guests became professional men, officials, professors, purveyors, we discussed books and current events – we dwindled into popularity.

I told her a little of all that, and made some attempt to sketch the past (truly, I wanted her to know a little about me), I told her about my academic career, I was proud of that for once done with politics, I had gone to graduate school in the Midwest and in five years had picked up a doctorate, an assistant professorship, an associate professorship. And two years later, back in New York, I had made full professor (the Clark Reed Powell Lecture). It came out of course in no formal way, story here, anecdote there, our mood drifted with the indolence of boats on a harbor swell, lifting down the spine of each small wave.

'Let's eat,' she said at last, and got out of bed to cook

us two small steaks, a bit of spaghetti, scrambled eggs. We ate – I fell on the food, I had lost all sense of how hungry I was – and when we were done, over the coffee and the new cigarettes, it seemed her turn to speak. Sitting at the table, her wheat-colored wrapper gathered about her (while I was offered a robe which must once have belonged to Shago Martin), I listened to Cherry talk about herself. She had been raised by her half-brother and half-sister. I remembered that. Her half-brother was eighteen the year her parents were killed in the automobile accident, her big sister was sixteen, she was four, her little sister was a year. Her older brother was admired by the neighbors because he worked at two jobs. He worked hard, he kept the family together.

'There was just one tiny flaw,' said Cherry. 'Brother was sticking it into sister every night.' She shook her head. 'I used to hear my mother and father talking to me on the way from school. "Tell big brother to stop his silliness," they would say. And when I got to be eight and ten, I came to know that people in town were on to what was going on. But it didn't seem to hurt our hard-ass little respectability. I used to play in the other girls' backyards and once in a while they'd come to mine. And my brother was on the way to being a reasonable success in town. It wasn't that he liked little sis and me. He sort of disliked us. But he knew what it could do to impress a town with six hundred churchgoers if he accepted his burden at eighteen. I mean he thought that way. Even before he was eighteen, he had big jaws, and a cigar stuck in them.'

'What does he do now?'

'Sheriff. Last I heard he was running for State Legislature. I was tempted to send him a photograph of Shago and me.' She looked away for a moment as if Shago had become real to her again. 'Well,' Cherry said, '*anyway*, we pretended we had kept our family secret, and were as nice as anybody – I mean we all came from good Southern families, all six hundred of us. In a town that size, all you need to be good family is to have a rich great-uncle you've never seen and be rich enough yourself to bring the outhouse into the house, but' — she took a sip of her coffee — 'big brother went off and got married, and that left big sis to take care. And she went potty. She used to be out each night with a different man — she was doing it for quarters and dimes — which left little sis and me disreputable. They still admired my brother — I guess all that incest taught him how to move politically — but my sisters and me were to be ostracized. I used to go to school by myself, come home by myself. Finally we had to leave town with big sis.' They went to live in Georgia, they went to live in northern Florida, the older sister got married, Cherry went through high school living in the home of a brother-in-law who was made progressively more nervous by her presence. Finally she had to leave her sister. She finished high school sleeping in a rooming house, working as a waitress. 'And of course,' said Cherry, 'I hung around the juke spots and cheap-hole nightclubs cause I had a bouncy little back-country voice and wanted to be a singer. That was the year I was so nice on that football star, but he decided to go away to college. I didn't answer his letter. I used to feel about the way you feel in a dream once you start to wake up. I guess incest brings back the dead.' She said this with such a finality of tone, such a dry old lady certain of her tonics and recipes, that I had no notion if it were her own idea, or a piece of folklore the village idiot could talk over with the town's first banker.

'Well, next I had a short stretch of young girl's bliss — a Navy flier. We were going to get married. Only it turned out he was married already. Crash. Then I met Daddy Warbucks,' she said, and stopped. 'Sure I should go on?'

'Yes.' I wanted to know more.

'Well, I lived with a rich man for a time. A rich older man. That's the quick of it. He picked me out in a nightclub

– he was a businessman passing through – and, well, there was something between us,' said Cherry. 'He took me to the next town.'

'Yes.'

'I stayed for several years. He was considerably older than me, but . . .'

'But what?'

'It was kind of carnal, beloved.'

We had a profit to spend. It was what we had gained from that last hour – so she would tell me the truth. If finally I could not bear to hear it, then, said her face, we had not deserved the profit.

'Yes,' I said. 'Carnal.'

'The trouble is,' said Cherry, 'I hardly saw him. He would install me in some pleasant apartment in some city or other, and then I might not see him for a week. I would get the impression he had been across the country back and forth three times.'

'Didn't you mind being alone?'

'No, I'd find the best singing coach around. And I did a lot of reading. I'd just wait for Daddy Warbucks to come back. It was a delight to talk to him. So long as I thought he was just a rich intelligent man with a family somewhere, it was all right. But one day I saw his picture in a news magazine, and realized he had not even told me his real name. I was ready to leave him then. But he convinced me to come with him to Vegas. He said if I were willing to live there, we could be together in public. So then I dug. Because in Vegas I naturally came to meet a few of his friends, and – click – they were the big dogs of the Mafia.'

'He was in the Mob?'

'He was wealthy. A very respectable man. He liked to gamble. Sometimes I would believe we were in town just for that. Sometimes I would come to the conclusion he might own some of Las Vegas. Because now when he would leave me for a week or often enough a month – my telephone didn't ring unless the call was from him. And that did not figure if he was simply a rich man who'd left his young lady behind. So I had to think I was either too unattractive to draw anybody near me, or Daddy was some special big dog. But very special. He was obviously not the type to be in the Mob, not in any way directly. You want some more coffee?'

'I'm fine.'

'I guess I am too.' She had been stopping at odd times in her account. There had been several pauses when she told me about her brother, and now there was one again.

'Of course, there's always been an argument,' Cherry went on, 'about "The Big Guy." Does he exist or doesn't he? You could have two big-time hoods discussing this, brother peas in the pod right down to the same number of carats in the diamond on their tiepin, but one would say, "The Big Guy don't exist, forget it," while the other would just about cross himself.'

'What did you decide?'

'I don't know. Sometimes I used to think Daddy Warbucks could be The Big Guy, nothing less. Then I would decide that was too farfetched.'

'What would you say today?'

'I think he wasn't Mob at all. But the Mob did very special jobs for him. Very large intricate jobs. Some of it was overseas. I had that impression.'

Another of her pauses came here. 'And then,' she said finally, 'I wasn't sure I wanted to know too much. Because there came a time when I wanted to get free of this man, and I didn't know how to do it. He wasn't the kind who would threaten or any of that discord, but I knew I'd get mangled on the way out, and the question was how badly.' She came to a full stop. 'Well, we parted as friends. We had a quiet little talk, and he passed me on to an acquaintance – with my consent. I figured this was the way to pay my dues. So I got the friend – the king of narcotics in L.A. I found out two days later. The friend had secret inclinations which could blast you to the moon. And he did threaten to kill me when I told him it wouldn't go. I got my guts together for that one. I finally stood up to somebody, even to even. "Better not," I told the gentleman, "or I'll make it a point to haunt you." These Mafiosos are superstitious as a witch. I had said the right thing. Only I didn't know it then. I couldn't sleep for the next two months waiting for the door to open. But at least I had the sense to stay where I was in town. One of the smartest men I knew once said, "Flee from a knife, but charge a gun," and this narcotics gent was strictly a pistol. If I'd tried to run to another city, I'd have gotten it in the back — which is a poor position from which to go out, for it makes the haunting less impressive.'

'What a pro you are.'

'Better believe it.'

'No, I'm impressed.'

'I was just a dry leaf waiting to fall off the tree. But I had good luck. So I was able to get myself together. Then I began to break in with singing dates in Vegas — because of my previous associations I had cartel — and I had a couple of nice years. I only went with men I liked, and there were a few I spent some time with, a couple of Italians with class whom I just did manage to find. Hoods, but I liked them. Italians are all so treacherous I used to feel virtuous next to them.' Pause. 'But then I knew it was time to get to New York.'

'Why?'

'Some day I'll tell you.'

'Tell me now.'

She pursed her mouth as though adding a bill. 'I'd picked up power in Vegas I didn't deserve. I didn't know what to do with it. Nobody in the Mob knows how much anybody else knows. In fact nobody knows how much he knows himself. So considering the men I traveled with, other people I hardly knew were ready to do favors. They thought I was more important than I was, and that helped to make me just a bit important. It's not exactly cool to brag on this, but I had the power to get people killed. It also occurred to me I could get killed myself, and this time I wouldn't know what for or who. It didn't put itself together. I may have been greedy, but I was full of scarcity – know what I mean? I grew up in a stingy town. When the food got too rich, I felt just like a skinny little Southern girl all over again.'

She sighed. When she started out, she explained, she always felt as if she had a small angel accompanying her. All orphans did – that was part of the economy of nature. And for companion, the angel had a whore, because the two got along with each other. 'I mean,' said Cherry, 'the tart would have herself a fling and the angel would say, "That's okay, honey, you're entitled to a bit of fun after all that misery."'

But in Vegas, the angel became an asset, it kept drawing people in. 'I've always been independent,' Cherry said, 'or at least I like to think so. I believe there's a side of me doesn't want anything from anybody, and maybe that's what those hoodlums liked. But then the other side of my character was swelling up like a frog – I was becoming as bad and evil as a colored madam. I was ready to make that angel hustle.' She looked wistful as she said this. 'And then, too, I had to keep an eye on my killer. There *was* a crazy killer right inside.'

'For certain?'

'Honest-to-God killer.'

'Maybe you borrowed him from your friends.'

'I'll never know,' she said. 'The ugly fact, if I was to trace it out, is that one or two men in Vegas are probably dead because of me. They were at the other end of a string, but I was vindictive enough about them to have been the one who pulled the string. I started thinking of that small-town hatred I had always considered beneath me, that envy and spite, and it was now a part of me. I came to the conclusion I'd flip out so far I'd not come back if I stayed in Vegas too long. So I decided it was the year for New York.'

'Did the angel bring you to Shago Martin?'

'No,' she said, and then, 'Yes,' she said. It was obvious we were thinking of her sister.

'Well, look how nice you are now,' I said.

'I'm a spirit now,' she said, and gave a tough sensuous grin full of her flesh.

'I should have had you on my program.'

'I could have set it straight. I would have told America some people got souls, and some are spirits.'

'I'm sure.'

'People with souls are the ones who make the world move,' she said in her Southern voice, the accent became as thin and precise as any little old Southern Baptist lady, 'and if they fail, but honorably, why then, God, as a mercy, or as a compromise, may it be, takes their soul away and makes them a spirit. That's a sad thing to be because you can't live with other spirits – too sad. So you have to look for somebody with soul even if they're mean and awful.'

'Like Eddie Ganucci?'

'He's awful. He's a sick old man who never had any class.'

'But the ones who have class are afraid of him?'

'Yes.' She nodded several times. 'Maybe that's another reason I left. It's not good to be around men who stand up most of the time, but know there's one thing they never stand up to.' She gave a radiant smile. 'I was sure you were going to back off from Romeo last night.'

'I was so far gone I didn't care if he beat me to death.'

'You were better than that.'

'Did Shago teach you how to sing?' I asked.

'He taught me a little bit. But I'm a lousy singer, I fear.'

That ended conversation about Shago. She stretched her arms and yawned prettily. I was very relaxed. Somehow I had been prepared for something worse in her story. So the mood was settling in again. Soon we'd be ready to go back to bed.

'Steve?' asked Cherry.

'Yes?'

'Did you kill your wife?'

'Yes.'

'Yes,' she said.

'You're a cunning little cutie.'

'No, baby, I knew you did it. Oh God.'

'How did you know?' I asked.

'I saw a man once just after he came back from a killing. You looked like he did.'

'How did he look?'

'Like he'd been painted with a touch of magic.' Her face crumpled. 'I was hoping I was wrong,' she said, 'but I knew I wasn't. Oh, I hope it's not too late for us.'

'Yes.'

'I'm afraid.'

'I am a little myself.'

'Do you have to be somewhere tonight?' she asked.

I nodded.

'Who is it you're going to see?'

'Deborah's father.'

'Barney Oswald Kelly?'

'You know his name?'

'I read the papers today.'

But I could feel her receding from me. There had been something wrong with what she said.

'You've heard of him before this?'

A look came into her face. We had the longest pause. It went on so long I could hear a ringing in the air.

'Stephen,' she said, 'I used to know Kelly.'

'You did?'

'He was the man who took me to Vegas.'

I had a repetition of that vision in Ruta's bed, of that city in the desert with its lights burning in the dawn.

'I don't want to talk any more about it,' she said. And as if revelation had stripped her naked, the wheat-colored wrapper came slowly apart, it opened with a grave movement.

'How the hell could you?' I broke out.

'He's an attractive man.'

'He's odious.'

'No, he's not.'

And he wasn't. In fact, he wasn't. It was different than that. I felt as if Kelly and I were running in the same blood. And that sensation of not belonging to myself, of being owned at my center by Deborah – that emotion which had come on me not five minutes before I killed her – now came back. I felt murder. It frightened me. The possibility that what I felt, when we made love, was a sensation which belonged to me alone, left me murderous. For how did one distinguish love from the art of the Devil?

But then like a child, I said to myself, 'The Devil has no wings.' Those roses which washed from the sea, that angel which went by the room . . . 'Do you think we made a child this morning?'

'Yes.'

There was no quiver in the air. If she were lying I was blind to the point of death, or she was a perfect invention of evil. Moments went by. A gentleness came back to me. 'Is it a boy or a girl?'

'I'll tell you one thing, mister,' she said, 'it's a boy *or* a girl.'

But there were operations we must get through. I had a lover's practical savagery. 'Let's go into all of it,' I said.

'We did.'

'There's more.'

I saw her temper rising, a flash of that sun-tanned sensual

pride with which she had sung her set last night. But something humble took her over. 'All right,' she said.

'You ever pregnant before?'

'Yes.'

'Kelly?'

'Yes.'

'What happened to the child?'

'I didn't have it.'

'Any other time?'

She was silent.

'Shago Martin?'

'Yes.'

'Afraid to have it?'

'Shago was afraid to have it.'

'How long ago?'

'Three months.' She nodded. 'Three months ago. And last week I broke up with him.'

Once, in a rainstorm, I witnessed the creation of a rivulet. The water had come down, the stream had begun in a hollow of earth the size of a leaf. Then it filled and began to flow. The rivulet rolled down the hill between some stalks of grass and weed, it moved in spurts, down the fall of a ledge, down to a brook. It did not know it was not a river. That was how the tears went down Cherry's face. They began in some tight knurled pit of grief, some bitter hollow, rose to her eyes, flowed down her face, dripped to her open breast, fell to her thigh, and collected in the grove – a teaspoon full of ten years' sorrow. 'You see,' she said, and now she began to weep, 'I thought I could never have a child. The doctor Kelly sent me to hinted something was wrong, and I never tried to find out. I just never got pregnant all those years. And then with Shago I did. He turned on me. He said I was a white devil – after all the time we spent together.'

'And you didn't want to have it by yourself?'

'I didn't have the guts. You see, I *had* cheated on him.'

'With Tony?'

'Yes.'

'Why?'

'Habit, I guess.'

'Habit, hell. Why with Tony? What does he have?'

She shook her head. She seemed almost in pain 'There's something sweet in Tony, believe it.'

'How can I?'

'I was aching so. Shago can be evil.'

That did it. She put her head on the table, and gave herself up to grief. I stroked her hair. It had been fine hair once, but hairdresser's tint had roughened the silk. As she wept I heard an echo from the little silence of each pause she had made as she talked. 'Lordy, Lordy,' she said at last, brought her head up and tried to smile. She had that look of naked relaxation which is shared by sex, grief, and the end of huge physical exertion. 'Give me a cigarette,' she said.

I lit it for her.

'How about me?' I asked. I was not far from a child with my desire for an answer. 'Do I manage to kiss the bruise? Is that what my sweet rep is?'

'Don't talk too much.'

'I want to know.'

'Something happened with you,' she said.

'What happened?'

She shook her head. 'Why do you insist? It's bad luck to go on. But you insist. So, listen, Stephen, you can have it, it happened with you. I had an orgasm with you. I was never able to before. Now, pick up on that.' But there was a delicate hint of gloom to her remark, as if it had happened with the wrong man at the wrong time.

'What do you mean, never?' I asked — the need was to make her repeat it.

'Never before. Every other way, yes. But never, Stephen, when a man was within me, when a man was right inside of me.'

'All those years?'

'Never.'

'Christ almighty.'

'I swear.'

'Can I believe you?'

'Yes, you can. Because I always had the feeling once it happened I would soon be dead. I know that's special and doubtless very crazy of me, but that's been my little fear.'

'And now you don't have it?'

'I don't know if I have it, or lost it, or what. All I know is I'm happy. Now, hush, stop trying to spoil it.'

There was a sharp little rap on the door. The sentinels had not warned us after all. The rap beat out a tricky little rhythm, as weighted inside as a drummer's tattoo on the rim of his snare. Cherry looked across the table at me with a face from which all expression was gone. 'That's Shago,' she said.

A key turned in one of the tumblers, then the other. The door came open. An elegant Negro with a skin dark as midnight was standing there. He looked at the robe I was wearing.

'All right,' he said to me, 'get dressed. Get your white ass out of here.'

7

A Votive is Prepared

I had seen Shago Martin in the final reel of a movie about some jazz musicians, and his photograph on slip jackets for his records – a handsome face, thin and arrogant, a mask. I had even gone on caravan once with Deborah to the Latin Quarter or the Copacabana, a rare excursion for the lady since there was nothing she found more unsettling than a large nightclub, but Martin was singing that evening and Deborah and her friends had come to watch. 'He's the most attractive man in America,' she told me when he went on.

'What do you mean, "most attractive"?' I asked. I was doing my best to be a young Harvard banker in from Boston for the night.

'Shago,' Deborah said, 'comes from one of the worst gangs in Harlem. I think you see it in his walk. There's something about him independent, something very fine.'

'He sounds loud enough to me.'

'Well,' said Deborah, 'he may be loud at times, but there are people who can hear what he is saying.'

There were few matters in which Deborah was bloody; music was one of them – she did not know bugger from beans – I had decided long ago that Shago was the most talented singer in America. Whereas Deborah and her friends had come to him lately. They had always respected him, too many experts said he was good, but they had never respected him thus famously; now the roulette of fashion came up double-zero: Shago was in. They were enchanted that he was oblivious to fashion; or at least oblivious to the shift in taste which made him fashionable this season in New York. He was singing only at the Copa and Latin Quarter these days – any other season this would have disqualified him forever – but now since it proved impossible to invite or attract him to the parties which made up the inner schedule of the season each week, everyone's desire for such an evening took on the proportions of a frontier war. Deborah and I were present that night because Deborah had stalked him (by telephone) into the promise to give an interview after his eleven o'clock set: she was going to hog him to a contract to sing at a charity ball coming up in four weeks and three days. But Shago was not in his dressing room when the set was over; he had left a note with his valet: *Sorry, lady, but I can't go that milk and charity shoot.* 'Oh, dear,' said Deborah, 'the poor man must be trying to spell shit.' She was, however, livid. The world was now more defined. In return for this raid on good feelings, Deborah got Shago good. I never knew how many phone calls it took, nor how many looks were dropped on how many marble floors: 'Do you really like the man?' but in four weeks and three days, by the night of the charity ball, no hostess I knew was keening for Shago. That was that. There was a base to Deborah's humor which smelled of old brass.

I used thereafter to keep his records, and I would play them. Actually, I did not enjoy him altogether. His talent was too extreme. He was not often evocative of the smell of smoke in a fog or the mood which is near a young girl when she comes into a room, he did not suggest that the nicest affair of the year was about to start, he did not make me think, as other singers often did, of landscapes in Jamaica, of mangoes, honey, and a breast beneath a moon, of tropical love and candy which went from dark to dawn, no, Shago gave you that, he gave you some of that, but there were snakes in his tropical garden, and a wild pig was off in the wilderness with a rip in its flank from the teeth of a puma, he gave you a world of odd wild cries, and imprisoned it to something complex in his style, some irony, some sense of control, some sense of the way everything is brought back at last under control. And he had a beat which went right through your ear into your body, it was cruel, it was perfect, it gave promise of teaching a paralytic to walk: he was always announced at places like the Copa as 'The Big Beat in Show Biz,' and the worst was that some publicity man was right for once, his voice had bounce as hard as a hard rubber ball off a stone floor, listening to him was cousin to the afternoon one played a match with a champion at squash – the ball went by with the nicest economy, picking up speed as it went, taking off as it blew by; so Shago Martin's beat was always harder, faster, or a hesitation slower than the reflex of your ear, but you were glowing when he was done, the ear felt good, you had been dominated by a champion.

The only difficulty was that his talent persisted in shifting. Deborah began to dance with spiritual delight at some of his later records. 'You know, I despise that man,' she would say, 'but his music is improving.' She was right. His voice had developed to the point where you could not always distinguish it from a trumpet or even on virtuoso occasions from a saxophone. Once off on a ride, his song seemed able to take a step between each step of the rapid elegant dance a jazzman's fingers could pick across the keys. But of course he had become too special – no average night-club audience could follow him. He was harsh. Some of his most experimental work sounded at first like a clash of hysterias. It was only later that one discovered his power of choice – he was like a mind racing between separate madnesses, like a car picking its route through the collision of other cars. It was harsh. The last I heard he was even singing at times in the kind of cabaret which closes on the fatal Thursday night when there is not enough in the cash register to pay the police their weekly protection. That was what delighted Deborah. That was what she heard finally in his music: he was no longer in danger of developing into a national figure.

Now, as he stood inside Cherry's door, he was wearing a small black felt hat with a narrow brim, his gray flannel suit had narrow pants, he wore short boots of some new and extraordinary cut (red-wine suede with buttons of mother-of-pearl) and a red velvet waistcoat to match. A shirt of pink silk took light from the vest, even as a crystal glass picks up an echo in the color of the wine, and his tie was narrow, black knit, with a small pin. With his left hand he held a furled umbrella, taut as a sword in its case, and he kept it at an angle to his body, which returned – since his body was tall and slim – some perfect recollection of a lord of Harlem standing at his street corner.

This was a fair sum to notice in the time it took him to open the door, come in, look at Cherry, look at me, see his bathrobe on my back, and tell me to get dressed and out, but I saw it all, my sense of time – like that hesitation before the roller coaster drops – was as long as the first breath of marijuana when the lung gives up its long sigh within, and time goes back to that place where it began, yes, I saw it all, had memories of Shago singing, and Deborah reading the note, I had one very long instant indeed as he looked at me. A wind came off him, a poisonous snake of mood which entered my lungs like marijuana, and time began to slow.

Then a curious happiness came to me from the knowledge Shago was capable of murder, as if death right now would carry me over just that moment I had known in Cherry when something went up and into the fall. So I smiled at him, no more, and pushed a pack of cigarettes in his direction.

'Get out,' he said.

Our eyes met and stayed together. There was an even raw gaze in his which stung like salt on the surface of my eyes. But I felt damnably abstract, as if my reactions had been packed away, were instruments in a case. When I didn't move, Shago turned to Cherry and said, 'He won't run?'

'No.'

'I be damn,' said Shago, 'you got yourself a stud who can stand.'

'Yes.'

'Not like Tony?'

'No.'

'Well, stand! you mother-fucker,' said Shago to me.

When I stood up, Martin opened his fingers. He had been holding a switchblade in his right hand, and it opened from his palm like a snake's tongue. The flick of the blade made no more sound than a stalk of grass being pulled from its root. 'I'll tell you,' said Shago, 'get dressed. I would not like,' he went on, 'to get cut while I was wearing another man's robe.'

'Put away your blade,' I said. My voice spoke out of that calm.

'I put it away, man, after I cut my initials on you. That's S.M. Shit on Mother,' said Shago. He turned his head to Cherry, his eyes a startling golden yellow in his black face. They were nearly a match to hers, and began to laugh. 'Oh Jesus,' he said, 'shee-it, shee-it,' and he held up the blade and flicked it closed. Like a magician. 'She's my honey,' he said to me, 'she my wife.'

'Was your wife,' said Cherry, 'till you were so evil.'

'Well, shit a pickle,' said Shago.

'Yeah,' she said, 'shit a pickle.'

They were like a man and woman balancing on a tight wire. 'Evil,' he cried out, 'evil,' he demanded, 'listen, Sambo,' he said to me, 'you look like a coonass blackass nigger jackaboo to me cause you been put-putting with blondie here, my wife, you see, dig? digaree? Evil! Evil? Why the white girl's evil, you see.' There was a tiny froth at the corner of his immaculate lips, a strain of red in the white of his eyes. 'What you doing with him?' asked Shago of her, 'he's fat.'

'He's not,' cried Cherry, 'he's not.'

'Keep wasting,' said Shago. 'He's a tub of guts.'

'Just go on talking,' I said.

'You say that?' he asked of me.

'Yes, I said that.' My voice was not as good the second time.

'Don't cut me, boy,' said Shago. The blade was out again.

'You're a disgrace,' said Cherry.

'Every nigger's a disgrace. Look at Sambo here. He's a disgrace to the fat white race. What you doing with him? Why he's a professor, he's a professor. He hugged his wife so hard she fell down dead. Ha, ha. Ho, ho. Then he push her out.'

'Close your knife,' said Cherry.

'Shee-it.'

'There's blood on your lip,' said Cherry.

'Not bleeding a bit.' He took his umbrella and flipped it behind him to the door. It made a muffled sound like a woman thrust aside. 'Her womb is full of blood,' he said to me. 'She had a kid and afraid to have it. Afraid to have a kid with a black ass. What about you, uncle, going to give a kid with a white ass, with a white diarrhetic old ass? Kiss my you-know-what.'

'Shut up,' I said.

'Get my knife, shit-face.'

I took a step toward him. I did not know what I was going to do, but it felt right to take that step. Maybe I had a thought to pick up the whiskey bottle, and break it on the table. The feeling of joy came up in me again the way the lyric of a song might remind a man on the edge of insanity that soon he will be insane again and there is a world there more interesting than his own.

Shago retreated a step, the blade held out in his open palm, his wrist dipping to some beat he heard in the mood. Looking at that blade was like standing on the edge of a high cliff, one's stomach sucking out of one, as one's eyes went down the fall. I had a moment when I remembered the German with the bayonet, and my legs were gone, they were all but gone; I felt a voice in me sending instructions to snatch the whiskey bottle and break it, break it now that he was out of reach and so could not slash me with the knife, not without taking a step, but the voice was like a false voice in my nerves, and so I ignored it and took another step forward against all the lack of will in my legs, took the step and left the bottle behind as if I knew it would be useless against a knife. My reflexes were never a match for his. What I felt instead was an emptiness in his mood which I could enter.

Shago took another step back and closed the blade. 'Well, Cherry,' he said in a cool voice, 'this cat's got val*o*r,' giving a Spanish pronunciation to the word. Then he put the knife away. And gave us both a sweet smile. 'Honey,' he said to Cherry, 'laugh! That's the best piece of acting I done yet.'

'Oh, God, Shago, you're evil,' she told him. But she had to shake her head. There was admiration despite herself.

'I'm just sweet and talented, honey.' He smiled sweetly at me. 'Shake hands, Rojack, you're beautiful,' he said, and took my hand.

But I did not like the feel of his palm. There was something limp and leathery to the touch. 'How's that for putting you on?' he asked of me.

'First-rate,' I said.

'Oh, beautiful,' he said. 'Such beautiful dozens. Such éclat.'

I was near to being ill.

'That's how Shago can sicken you,' Cherry said.

'I'm a sick devil, no doubt of that,' he said with charm.

And his voice was beginning to take a few turns. Accents flew in and out of his speech like flying peacocks and bats. 'Haul ass, the black man is on the march,' Shago said to me suddenly, 'and he won't stop until his elementary requirements are met. Ralph Bunche. Right? "Take your hand off my fly," said the Duchess to the Bishop cause she was a Duke in drag. Chuck, chuck, chuck.' He looked at me with eyes which were suddenly wild as if the absence of rest had set them racing like cockroaches under the flare of a light.

'Shago, what are you on?' Cherry asked.

'*Yeah.*'

'Oh, no.'

'Well, that's how it is, sugar. Come and cry with me.'

'You're not. You can't be on again.'

'Now, honey, couldn't you tell? When I came in the door with the street corner bit. Up in Central Park! *Sambo!* I mean I don't go for that sauce, sugar. You know that. I'm too pretty to rumble, and that's a fact. Rojack,' he said in my direction, 'I love you, you're so gruesome. Put some gravy on the bread.' And he began to cackle. 'Why, bless bless, my Cherry, if I got to lose, I got to lose to a square with heart, I mean he's all that heart and no potatoes, just Ivy League ass. Harvard, I presume, Doctor Rojack.'

'You're not on horse,' Cherry said.

'Stone out of my mind, baby.'

'But you're not on horse.'

'About to take the needle. My steps were leading me there.' He tapped his feet in a tricky little riff. 'So I came to see you. You can help me stop.'

She shook her head. She was mute.

'Honey,' he said, 'you're still creaming for me.'

'I'm not. Go away, Shago, go away.' She kept her face averted from both of us.

'It's never over,' said Shago. 'I said to you once: honey, we see each other ten years from now, we still make it.

188

You hear?' he said to me, 'it's never over with her and me. You got nothing but the whiskey and the embers. All those piss-wet embers.'

'You won't know,' I said. But there could be truth in what he said, I thought suddenly.

'Man,' he said, 'let's get cool and enjoy each other. I can live without my Cherry. I've had movie stars. I put them in my scrapbook. That's cool. Let's keep it that way. You ask her how many time I throw away my cool.'

'What are you on?' she repeated.

'Shit and shinola. Listen, baby, take a vacation from all this. I'm cool, now, I'm back in my cool.'

'You just waved a knife.'

'No, I'm back with the living. I swear. Here to entertain. I mean I read the scene. You and me, husband and wife except for the ring – but we *know* each other, we didn't make it. I could cry. But still I got to wish you the best. The best, Rojack, the best, Cherry.'

'Make him leave,' Cherry spoke out, 'please make him leave.'

'No, no, no,' said Shago.

The blade was out again. He held it point up, his head looking down on it like a priest with a candle. 'Throw away the restraints,' he said, 'throw them away.' She got up from the chair where she had been sitting since he entered the room and holding her wheat-colored wrapper about herself with both arms, she walked up to him. 'Put that stick away,' she said.

'No. Tell him about the Freedom Rider bit.' But as if her presence close to him, her proximity to that knife, was vertigo for him, he closed the blade, put it back in his pocket and stepped away from both of us. Some spasm of language began in him.

'Contemplate this,' he said to me, 'I did the Freedom Rider bit. Like I was running for President of the black-ass USA. That's the Dick Gregory bit, not mine, but I did it.

I did it. And I mean I got nothing but elegance to sell, plus a big beat. And that big beat comes from up High, it don't come from me, I'm a lily-white devil in a black ass. I'm just the future, in love with myself, that's the future. I got twenty faces, I talk the tongues, I'm a devil, what's the devil doing on a Freedom Ride? Listen,' he said, building up force as he went, 'I'm cut off from my own lines, I try to speak from my heart and it gets *snatched*. That's Freedom Ride. Why,' he said, with no sense of going off in another direction, 'you seen my act, I remember you, you brought your wife back to me, that battleship with the pearls around her neck, you think I forget, I got elegance, man, and elegance is nothing but memory. I mean I got elegance when I do my act.'

'Yes,' I said.

'And I spit in your wife's face.'

'Metaphorically.'

'Metaphorically. Yes, I did. And I said to myself, "Man, you're spitting in the face of the Devil."'

'I didn't know you thought twice about it.'

'Kiss me, sweets. Didn't know I thought twice about it. Why I knew your wife was society bitch. That's a *bitch*! I knew what she was promising, all that White House jazz, mow my grass, blackball, you're so sexy – think I like to pass that up? But there was your wife asking me to sing at her charity ball for no, for her smile. I said to myself, Why, lady, you wouldn't give half a buck to the poor nigger woman who wipes your mess in the ladies' latrine. A quarter, that's what she'd leave, right?'

'I don't know.'

'Fire when ready, Gridley, we have seen the whites of their eyes.'

I began to laugh. Despite myself. Finally Shago laughed. 'Yeah, man, it's *so* funny. But I was at the big divide. Pick it up. They were ready to pick me up, make me a society singer, I'd had it with that Village shit, I'd had it with that Mob shit, that big-time shit, "What a nice suit you're wearing tonight, Mr Ganucci" – no, I wanted the society shit cause I was right for that, but I took one look at your wife and I gave it up. I'd played it cool all the way, passed up their parties, "No," I'd have my flunky say, "Mr Martin does not attend parties," I was a virgin, and had them eating in the crack, I was old Buddha's ass on the stairs, but it was too much, that wife of yours – she *cooed* to me, "Mr Martin, you know I can make you change your mind," yeah, you bet she could, till I got a good look at her sitting with you in the front, eating me, man, I could feel the marrow oozing from my bones, a *cannibal*. So, I told her what to do. Pus and dandruff to you, Peter the Great – Shago Martin ain't adding his tit to your milk and charity.' He shook his head. 'That was the end of society shit, *yeah*, but I was right for them, I was the cup of tea they'd been brewing. They knew it. Cause I can do the tongues, all that cosmopolitan *dreck*, bit of French, bit of Texas, *soupçon* of Oxford jazz – I promise you,' he interpolated with a perfect London voice, 'that we'll have masses of fun and be happy as a clam, why,' he said, snapping his fingers, 'I can pick up on the German, Chinese, Russian (*Tovarich*, mother-fucker, I can do a piece of each little bit, St Nicholas Avenue *upper* nigger, Jamaican, Japanese, Javanese, high yaller sass – I just call on my adenoids, my fat lips and tonsils, *waaaaah*, I can do a *grande dame*; anything from a gasbag to Tallulah Bankhead, "*Out*, you pederast," it's all shit, man, except for the way I use it cause I let each accent pick its note, every tongue on a private note, when I sing it's a congregation of tongues, that's the spook in my music, that's why they got to buy me big or not at all, I'm not intimate, I'm Elizabethan, a chorus, dig?'

'You're just an old dynamo out on the moon,' said Cherry. Tenderness for him was back in her voice. Acid entered me.

'When I start talking, I hear motors. I'm a devil, see. I used

NORMAN MAILER

to watch your television. You're a white ass. Her and me used
to sit on that sofa and watch your television. "What a sweet
white ass" I would say to her. We would laugh.'

'Now *you're* on a television show,' I said.

'Yeah. Right in the hour where you used to be. Channel
Forty-one. They're so poor they don't pay the camera.
Have some hash.' He took out a cigarette rolled tight as a
toothpick, lit it, offered to pass it to me. I refused. There
was an unfamiliar pressure at the back of my neck, an
accumulation of I did not know what, but it was from the
last half hour, and it warned me to say no. I took a swallow
from my whiskey glass.

'For you, girl.' He held it to her.

'Uh-uh.' She shook her head. 'Uh-uh.'

'You pregs again?' he asked. And at the expression on
her face, he whistled, laughed, made a small demonstration.
'Shee-it,' he cried out, 'you can't tell, you can't tell that
fast. That's a mistake made by many. You don't know,
girl.' But the shaft was in. I saw something in his eyes as
the marijuana took hold, he had not been ready for this.
He had the expression of a big fish just speared – the flank
of the eyeball showed horror; something in the past had
just been maimed forever. He was suffering not from the
possibility that she was pregnant but that she had had an
experience with me which made her believe she was, and
he knew all about that.

'Listen, baby, you don't leave me,' he said. 'I'll cut out
your heart. You got nothing but spade in you, and I'm left
with that Southern shit. I'm a captive of white shit now,'
he said looking at me, his eyes blank as a prison wall. 'I
bathe in the flesh, you ass,' he said again, 'I keep it for
myself, all that white stinkeroo, all of it, but she ain't
white, no she ain't, not my girl, she got my black in her.
Yessirree, boss, thanks for that thin dime. Listen, man, I
made her knock the kid cause it was nigger, you see, black
as me, and I'm a white man now.'

'You black-ass ego,' she said, 'You're not white, you're just losing your black. That's why you still got your spade in you and I got my white in me. Because I don't look back. When something's done, it's done. It's *over*.' Some whiff of marijuana must have entered her nose for she talked with a strong male voice, some small-town Southern mill boss or politician – her brother, I realized then. 'Do you think?' she cried out, 'we built white shit and progress by saying "Forgive you one more time." Well, we didn't, you ass, we didn't. It's done, Shago. Out of here.'

'Man,' he said to her, 'take your devils and banish them down to us. We're the mirror of your ass.'

'Come on, baby,' said Cherry, 'don't lose all your cool.' Her face flushed, her eyes bright, she looked eighteen, tough dittybop beautiful, eighteen. They stood glaring at one another.

'Cool! Baby, I got cool this professor of yours and you couldn't locate in twenty years. Listen, you,' he said to me, 'I should have brought my army down here. We could have put toothpicks under your nails. I'm a *prince* in my territory, *dig*? But I came alone. Cause I know this bitch, I know this Mafia bitch, she's made it with hoodlums, black men, some of the class, now she picks you, Professor, looking to square out, she's looking for something luke and tepid to keep her toes warm. You kissing them yet, you jackass?' And with that he walked over to me, put his fingers on my chest, gave a disdainful push, 'Up your ass, Mother Fuck,' and turned around, leaving the scent of marijuana on my clothes. The pressure back of my neck let go of itself and I was a brain full of blood, the light went red, it was red. I took him from behind, my arms around his waist, hefted him in the air, and slammed him to the floor so hard his legs went, and we ended with Shago in a sitting position, and me behind him on my knees, my arms choking the air from his chest as I lifted him up and smashed him down and lifted him up and smashed him down again. 'Let me go, I'll kill you, bugger,' he cried out, and there was a moment when I could have done that, I had the choice to let him go, let him stand up, we would fight, but I had a fear of what I heard in his voice – it was like that wail from the end of the earth you hear in a baby's voice. My rage took over. I lifted him up and stomped him down I don't know how many times, ten times, fifteen, it could have been twenty, I was out of control, violence seemed to shake itself free from him each time I smashed him back to the floor and shake itself into me, I kept beating the base of his spine on the floor, the shock going up to his head, I had never had an idea I was this strong, exhilaration in the fact of the strength itself, and then he went limp and I let go, stepped back, he fell back, the back of his head struck the floor with the blunt dud of an apple dropping from a tree.

Shago looked at me from the ground and said, 'Up your ass.'

I almost kicked in his head. Close as that. Instead I picked him up, opened the door, manhandled him to the hall. There he put up resistance, and when I got a whiff of his odor which had something of defeat in it, and a smell of full nearness as if we'd been in bed for an hour – well, it was too close: I threw him down the stairs. Some hard-lodged boulder of fear I had always felt with Negroes was in the bumping, elbow-busting and crash of sound as he went barreling down, my terror going with him in the long deliberate equivalent of the event which takes place in an automobile just before a collision – and into the smash itself. The banister quivered as he hit, he looked up at me from the bottom, his face bleeding from cuts, welts springing out, his head near to misshapen like the Negro I saw in the precinct, and said, 'You shit-ass,' and started trying to climb the stairs on his hands and knees which released still another core of rage in me as if it were doubly intolerable that his will would not break – I knew this was how children came to kill little cats – and I met him on the fourth stair from the bottom and ran into one weak punch he threw which caught me a glint of pain on the chin (and was bleeding later from the mark of his ring) and then rushed him across the landing and down another flight of stairs, back another landing, down another flight of stairs, the eyes of the Puerto Ricans on us from the crack of every door, me holding him with two grips on his gray conservative suit as if he were a bag of potatoes I could bump along, and when on the last flight of stairs he tried to bite me, I threw him down the run again, and waited while he lay still.

'You had it?' I called down, like some whiskey-flushed Episcopalian minister of doom.

'Shit on your mother,' he said, getting to his hands and knees.

'Shago, I'm going to kill you,' I said.

'No, man. You kill women,' he said. It was a speech, but he said it so slowly that my breath flowed back and forth five, six, eight, ten times. 'Why, shit,' said Shago, 'you just killed the little woman in me.' Then he made an attempt to climb the stairs, but his leg buckled, he sat down on the floor, he vomited from the pain. I stood where I was, waiting for him to finish. 'All right,' he said at last, 'I'm going.'

'Shago, can I get you a cab?'

He laughed like a fiend. 'Well, buddy, I fear that's your problem.'

'All right,' I said.

'Crazy.'

'Good night, Shago.'

'Say, dad,' he said, 'I'd rather they eat me outside than that you get me a cab.'

'Okay.'

Now he smiled. 'Rojack?'

'Yes.'

'Tell you something, man. I don't hate. Never. That's it.'

'That's it.'

'Tell Cherry, her and you, I wish you luck.'

'You do?'

'I swear. Yes, I swear. Luck, man.'

'Thank you, Shago.'

'Sayonara.' He got up from the floor and put together a series of moves to get through the door to the street, progressing like a fly without wings and three legs torn off.

I could hear a child crying. Through the crack of the door, her mother glared at me. But I came up the stairs to a titter of appreciation from the Puerto Ricans. Suddenly I realized I was wearing nothing but my bathrobe. Yes, I would have made a champion sight getting him a cab. I swayed once, feeling a bout of misery again. There was the kind of panic which comes from a dream where one is killing cockroaches. They were about me, literally; I saw several run off in jagged directions to follow their mysterious trail – that line of pure anxiety – which one sees in the path made by a car driving over a lake of ice. But who was the driver in the cockroach? And the dread I had escaped since I returned from the police station and Cherry had been there to open the door, now flew in silent as the shadow of a bat, and my body was like a cavern where deaths are stored. Deborah's lone green eye stared up at me. It had all gone wrong again. I could feel the break in the heavens. If I could have taken some of it back, I would have returned to that moment when I began to beat Shago to the floor and he dared me to let him go.

It looked as if Cherry had not moved from the bed. She was lying on her back, and she did not stir when I came in. Her face had gone too pale, and although she had not been crying, her lids were red, her eyes had a washed-out look. I reached to touch her hand; a mistake – her skin gave back no life.

I sat down to have a drink, and finished it in three nips. Perhaps ninety seconds went by before a new drink was in the glass. This one went more slowly, but I was on whiskey again. I was on the habit when whiskey felt equal to blood.

'Like a drink?' I asked her.

She did not reply. I took my next nip with the idea of leaving. It was close to midnight, I was due soon at Barney Kelly's, and I would find no fortification for that event sitting here.

But she looked up and said, 'I don't feel right.'

'You don't look well.'

'Well,' she said, 'you look about as good as you looked when I met you on the street.'

'Thank you,' I said. She looked no more and no less than a tired nightclub singer. I got up from my drink, and spent the next five minutes getting dressed.

'I guess you're good at one-night stands,' Cherry said at the end of this.

'Sometimes I am,' I said.

'You feel good, don't you?'

'A part of me feels good. I won a fight. I can't help that. I always feel good when I win a fight.' Then I almost laughed at the ease with which I said it. The dread had begun to be muted in the whiskey, but it would be back, it would certainly be back.

'Don't forget,' I said, 'he had a knife and I didn't.'

'That's true.'

'I thought of turning him loose, but there was the knife.' I could hear something false in my voice.

'In a real fight, Shago wouldn't have used it.'

'He wouldn't?'

'There's something clean about Shago,' she said.

'You sure?'

She began to cry silently. I knew what it was. I had sealed the past in a vault – but if I ever opened the doors . . . the memory of Deborah pregnant came floating up. I could not mourn Deborah. I could not begin to mourn Deborah or my mind would ride off with me. There was nothing so delicate in all the world as one's last touch of control. 'I'm sorry you and Shago didn't make it,' I said to Cherry.

She was silent. After a long silence, I finished my second drink and started on a third. 'There's something I could tell you,' she said. But she didn't have to. I felt the thought rise in her and drift over to me. They had looked very good standing next to one another – she did not have to explain a thing. 'Yes, I know,' I said. It was rare to be in love, but to believe that you could not find a better purpose in your life – that was rarest of all. 'Yes, I know,' I said, 'you used to think the whole country depended on you and Shago.'

'It was a crazy idea but I used to think something would get better if Shago and I could make it.' She looked unhappy again. 'I don't know, Steve, it's not good to think too much – at least the way I do. Cause I always end up with something like the idea that God is weaker because I didn't turn out well.'

'You don't believe everything is known before it happens?'

'Oh, no. Then there's no decent explanation for evil. I believe God is just doing *His* best to learn from what happens to some of us. Sometimes I think He knows less than the Devil because we're not good enough to reach Him. So the Devil gets most of the best messages we think we're sending up.'

'When did you begin to have ideas like this?'

'Oh, I got them in places like Houston and Vegas, reading books and waiting for Barney Kelly to come back. Why?'

'Sometimes I think in the same way.'

We were silent again.

'Stephen,' she said at last, 'we can't leave it here. I'm not in love with Shago any more.'

'You're not?'

'Shago killed the most beautiful idea I ever had about myself. Shago killed that idea. Sometimes I felt I wasn't living with a man but with a creature. And the Devil had a pipeline into that creature and took all the hate in the country and piped it into him. Remember when he was talking about the Freedom Rider bit?'

'Yes.'

'Well, he went down South for some organization. And he took his abuse with the others and had his picture in the paper, and spent two days in jail. The only thing – all that non-violence made those boys violent. When they got back to New York they had a party, and one of them flipped out, I fear, and told Shago he was a headline-hunter and had no heart in the movement cause he went around with me. Well, the fight was stopped before they got outside. But Shago was afraid and his friends saw it. He started putting everything down. Everything was bad, and I was bad, and well, he lost his dignity. I had been faithful to him for two years but he was so evil that when I decided to start with Tony, I'm afraid I offered a considerable first night.'

Now I could know again why women never told the truth about sex. It was too abominable when they did.

'Do you have to tell me?'

'Yes, I have to tell you. It's either that, or go back to my shrink.'

I thought of Ruta. 'All right, I'm listening.'

'Well, I thought I was in love with Tony. I *had* to think that. And Shago popped up as he did tonight.'

'Here?'

'No. You're the only man besides Shago I've taken here.' She lit a cigarette. 'No, Shago came in on Tony and me in the other place. Shago had connections in Harlem and Tony was afraid of those connections because Uncle Ganucci had arrangements pending with them. So Tony faded. Just puke, honey. It's a dull story. And I felt like puke. Because Shago got something back by seeing Tony was afraid of him, but it was a rotten recovery. He made me so filthy these last two months that when you were with him in the hall, I had a thought. It was: throw that nigger down the stairs.'

'Yes.'

'Throw that nigger down the stairs! Shago was the only man I ever knew who could make something in me turn over when he came into a room. I don't know if I'll ever feel that again. I think you get that only with one man.'

'Yes,' I said. Would I be good enough to take every last truth she had to offer? 'Yes,' I said, 'I know what you mean. I had something like that with Deborah. Still,' I said flatly, 'we have something else.'

'Yes. Yes we do . . . Oh, honey, here we are.'

'Too late to save the country.'

'Stephen, I want to become a lady.'

'Come on, cup-cake.'

'No, a real lady. Not the kind who's on committees or goes shopping. A real lady.'

'Ladies like to be wicked and wasteful.'

'No, a *lady*. Some day you'll see what I mean. You bring out the lady in me. I've never felt so nice. While you were away at the police station, I had the feeling that something would send you back to me because we could be good so many ways. Then I saw you fight Shago. You had to fight him, I know that – but still – I was sick. "Oh, Lordy," I thought, "it's the Mafia all over again."'

'Well, it was,' I said. I was thinking of Tony.

'Steve, I don't know if we're any good,' she said, 'or just as low-down and dead as two shits. I want us dead if we turn into that.' The look of a child touched by an angel came back to her. 'I want it to be all right.'

But the memory of the fight lay between us. We had talked forward, we had talked back – there was a hint of that time when we might be married and talk too long for too little, while beneath all surface of the marriage, like the corpse of a memory buried alive, some flaw would continue to rot at the center. 'Oh, baby, the fight left a hole,' she said.

Yes, love was a mountain which was climbed with a good heart and a good breath: one was brave and the other was true. The ascent was not yet begun, and I had been ready to betray. What we had was spoiled in part already; like all love which is spoiled we were now locked together a little more. Because she kissed me then, and the sweet which comes from a rare grape was in her mouth, but then something more, some hint of fever and a sly bitch, a sly wild bitch still years away from her, but coming to me from out in the future and something coming out from the years of her past: there was less of loyalty between us now, and more of the hot hair of the itch.

I finished my drink. In a minute I would have to go.

'Will you be all right?' I asked.

'Yes.'

'Will Shago come back?'

'I don't believe so.'

'Downstairs,' I said, 'Shago said to wish you "good luck."'

'He did?' She seemed thoughtful. 'Well, if he comes back, he comes back.'

'Will you let him in?'

'If he comes, I have to let him in. I'm not going to run from Shago.'

'I'm not so sure I'm going to see Kelly then.'

'You have to,' she said, 'or we won't have any idea what is in his mind. I don't want to wonder about that.'

'Yes.' In fact, I had a desire to go, half a desire. It might be better to go away for a while. We were beginning to feel good again, but the mood would not last if nothing was gambled.

'Sugar,' she said.

'Yes.'

'Watch the booze when you're with Kelly.'

' "Take your hand off my fly," said the Duchess to the Bishop.'

We laughed. We had come a little of the way back. 'Angel,' I said, 'do you have any money?'

'Close to four thou.'

'Let's buy a car and go away somewhere.'

'I'd like that,' she said.

'We could go to Las Vegas,' I said.

'Why?'

'Because if you're going to be a lady and I'm going to be a gentleman, then I have to win your love in every way.'

She took a quick look, and saw I meant what I had said more than I did not: so she smiled. 'Divine,' she said. And held out a finger. 'We'll make a fortune in Las Vegas. I win at the tables.'

'You do?'

'Not when I roll,' she said. 'You have to restrain me when I roll, cause I lose then. But when the men come up and take the dice, I come close to being a Power. Because I always know who's going to win and who will lose.'

'Well, I'm sixteen thousand in debt,' I said, 'so you better be good.'

'Your debts are dissolved,' she said. And she walked me to the door, and gave a soft plump kiss for goodbye, and nipped my lip and promised me with her tongue. Then she saw me looking at Shago's umbrella, and handed it to me. 'Now, you got a stick,' she said.

I descended the stairs, hearing no echo of my journey down with Shago, but in the hall at the foot of the last landing was the puddle he had left. I wanted to pass; my preference was clearly to ignore it, but instead I laid the umbrella aside and searched in a trash can behind the stairs

until I found a few pieces of sodden ill-scented cardboard
with which I did my best to scrape that pottage, making
several trips back and forth, the while I gagged. The odor
of his stomach, certainly no better than mine, was not free
of poverty — it had the hint of cheap Negro hash-houses
with their frying fat and the gamy near-rot of chitterlings.
I did the job slowly, with my fingertips. I had no desire
to see Barney Oswald Kelly in less than mint condition,
but it was a brutal work no matter how, for I was thinking
despite myself of student sit-ins and Negroes shot in the
night, and — any nearness to moralizing about the victim
on the stairs was shut off by a whiff from the job. So I
worked away, scraping slowly and carefully with my damp
cardboards, expiating a host of — I no longer knew what.
Primitive feathers of thought stirred in my brain. I had
some savage notion that spirits might rise from the food
we threw back. There had been a time when I thought
something exceptional was in my reach — which is to say
it would have taken genius to give lucid presentation of
what was sometimes near the edge of my thought; now
the farthest of my ideas depressed me, for madness was
attached to mining them. A scholarly example — here is
comedy if you wish it — some sense of the sinister was left
as I ended the work, went out to the street, called a cab,
and on impulse told him to go first to Central Park and
there drive about. For no demons resided in the vomit,
only torture and funk, and I had an impulse to go back —
if there were demons in Shago, they were in him still, so
said my instinct — was it all that routine to leave Cherry
alone? But my fear of Kelly whipped up again, and spoiled
the choice.

I must have fallen asleep on the ride. When I looked
out we were almost in Harlem and again I had a moment
where I could have believed I was dead. The cab driver
was silent, the streets were wet, and the vehicle was like
a hearse. The handle of the umbrella seemed alive to my

fingers. I had a thought. It suggested I should go into Harlem this night and drink until closing. That was right. That was the way to pay for it. There had been nights when I had done this. After very bad nights with Deborah I had made the rounds and walked down back streets and toured from bar to bar, but nothing had ever happened. The waiters had been polite, the drinkers had been polite, the streets were quiet. Even the hookers had done no more than cast an eye. I had spent some of the politest nights of my life in Harlem, and yet now – no, I believed in Africans and demons. If tonight I entered those bars the sound of Shago's fall would reverberate from my mind and I would not escape some evil incident. 'Do you want your love to be blessed?' said my mind, 'go to Harlem.'

Something was wrong, very wrong. It had been right for a little while, for an hour with Cherry in that room it had been almost right, I had felt safe, and now it was bad again – some air of hurricane lay over my head. Once again I wished to rush back to her – she was my sanity, simple as that – and then I remembered the vow I had made in her bed. No, if one wished to be a lover, one could not find one's sanity in another. That was the iron law of romance: one took the vow to be brave.

Therefore, I must go to Harlem. One could see Kelly later. Or was that still another excuse? Was it Kelly I feared the most; would I waste the early morning hours in one uptown bar after another, my bankroll ($75) safe, my person safe, neither mugged, nor accosted, nor even recognized as the latest white man to give up the guilt; would I come to understand at four in the morning, all bars shut, that I played a trick on myself to skip an encounter with the real fear? 'Go to Kelly,' said a voice now in my mind, and it was a voice near to indistinguishable from the other voice. Which was true? When voices came, how did you make the separation? 'That which you fear most is what you must do,' said my mind. 'Trust the authority of your senses.' But I had taken too long to decide: I had no senses. I was now nothing but fear. 'A curse on the logic of the saints,' I thought, and the taxi, making the circuit of the Park, passed the rain-washed exit to 110th Street and Seventh Avenue; we were turning back to the center of the city. Too late for Harlem. Was it woe I knew, relief, or some nausea of the cells? The handle of the umbrella felt sullen in my palm.

I opened the window, receiving a mist of rain on my face, and breathed deeply. The air was almost clean of smog, the whiskey was burning away, guttering in my stomach like the dregs of liquid in a spirit lamp. Did it matter where I went? If there was a dislocation to the heavens, it followed me: I would meet something tonight – was that not the odds? And the voice again: 'Still it would have been better to choose.'

I had been in states like this before. Possessing the salt of Mohammed or Buddha I could have founded a religion. Doubtless. It is just that I would not have had too many followers. Comfortless was my religion, anxiety of the anxieties, for I believed God was not love but courage. Love came only as a reward.

The metaphysics, however, was vast – buried in the twenty volumes I had not written. And I at this moment was buried in fear. I no longer had the confidence my thoughts were secret to myself. No, men were afraid of murder, but not from a terror of justice so much as the knowledge that a killer attracted the attention of the gods; then your mind was not your own, your anxiety ceased to be neurotic, your dread was real. Omens were as tangible as bread. There was an architecture to eternity which housed us as we dreamed, and when there was murder, a cry went through the market places of sleep. Eternity had been deprived of a room. Somewhere the divine rage met a fury. I shivered in the open window of the cab. What was it Shago had said? 'Man, I was spitting in the face of the Devil.' He was wrong. It was the Devil's daughter. And the memory of Barney Oswald Kelly came back. For we were approaching the Waldorf and I could feel his presence in a room near the top of the Towers.

8

At the Lion and the Serpent

The taxi turned around on Park Avenue, came up to the canopy, the doorman said good evening and gave a smile. I had passed him five dollars one blizzard of a night long ago when he managed to produce a cab for Deborah and me; the gift was old, but he remembered, and I, remembering that evening, had a sudden unaccountable urge not to enter by the main lobby, not at this late and empty hour. It was raining harder now, a cold rain which gave a hint of ice underfoot; I opened Shago's umbrella. The spars slid up the mast with an intake of breath, a grating swooping asthmatic sound as the cloth filled out. A voice came through the handle and into my palm — so it seemed. 'Go to Harlem,' said the voice. But I was on my way to the Towers. There was a private entrance on Fiftieth Street not a hundred feet from the corner, and I would take an elevator there, and avoid the lobby.

The street outside the side entrance was decked, however, with three limousines double-parked and a squad of motorcycle policemen stood at the door. I had a moment of panic — they were there for me, they must certainly be there for me — it took the time to light a cigarette before I recovered sufficiently to walk through the file and through the door; then up in the foyer against still another eight, each man more than six feet two, handsome as a prize herd of test-tube bulls. Their herder (I almost bumped into him) was a small plump detective from the

Commissioner's office, well-dressed, with a round petulant face and a fresh carnation. He was waiting by the elevator and as I approached he did two things at once: he managed to avoid looking at me, yet succeeded in studying my clothes. There was something wrong with me, he knew that – some remnant in his memory of my picture in the paper. But he gave it up, and turned to the elevator girl. 'She'll be coming down in three minutes. In about one minute I'll be going to the floor with you.'

Then I knew the police were there to escort the First Lady to her limousine or there to take a visiting princess out to a nightclub – some woman of huge institutional importance was about to descend – and I had no desire to wait. The air had the virile blank intensity of a teller's cage. So I went out again, opened my umbrella, took the short trip back to the main entrance, smiled at the doorman, and climbed the marble steps into the lobby of the Waldorf, a mountaineer's fatigue coming into me with this ascent. A pain gripped me in the angle between my shoulder and my chest, a pain so bright it gave promise of severing the nerve – there was nothing to save me but the pain itself – it reached to climax, opened an iron glove, ebbed, went away, and left me staring at the lobby of the Waldorf. But for a moment I had died and was in the antechamber of Hell. I had long had a vision of Hell: not of its details; of its first moment. A giant chandelier of crystal above one's head, red flock on the walls, red carpet, granite pillars (as I proceeded) now a high ceiling, was it gold foil? a floor of white and black, and then a room of blue and green in whose center stood a nineteenth-century clock, eight feet high with a bas relief of faces: Franklin, Jackson, Lincoln, Cleveland, Washington, Grant, Harrison, and Victoria; 1888 the year: in a ring around the clock was a bed of tulips which looked so like plastic I bent to touch and discovered they were real.

I needed a drink but the Peacock Lounge was closed.

One old woman in ermine came trailing by, and left a perfume behind, faint as the ghost of a jewel box. I had to quit the clock. But back in the lobby, the Waldorf looked like one of those silent rooms in the Casino at Monte Carlo, one of the dead and empty spaces which collect about the exit of a man who has lost a million in an hour. I had thought to mount the stairs to Kelly's apartment, all thirty-plus flights, a passing thought, but it would not quit me. I had some sense this was what I must do, it might be the equal of going to Harlem. Yet I could not begin. It seemed too heroic to mount those fire stairs, go through locks and ambushes, up through vales of anathema exuding from the sleep of the wealthy; and night detectives to be encountered. I could see my picture in the paper, professor-picked-up-as-prowler. No! Yet I was certain it was better to walk those stairs, ascend through fear and fever, even fail in some exhausted spasm of the heart, than be whipped along by elevator through the belts of psychic magnetism which guarded the tower.

In an alcove of the main floor, one flight above the entrance from the street, was a continuation of the private cars. While I waited, I went into a study of the doors, a frieze of nymphs and willowy dryads with stainless-steel hair and slim steel breasts. The elevator stopped with a strain of annoyance, as if, at this hour, visitors would not be walking through the lobby. I gave the operator – a sturdy turnip of a woman – the name of Barney Kelly, and she studied me like a police matron.

'Mr Kelly expecting you?'

'Indeed he is.'

While we ascended, I felt the air burning from the shaft and some rich exhaust went out of my lungs as if I had fallen asleep in a room with a fire and awakened from a long sensual dream to discover that the fire had consumed the oxygen and my satyr's heaven was compounded of suffocation. Up we went, rocketing the stories of the

Waldorf, while the umbrella in my hand quivered like a rod, a dowsing rod, as if here, here, we had just passed some absolute of evil to the left, and there to the right an unknown concentrate, crypts of claustrophobia, abysses of open space, now through a distillate of gloom – what depression surrounded the rich – and some compass of direction went awry in my mind; I had the physical impression we were moving through a tunnel rather than rising in a shaft; once again I felt something begin to go out of the very light of my mind, as if the colors which lit the stage of my dreams would be more modest now, something vital was ready to go away forever even as once, not thirty hours ago, I had lost some other part of myself, it had streamed away on a voyage to the moon, launched out on that instant when I had been too fearful to jump, something had quit me forever, that ability of my soul to die in its place, take failure, go down honorably. Now something else was preparing to leave, some certainty of love was passing away, some knowledge it was the reward for which to live – that voice which I could no longer deny spoke again through the medium of the umbrella. 'Go to Harlem,' said the voice, 'if you love Cherry, go to Harlem – there is time.' Then I knew how afraid I was of Harlem, and argued with that voice, saying, 'Let me love her some way not altogether deranged and doomed. It makes no sense to go to Harlem. Let me love her and be sensible as well.'

'The sensible are never free,' said the voice.

'Let me be free of you.'

'Free as you wish,' said the voice, and something departed from me, some etched image of Cherry's face turned to mist. And the handle of the umbrella peppered my palm, I almost tottered. For the elevator decelerated with a plunge of sinkers at my chest; we were there.

I went down the hall, a long hall with a carpet of civilized brown, much milk in it, and pale green walls, light as a new leaf. Kelly's door was familiar, it had a medallion beneath the knocker, a miniature of the coat of arms of the Mangaravidis and the Caughlins, quarterly, 1 and 4, gules, a lion rampant; 2, 3, sable, serpent argent, crowned azure, vorant a child proper – so Deborah had delineated the blazons. And the motto: *Victoria in Caelo Terraque.* For a moment I began to shake, as from a chill. Not from the motto (yes, from the motto, too) but from the memory of the half-dozen times I had come to this door. Then I lifted the knocker.

Ruta answered. She was wearing an expensive black silk with a string of pearls, and her face stared back at me, piquant and painted, inquisitive, rapacious – some energy returned to my blood – the blood no longer felt as if it would flow away to the moon, no, some pig's riot gave promise of existing still, and I stood at the door, giving a full stare at her, while a provisional sanity began to form.

'You look well,' I said.

She smiled. Two or three hours plus a full twenty-four must have gone by since she quit the precinct, but she had found the time to go to a beauty parlor, the best beauty parlor in New York no doubt. Now the red in her hair was perfect as the red and brown of a fine wood with a lick of flame, the soft lick of a flame, and the red of a rich clay to support the fire and the wood.

'Good evening, Mr Rojack,' she said.

The last time I had been this close, Ruta's hair was half down her neck, the roots had shown, lipstick was half off her mouth, clothes up, off, to every side, her clump in my fingers and both of us dripping ozone in the haste of making love while standing up. A host of the heats came to me on a whiff of my own odor now and the hint was there again between us. Her pointed nose, sensitive to mood as the antennae of a cat, tilted to the side and looked at the unprotected space between my cheek and my ear.

'Well, bless you for being so good with the cops,' I said.

'Oh,' she said, 'you are much too kind.' We were thinking that she had been not so very good after all, not with the cops. 'But, in fact, I tried to do you no harm. After all, I do not dislike you.'

'I would count on it that you didn't.'

She stirred in the attention between us. 'Of course not,' she said, 'of course. But what woman enjoys the just liking a man? That is all *crap*.' Then she smiled sweetly as if to think of secrets. 'Between us,' Ruta said, 'your father-in-law had something to do with getting you off.'

'I wonder why?'

'You must ask him yourself.' She looked, for an instant, about to offer me more, but her expression moved on. 'Look,' she said, 'it is disturbed here tonight. There have been people all evening. Now two are left. I tell you in secret they are horrible.'

'Let's go in nonetheless.'

'You would not like to see Deirdre first?'

'She's back from school?'

'Of course she is back. She waited until midnight for you to appear. Then her grandfather sent her to bed. She is up, however.'

I had a pure woe, as if an airplane dropped suddenly. The route was too round about. I had forced my nerve to be ready for Kelly; now such preparation would be lost. Memories might begin. I did not want them. Indeed I had met Deirdre on the day I met Kelly, here in this suite nine years ago, and the recollection was not pleasant. Deborah had too been terrified of her father. Her lips quivered when Kelly spoke to her. I was never to see her so useless again, and thus had a hint of the shame she felt in marrying me.

Only Deirdre had been able to save a part of the meeting. She had not seen her mother in more than a month, she had been sent from Paris to visit Kelly six weeks ago, but it was my face she ran to across the room, there in front of her mother and grandfather.

'*Moi, je suis gros garçon,*' she said to me. For a three-year-old, she was very small.

'*Tu es très chic; mais tu n'as pas bien l'air d'un garçon.*'

'*Alors, c'est grand papa qui est gros garçon?*'

We laughed. It was the only laughter of the visit.

Now Ruta took me up from the memory by putting her hand on my arm. 'I don't know,' I said to her, 'if I can bear to see Deirdre.'

'Pay cash,' said Ruta.

She drew me to a bedroom. 'Look,' she said, 'I will try to wait for you. There's something I want to talk about.' She gave another smile, reached across to open the door and said, 'Deirdre, your stepfather is here.'

There was a flight from the bed. A thin figure, a wraith with arms, hugged me hard.

'Turn on the lamp,' I said. 'I want to see what you look like.'

Actually I had a fear of being in the dark with Deirdre, as if my brain would be too vivid. But with the lights on, there were no pictures of the night before. I was suddenly happy to see Deirdre. For the first time since entering the hotel I felt back in myself again. 'Well, give us a look,' I said.

She had grown since I had seen her last at Christmas, she was going to be tall and very slim. Already I could no longer kiss the top of her hair. Soft as a bird's feather, Deirdre's hair offered the suggestion of a wood where birds were nesting. She was not a pretty child, she was nothing but eyes – she had a thin triangular face with a chin much too pointed, a mouth as wide as Deborah's and a nose whose nostrils were too chiseled for a child – but eyes she had! Enormous, and stared at one with a clear luminous look, an animal's fright, some creature with huge eyes.

'I was afraid I wouldn't see you,' she said.

'Of course you would. I wasn't going to disappear.'

'I can't believe any of it.' She always spoke like an adult. She had one of those charming accents which belong to

213

children who have grown up in a convent; something disembodied in her voice invoked the precise breathless tone of her nuns.

'Mummy doesn't feel dead.'

'She doesn't.'

Tears came to Deirdre's eyes like a tide welling into two hollows of sand. 'Nobody mourns her. It's awful. Even Grandfather is in a state.'

'He is?'

'Cheerful.' She began to cry. 'Oh, Steve, I'm lonely.' She said this in the voice of a full widow, then kissed me with a pure flesh of grief.

'The shock must be worse for your grandfather than anyone else.'

'It's not shock. I don't know what it is.'

'Is he numb?'

'No.' Grief passed her by like a wind. She was thoughtful again. Suddenly I knew that the nerves were shattered: her skin kept her intact, but the nerves spoke in separate broken bits. One bit wept, another had a thought; a third was dumb. 'Once, Steve, when I came here with Mummy, Grandfather was in a very good mood. He said, "You know, children, a celebration is in order. I made twenty million today." "That must have been a bore," Mummy said. "No," he said, "this time it wasn't because I had to take a big chance." Well, that's how he is now.' She shivered again. 'I hate being here. I was writing a poem when they told me this morning. Then there was nothing but Grandfather's limousine to take me back.'

She was an exquisite poet.

'Do you remember anything from the poem?'

'Just the last line now. "And share my fools for bread." That's the last line.' A small look opened its arms to me. 'Mummy doesn't feel dead yet,' she said.

'We've talked about that, haven't we?'

'Steve, I used to hate Mummy.'

'Girls sometimes do hate their mothers.'

'Certainly not!' She was directly offended by my remark. 'I came to hate her because she was awful to you.'

'We were awful each to the other.'

'Mummy told me once that you were a young soul and she was an old one. There was the trouble.'

'Do you know what she meant?'

'I think she meant she had had other lives. Maybe she was there during the French Revolution and the Renaissance, or was even a Roman matron watching Christians be tortured. But you were a new soul, she said, and hadn't had a life before this one. It was all-absorbing, but she had to go on to say you were a coward.'

'I think I am.'

'No. People with new souls have terror cause they can't know if they'll be born again.' She shivered. 'I'm afraid of Mummy now,' she said. 'When she was alive, I used to love her a little – once in a while when she chose to be nice, so nice. Still I was really terrified of her. When she separated from you, I told Mummy what I thought – we had a scene. She pulled open her negligee and showed me the place on her stomach where she had a scar.'

'Yes, I know the scar.'

'It was awful.'

'Yes, it was very much there.'

'She said, "I got this nifty little Caesar giving birth to you, pet, so don't complain. Caesars always turn out to be more trouble than anybody. In your case, Deirdre, you have turned out a bat." And I said, "You have a cross on your belly." Which is true, Steve. She had a horizontal wrinkle in the middle of her belly, and the scar from the Caesar ran right across it.' Something strangled in her, some wistful desire to be less extraordinary. 'Steve, those few minutes were disaster. Mummy had to say it again. She repeated, "I'm sorry, Deirdre, but you *have* turned out a bat." And I was very hurt – because it's true, that's what I look like. You know Mummy. Once she says something to people, you're put away like an insect on a pin. You never escape. I knew for the rest of my life I would always see myself that way. Oh, Steve. I said to her, ''If I'm a bat, you're Dracula's wife,'' which was fantastic to say because I wasn't talking about you at all, it was Grandfather, and Mummy knew I meant him. Well, then she became very silent, and began to cry. I'd never seen her cry. She said our blood was all filled with vampires and saints. Then she said she had only a little while to live. She was sure of that. She said she really did love you. You were the love in her life, she said. We both began to cry. We were closer than we'd ever been. But of course she spoiled it. She said, ''Well, after all, he's *virtually* the real love in my life.'' '

'She said that?'

'I told her she was a beast. She said, ''Beware of beasts. There's a species which stays alive three days after they die.'' '

'What?'

'She said that, Steve.'

'Oh, no.'

'I don't feel as if she's dead yet.'

It was as if a door high above us had closed. I looked around the room. 'I'm going to end as a lush, I swear, dear child.'

'You can't. Promise you won't take a drink tonight.'

It was an impossible request – I could not sit in wake on the liquor I had drunk already; yet I nodded.

'It's awful to break a vow,' she said seriously.

'I'll stay off the sauce. You get back to sleep.'

She got into bed like a child. She was a child again.

'Steve,' she asked, 'can I come live with you?'

'You mean, at once?'

'Yes.'

I was silent for a moment.

'Do you know, Deirdre, it may take a while.'

'Are you in love with a woman?'

I hesitated. But one could tell Deirdre anything. 'Yes,' I said.

'What is she like?'

'She's kind of blonde and sort of beautiful. She has a funny sense of humor and she sings in nightclubs.'

'She does?' Deirdre was enthralled. 'Oh, Steve, a night-club singer. It's stellar to find a girl like that.' She was profoundly impressed. 'I want to meet her. Can I?'

'Maybe in a few months. You see, we just began last night.'

She nodded her head wisely. 'People want to make love after a death.'

'Hush, *gros garçon*.'

'I'll never be able to live with you, Steve. I know that now.'

A cloud of sorrow concentrated itself into a tear, one pure tear which passed on the mood from her narrow chest into mine. I was in love with Cherry again. 'Bless you, pet,' I said, and then to my surprise I began to cry. I cried for Deborah for a little while, and Deirdre cried with me.

'It's going to take years before it feels the least bit real,' said Deirdre. She gave a wet adolescent kiss to my ear. ' "Forests are conceived in sorrow," ' she said. 'That's the first line of my poem about fools and bread.'

'Good night, Deirdre baby.'

'Call me tomorrow.' She sat up in sudden agony. 'No, tomorrow's the funeral. Will you be there?'

'I don't know.'

'Grandfather will be in a fury.'

'Angel, trust me on this. I don't think I can go to that funeral. I won't drink tonight, but don't expect me at the funeral.'

She lay back and closed her eyes with a tense flutter of her lids.

'I don't think your mother would want me there. I think she would rather I thought about her in my head. That's better, I think.'

'All right, Steve.'

It was the way I left her.

Ruta was waiting. 'Well,' she said, 'was it very bad?'

I nodded.

'You should not go around killing mothers,' said Ruta.

I made no answer. I was a fighter who had taken too many. The smile was on my face but the end of the round would be welcome, and a drink for the next round.

'Listen,' Ruta murmured, 'you and me, we will talk later. He's getting impatient.'

We went down the hall of the suite to a sitting room. Kelly was there and an old woman I recognized. She had the reputation of being the most evil woman ever to live on the Riviera, no small reputation. And Eddie Ganucci was there. But I had no more than taken them in when Kelly was on me. He put out his arms and gave an embrace, a powerful bewildering embrace, for he had never done more than shake my hand all the years I had been married, but now he held me with some deep authority of feeling. There had been times when Deborah greeted me this way, invariably when I arrived alone and late at a cocktail party and she was drunk. She would hug me then with gravity, her body immobile for many long seconds as if she had been guilty that afternoon of filthy infidelities and was expiating them now by a show of devotion. But there had always been a hint of mockery in the depth of the gravity she assumed, as if standing before a dozen or a hundred people she promised an allegiance I would never find at other times. On rare moments when the icy treacherous tone I heard in so many of our fornications had worn to the distaste of final exhaustion there would come again a moment when to make love to Deborah was like a procession through a palace, each stroke a step upon a purple walk. I was trapped in such an embrace now, I could feel the beating of Kelly's heart, some mighty sense of the powers in a cavern, and then — precisely as I used to feel with Deborah — there was an intimation of treachery one could recover only in a dream as if alone in a room, windows shut, a paper had blown from the table. Beneath a toilet water of punctilio and restraint (a mixture of cologne and limewater which Deborah liked to borrow) a deep smell came off Kelly, a hint of a big foul cat, carnal as the meat on a butcher's block, and something else, some whiff of the icy rot and iodine in a piece of marine nerve left to bleach on the sand. With it all was that congregated odor of the wealthy, a mood within the nose of face powder, of perfumes which leave the turpentine of a witch's curse, the taste of pennies in the mouth, a whiff of the tomb. It was all of Deborah for me.

'Bless, bless,' said Kelly in a muffled voice. And released me with the deft little push of a banker sending you ahead of him through a door. There were tears in his eyes, and looking at him, there were tears in mine, for he had some of Deborah's face, the wide curved mouth, the green eyes with a needle's point of light — some of the love I had never been able to give to her came rising up in me now, so that our embrace done, I had a desire to hug him again and truly, as if there were a comfort to be found in his flesh, as if indeed it was Deborah and me on one of those rare occasions when having fought to a bruised exhaustion we would grasp each other in a kind of sorrow, my sense of myself as a man all gone, her sense of herself as a woman equally gone, both of us reduced to the state of children in a tearful misery, in that soreness of the heart which looks for balm and makes the flesh of man and woman equal for a moment. And in that way, the embrace finished, I could have hugged him for a moment, his presence more real to me as an embodiment of Deborah than of himself. But my emotions were like Deirdre's I realized suddenly —

their continuation was shattered — if it was grief I felt, it had gone off like a small bomb. I was stiff and cold in the next moment, and wary of him, for the tears wiped from his face with one elegant pass of his handkerchief, he put one look into my eyes, like a tracer of light it leaped into me, and he had the secret — if there had been a doubt in his head, there was none now: he knew what I had done to Deborah. 'Well,' he said, 'oh good God, well, what a ghastly hour this is for all of us.' And I could feel his emotion retreat. Like a bull I had charged into the warm billow of a cape, and now was wrenched about to find nothing but the air.

'Forgive me,' he said to the guests.

'Oswald, of course not,' said the lady. 'I know *I'm* about to leave. You want to talk to your son-in-law. Naturally.'

'No, I won't hear of leaving,' said Kelly. 'Not for a little while. Let's have one drink.' And he made the introductions. 'You met Mr Ganucci — he was telling me how the two of you were thrown together. That must have been fun. And Bessie — you know Bess?'

I bowed my head. Her name was Consuelo Carruthers von Zegraide Trelawne and she was a distant cousin of Deborah's mother. She had been a great beauty once — she was still a great beauty. There was a grand profile, and violet-blue eyes, a hair tinted in balance between mercury and bronze. Her skin was the color of cream and there was a flush of strawberry make-up on her cheek. But her voice cracked.

'Deborah and I visited you once,' I said.

'Of course, I was telling Oswald about it tonight. Oswald, if I'm going to drink, give me more of the Louis Treize.' Ruta got up immediately and went to the table to make her a drink. Bess turned to me. 'You've improved since I saw you.'

'Better a little, worse a little,' I said. I was trying to remember what Bess had done: there was an episode in her legend which was notorious – it was one of the worst stories I had ever heard – but my memory would not produce it.

'Oh, bother, don't try to talk,' she said.

'Watch the brandy on our heart,' Kelly murmured.

'I don't want to hear about brandy,' Bess said. 'I drink Scotch with bores, coke with great-grandchildren, and save brandy for ghastly hours.'

'Please stop it, Bess,' said Kelly.

'No. Weep, both of you. Scream your heads off. The most heavenly girl in the whole glorious world has been plucked from us. I can't keep it in.'

'She was a peach,' Ganucci said in his hoarse voice.

'You hear,' said Bess, 'even this old wop can tell you.'

Kelly put his head in his hands for a moment, and then raised his face. He was a big man with a smooth body and very white skin, not pale but white, a full buttermilk white with shadings of pink, all flesh. One had the impression he was a bit wide in the middle, but the transition was so smooth his body looked to have a perfect shape for his head. He had a large head which began with a small pointed chin, went up to an urbane button of a nose, and on to a broad forehead. Since he was half bald, the length of his forehead seemed equal to the distance from his eyes to his chin. He looked at times like one of those very handsome babies who at the age of three months come out a stout hearty fifty-five years old. Actually he was sixty-five, and physically impressive, for he gave off the fortified good humor which is to be found in the company of generals, tycoons, politicians, admirals, newspaper publishers, presidents, and prime ministers. He had in fact a pronounced resemblance to a particular president and particular prime minister, but then for fact Kelly had two separate manners, one, British; the other, American; you had to learn to distinguish. The British was clipped, jolly, full of tycoon; he might have you knifed but dependably you would receive

NORMAN MAILER

a full twinkle as the order went down. The American was
hard in the eyes – they turned from green to gray, and
his face went cold – those eyes would buy you, sell you,
close you out, walk past your widow; they measured you
face to face, they were dirty Irish – they would put dirty
sand in your concrete.

His voice, however, was rich, an instrument; it purred
with good fun. Only at the end of a sentence would he
give a turn to the meaning and put you away. I had heard
people say he had the charm to capture anything alive if
he liked it – he had never liked me. 'Have some brandy,
Stephen,' he said now.

'I've been doing little but drink.'

'Shouldn't wonder. I've had a quantity myself.'

In the silence which followed he waved Ruta aside, went
to the bar, put a little Rémy Martin into a large snifter and
passed it to me. As he did, his nail gave a glancing tick
off mine, and left an electric sense of loss much as if a
beauty had brushed my hand and delivered a message to
my back of fine mysteries yet to discover. I held the glass,
but the promise to Deirdre was on me; I took no sip. Now,
another small silence developed. So I sat there holding my
glass, living in the pall which comes the moment there is
silence at a wake; that happiness which arrived for a while
talking to Deirdre now disappeared.

'You know, Mr Kelly,' said Ganucci, his voice whispering over its way like a fist rubbed down the bark of a tree,
'I started as a poor man.'

'By God, so did I,' said Kelly out of a reverie.

'And I've always felt like a poor man,' said Ganucci.

'Don't know that I have,' said Kelly.

'I still feel like a poor man in this regard – I love class.
Your daughter had the class of the angels. She could treat
you as an equal, simple as that. That's why I came to pay
my respects tonight.'

'I'm honored that you're here, Mr Ganucci,' said Kelly.

'That's nice of you to say. I know there've been all kinds of people here this afternoon and this evening, and you must be tired, but I came here to tell you this: I'm a big man in certain people's eyes, only I don't kid myself, you're a bigger man, you're a very big man. I came to pay my respects. I'm your friend. I would do anything for you.'

'Darling,' said Bess to Ganucci, 'you've written your letter. Now mail it.'

'Darling,' said Kelly, 'is this the night to be rude to Mr Ganucci?'

'I'm ready to explode,' said Bess.

The telephone rang. Ruta got up again to answer. 'It's Washington,' she said.

'I'll take it in the other room.'

The moment Kelly was gone, Ganucci said, 'I'm not even rude to the little colored fellow who shines my shoes.'

'Well, he's the future, darling,' said Bess.

'That's right,' said Ganucci, 'and you and me are dead.'

'Some of us are more dead than others, pet. There are weeds and roses through all the world.'

'No,' said Ganucci again to Bess, 'you and me are dead.'

'Weeds and roses,' Bess replied.

'You know what the dead are,' said Ganucci. 'They're concrete. You'll make a good bump on Route 4 in New Jersey.'

'Is that the one which starts to go to Tuxedo Park?' asked Bess.

'Yeah, that's the one.'

'Dreadful road,' said Bess.

Ganucci started coughing again. 'Listen, please don't call me a wop.'

'You *are*.'

Kelly returned. 'It was Jack,' he said to me. 'He said to send you his regards and commiserations. He also said it was an awful shock to him, and he knows you must be feeling awful. I didn't know you knew him.'

'We met in Congress,' I said.

NORMAN MAILER

'Of course,' said Kelly.

'As a matter of fact, I met Deborah because of him.'

'Yes, yes now it's back to me. I remember she even said something to me about you then. She said, "You better watch out – there's a half-Jewish fellow I'm crazy about." "More power to you," I said. Would you believe it – I was opposed to Jack at the time. I was wrong. I was so damn wrong. And wrong about Deborah. Oh, Christ,' he bellowed suddenly, in a shock of sound, like an animal receiving the blow of a bullet. 'Excuse me,' he said, and left the room once more.

'Well, now we'd better be going,' said Bess.

'No,' said Ruta, 'he'll be very upset if you're not here when he comes back.'

'You know him well, do you, dear?'

Ruta smiled. 'Nobody knows Mr Kelly well,' she said.

'Nonsense,' said Bess. 'I know him inside out.'

'Is that so, Mrs Trelawne?' Ruta asked.

'Darling, I was his first big fling. He was only twenty-four, but a treasure chest. I got to know him. How I got to know him. Inside out. I'll tell you, my dear,' she said to Ruta, 'he won't marry you.'

'Oo la la, Mrs Trelawne,' said Ruta.

'Be a honey, and put a cold compress on his neck. Tell him I have to go.'

The moment Ruta was gone, Bess turned to me and said, 'Watch out, baby boy, Barney's up to mangling you tonight.'

'Barney Kelly don't go in for blitzes,' said Ganucci.

'No, Mr Ganucci. You don't either, I'm sure. You just make a little money on dope and prostitutes and dropping wops into boiling asphalt,' said Bess.

'Passé,' said Ganucci, and coughed.

'Very afraid of popping off, aren't you?' Bess said next.

'The dead,' said Ganucci, 'are concrete. They're part of the sidewalk. That's the way it goes.'

224

'No, *tesoro*, you'll go through an accounting. They'll bring you to your patron saint, and your saint will say, "Eddie Ganucci is unspeakable. Hang him on a hook."'

Ganucci sighed. His stomach made an unhappy sound, something kin to the leak and gurgle in an old washing machine when the water is being changed. 'I'm a very sick man,' he said gloomily.

It was all too unhappily true. He sat there in a funk of gloom, we sat in silence, and a pestilence came up from Ganucci, a ripple of the worm of life trapped in a cement given off by itself. Death had already invaded him. Just as one hears in the yawp of a bird seized by a larger bird one squawk of agony sucked in from the nerve of nature itself, so now Ganucci gave off an essence of disease, some moldering from the tree of death. I knew his smell up close would be an event, one of those odors to which there is no end, a gangrene in the firmament. I wanted a drink, wanted it with my tongue against my teeth; as if alcohol, and alcohol alone, could clean the particles which traveled from Ganucci's breath to mine.

'Let *me* tell a story,' said Ganucci. 'I had a parrot once friends gave me. They taught the parrot how to talk. "Eddie Ganucci," that bird would say, "you're full of it, you're full of it," and I'd say, "Polly, that kind of talk is going to get you the oven some day." And the parrot would say, "Ganooch, you're full of it. You're full of it." And I'd say, "Polly, keep talking and you'll find the way," and the parrot said, "you're full of it," and got sick and died. That's a sad story.'

Bess had her handkerchief out. 'The room is absolutely foul,' she said. I went to the French windows, opened them, and stepped out on the terrace. It was a good respectable terrace, perhaps thirty feet long and twenty feet deep, and I walked out to the end of it and looked over the parapet, a stone railing about forty inches high, taking the gift of looking down to the street, all thirty and more stories of vertical fall, a swoop and stop, drop and ledge, fall again, down some eternity of measurement to the wet pavement below, and a desire started up in me again, faint as the first tuning of a bow in an empty hall. The moon was pushing through scud, and drifts passed over its face. I knew the longer I stayed at this parapet the more I would be tempted – fresh air lifted to my head like a lyric, I could not have enough of it. And I had a sudden thought, 'If you loved Cherry, you would jump,' which was an abbreviation for the longer thought that there was a child in her, and death, *my* death, my violent death, would give some better heart to that embryo just created, that indeed I might even be created again, free of my past. The wish to jump was clean, keen and agreeable, nice as the nicest things I had done, and I could not quit yet – I had the feeling that to go back in the room would be equal to deserting what was best in me: I had a thought then to get up and stand on the parapet, as if to dare the desire by coming closer to it would be logical, and the dread which followed this thought had a pure thrill like the moment in adolescence when one realizes one is finally going to get it, get sex – but what a fear! I was trembling. And then as if I were entering a great calm, like that calm I found the moment I began to run up the slope of the hill in Italy, I stood on a deck chair, and took the half-step up to the parapet. It was a foot wide, room enough to stand, and I stood on it, my legs a jelly, and felt some part of the heavens, some long cool vault at the entrance, a sense of a vast calm altogether aware of me. 'God exists,' I thought, and tried to steal a look down the fall, but was not ready, not so much of a saint was I, the street rose up with a crazy yaw of pavement and I looked away, looked back at the terrace just a step down on the other side, was about to get off, and had a knowledge that to quit the parapet now was too soon – the desire to jump would be only more powerful. 'But you do not have to jump,' said the voice in my mind, 'just take a walk around the parapet.'

'I cannot take even one step,' I answered.

'Take one step.'

I pushed my foot forward, scraping it forward inch by inch; my will, divided against itself, was quivering from the effort: I looked ahead and was frozen. For I was in the middle, fifteen feet from the corner of the terrace, fifteen feet of walk on a parapet one foot wide, and a fall of thirty stories on my right; then I would have to turn the corner, and walk another twenty feet back to where the terrace ended at the wall of the suite. It was beyond my strength. Yet I took another step, still another. I could do it perhaps. And then the wind came up with a sudden blast – like the impact of a trailer truck as it goes by – and I almost lost my balance: the fall to the street was sharp as a blade, Shago's blade, and I jumped off, back to the terrace, and looked at the French windows to see Kelly standing in them. 'Here,' he said, 'come on in.'

His face made visible by the light of the room, there was nothing in his expression to indicate he had seen me on the parapet, and perhaps he hadn't, perhaps he had come out an instant after I dropped back, or had been unable to see for the first moment in the dark, but there was a grin on his face, one hard hearty grin like the look of a man who has penetrated a riddle. And as we went inside, a force came off him, clear as a command. It was telling the others to go. Free as a free flight of paranoia through the storm, the lights in the room dimmed on this thought, then came up again.

'Yeah,' said Ganucci, 'it's late. Want a ride in the elevator?' he asked of Bess. Her face was a staging of masks, a collapsing of cakes and powders until the bone stood out. It was just a glimpse, some vision perhaps of how she saw herself, but the war looked to have been fatal. 'Yes, I'll go,' she said to Ganucci.

Kelly stood at the door. He would walk them to the elevator.

Ruta was nervous when we were alone. She had obviously a great deal to say and very little time to say it in. But I was breathing relief. The three steps on the parapet had left me weak, yet the weakness was agreeable, I felt as if I had come up out of a deep sleep. Of course whatever I had accomplished on the parapet, there was the muted uneasiness of knowing it had not been finished. But I was back at least in the room, Kelly was gone for a minute or two, there was respite: on this hearth, at this moment, Ruta was nearly equal to an old friend. But then a look from her sharp as a whiff of ammonia awakened me completely.

'Ruta, your double life seems to be over.'

'That is too bad,' she said. 'I like a double life.'

'You didn't mind picking up after Deborah?'

'Oh, your wife was not neat. Rich girls are pigs. But I am not just a maid, you know.'

'No, I should be aware of that.'

'Of course, I am nothing official. I just have concentration to do a job. Barney wanted me to do it, so I did it. I kept an eye on things.'

'Just what?'

'Oh, some of your wife's activities.'

'But how long have you known Barney?'

'Some years. I met him in West Berlin at a nice party. Never mind.'

'And now you are . . .' I was about to say, 'a most extraordinary little spy.'

'Nothing at all. I help Mr Kelly.'

'But Deborah was dabbling with spies – was she really?'

'An absolute amateur.'

'You don't expect me to believe you?'

'She had no real standing,' Ruta repeated with pride.

'Nonetheless,' I said, 'Deborah must have caused some worry.'

'Oodles of worry,' Ruta said. 'Last night there must have been electricity burning in government offices all over the world.' She was talking of a fine meal – gluttony in her voice at all that electricity. 'Yes, they had to let you go. Since nobody can know if you know a little or a lot, a real investigation would be ending *der Teufel* knows where.' She could not avoid a small smile. 'But you are the *Teufel*,' she went on, 'you take what you want.'

'Ruta, you haven't told me a thing.'

'And if I told you, then would you help me on something?'

'I would try to answer your questions as well as you answer mine.'

'Yes, that may be good.'

'What was Deborah up to?'

'Nobody knows.'

'Now, what do you mean?'

'Nobody knows for certain. It's always like that. Believe me, Mr Rojack, the more you learn the more you know there are never any answers, just more questions.'

'I'm curious to hear a fact or two.'

'Facts.' She shrugged. 'You may know them already.'

'She had three lovers – that I know.'

'You don't know who they were?'

'No.'

'Well, good. Let me tell you. One of them is an American who's more or less special.'

'In the government?'

'Pretend I didn't hear the question, Mr Rojack.'

'And another?'

'Another is a Russian who's attached to the embassy at Park Avenue. The third is an Englishman who is a liquor representative for some Scotch firm and used to be in British intelligence during the war.'

'Still is, you may be certain,' I said.

'Of course,' said Ruta.

'That's the lot?'

'She may have had something to do with a fellow named Tony who was up to see her once or twice.'

'Did she like Tony?'

'Not too much, I would say.'

'What was Deborah actually up to?' I asked.

'If you want my real opinion,' said Ruta.

'I do.'

'She was out to embarrass her father profoundly. She wanted him to come to her, to beg her to stop all her amateur espionage before all the important people in the world decided Barney Kelly was up to something bad, or could not control his daughter.'

'But what was Deborah interested in?'

'Lots. Too much. Believe me, everything and nothing. She was a gossip center and she pretended to be important. If you really desire my personal opinion, I think it gave her tremendous sexual excitement. Some women like horseback riders, some go for ski jumpers, there are women who are interested in nothing but Polish brutes, and Deborah had a *petite faiblesse* for the best agents. Whatever it was, it was very bad for her father. He suffered very much over this.'

'All right, Ruta, thank you,' I said. Despite three separate spasms of jealousy for three lovers, there had been a small intoxication in the center of the pain to be learning something at last.

'Still,' said Ruta, 'I have not asked you what I wanted to ask.'

'Please do.'

'Mr Rojack, why do you think I work for Mr Kelly? What do you think I look for?'

'Marrying him.'

'Is it so obvious?'

'No. But I trust Mrs Trelawne.'

'It stands out then – my ambition?'

'A little, perhaps. Of course you're very smart.'

'I am obviously not smart enough to hide it. That is, I am smart enough, but I have not had sufficient advantages. So I would like assistance.'

'An assistant?'

'A partner. To advise me.'

'Bess is right, my dear. He's not going to marry you.'

'You're talking like a fool, Mr Rojack, and you are not a fool. I'm not such an egomaniac that I don't think Mr Kelly can't buy and sell a girl like me ten thousand times. But I know something.' Her eyes now protruded slightly – Germanically – as if the pressure of her idea was back of them.

'Do you really know something?' I asked.

'A great deal. I have a chance he will marry me. If I can play the cards.'

'What do you propose to pay your consultant?'

'You told me you were hard as nails. I believe you. I would not try to trick a man like you. Besides,' she said, 'you can trust me.'

I was enjoying this. 'The trick,' I said, 'is to keep a sense of proportion. Why should I ever trust you? I certainly couldn't trust you with the bulls.'

Bulls? Bulls? Her lack of this word irritated her like the search for a missing tool.

'The police.'

'Oh,' she said, 'last night! You half-promised to make me a baby. I didn't necessarily want a baby, but you promised, and then you didn't. That is a very little thing, but it does not create undying loyalty in a woman.'

It did, however, create a recollection of our evening together. 'There was a second time,' I said.

A sneer went to Ruta's mouth. 'Yes, the second time,' she said. 'It burned.'

'I'm sorry,' I said.

'Usually it burns.'

'Perhaps you have an infection,' I said.

'Ha, ha,' said Ruta, 'that is just what I need.'

'Isn't Kelly taking his time?' I said suddenly. But suddenly I had felt his absence.

'He went to look in on Deirdre, I would suppose.'

I was tempted to ask if there was any way he could be listening. The room did not have that stricken air which recording devices brought to a mood, but then . . . 'Is there any equipment?' I asked.

'He had it taken out.'

'He did? Why?'

'Because one day I had the rare good fortune to find his private cabinet in the bathroom unlocked and so was able to listen to him while he was having a conversation in the library. And I was enough impressed to turn on the tape recorder in the private cabinet.'

'That was the day when you learned what you learned?'

'Yes, that was the day.'

'It's good enough to get you to marry him?'

'Maybe yes, maybe no.'

'It's probably good enough to get you hurt.'

'Oh,' she said, 'I have copies of the tape well secured.'

'One wants to treat you well,' I said.

'Thank you,' she said. 'But that does not produce my assistant.'

'Tell me your information. Who knows what that will produce?'

She laughed. 'Who knows? It is so good you must trust me.'

I laughed. 'Perhaps I don't have to trust you. Perhaps I have an idea of your information.'

'Perhaps you do.'

A bolt. I did not know what she was talking about; yet I had an intimation that I did, as if once again, somewhere deep within, a messenger was setting out. But now I did not want to talk. Which is to say there was some injunction in my brain not to proceed. It was as if I had spent my life living in a cellar, and now lights were being installed.

But I had lived too long without them. The desire to go outside and walk on the parapet came again.

'Let's put brandy on the curse,' I said. Something had certainly happened. Quietly, mildly, without a backward look at Deirdre, I had decided to drink.

We were drinking thus quietly – each waiting for the other to speak first – when Kelly came back.

'Is Deirdre still restless?' asked Ruta.

'Very much so.'

'I will see if I can get her to sleep,' Ruta offered.

Now Kelly and I were alone. He reared back his head as if to search my face. 'Have a talk?'

'All right.'

'You can't imagine this day.' He rubbed his eyes. 'I suppose you've had your moments, too.' I did not answer.

Kelly nodded once. 'Carloads of people here. Friends, enemies, the lot. I've just left word downstairs – no one is to be let up. But then it's probably too late anyway. What time do you have?'

'After two.'

'Thought it was close to dawn. Are you all right?'

'I don't know.'

'I don't really either. I've hardly felt a thing all day. Burst into tears once. What with all the people here, I was somehow expecting Deborah to pop up for a drink, when wham!' he said softly, 'it hit me – no more Deborah.' He nodded. 'You're still numb, aren't you, Rojack?'

'There was bad blood between Deborah and me, I can't pretend.'

'To your credit to admit it, I suppose. I always thought you were mad about her.'

'I was for a long while.'

'Hard not to.'

'Yes.'

'All the world's certain you did her in. I spent the day telling people you didn't.'

NORMAN MAILER

'Well, I didn't.'

'I wasn't sure myself.'

'No, I didn't kill her.'

'That's good. That's just as well.'

'Yes, it is, considering the favor you did me.'

'Let's enjoy our drink,' Kelly said. 'I'm numb, too.'

In the silence, I helped myself to another brandy. I had been dragging sobriety after me; with the first taste of the new drink, I topped a hill: all the weight of my psyche was pulling me down the slope. I was suddenly drunk again, drunk clear through my mind – I wanted to tell him the truth.

'In fact,' he said, 'it wouldn't matter so much if you *had* killed her. I'm just as guilty, after all.' He rubbed his nose vigorously. 'I was a brute to her. She visited that brutishness back on you. So it comes to the same thing in the end, doesn't it?'

I could not think of an answer to this. Indeed, I had no idea what Kelly was up to.

'You haven't said a word about the funeral,' he said.

'No.'

'Well, let me tell you. It's going to be a small funeral, and we'll bury Deborah in a nice place I've picked – you were nowhere around this morning so I had to decide on it. It won't be hallowed ground of course, but it will be peaceable.'

We exchanged a stare. When the silence which came off from me did not falter he added, 'You're going of course.'

'No.'

'Is that what Deirdre was upset about?'

'I would think that's what it was.'

'Well, I want you to be there. I can't conceive of an explanation otherwise.'

'You can tell people I'm too broken to show.'

'I don't intend to tell them anything. I want you to stop being a bloody fool. You and me are going to stand side

234

by side at the funeral. Otherwise, it's hopeless. Everyone will be convinced you're a murderer.'

'Can't you understand,' I said, 'that I really don't care what people say. It's gone a little too deep for that.' My hand was trembling. To steady myself, I said, 'Besides, even if I go, they'll still say I did it.'

'Bother them all, there's a critical difference in the way it'll be said.' He was altogether calm as he spoke, but a vein in his forehead gave a jump and began to pulse. 'I never thought I'd have to explain to you,' said Kelly, 'that it doesn't matter what is done in private. What is important is the public show – it must be flawless. Because public show is the language we use to tell our friends and enemies that we still have order enough to make a good display. That's not so easy if you consider the general insanity of everything. You see, it doesn't matter whether people think you killed Deborah, it matters only whether people are given the opportunity to recognize it's been swept under the carpet, and you and I together are in control of the situation. If you don't show, it will cause so much talk that you and me will never be able to get to the real thing.'

'Which is?'

'That we become friends.'

'Kelly, I realize this has been quite a day for you . . .'

'I have confidence. We're closer than you expect.' He looked about. 'Come, let's go into the library.' It was the largest chamber in the suite and served as an omnibus bedroom, sitting room and antique gallery for Kelly. 'Come on,' he said, 'we can talk better there. It's a better place for what I have to say. You see, I want to tell you a long story. A long Godawful story. And the library is the place for it. It may not be your favorite room, but it certainly is mine. It's the only thing still belongs to me in New York.' He had in fact a town house in the East Sixties but never entered it. The house was occupied as a sort of hospital by Deborah's mother who was bedridden, profoundly separated from Kelly and had not spoken to Deborah since we were married.

'Very well. We might as well go in,' I said. But I did not want to. The library was a poor room for tonight.

In there, was a turn of mood as precise as the instant of entering a royal chapel, some dark chamber with reliquaries and monstrances; indeed, just as one went in, there was a silver monstrance before a screen, silver-gilt, set with stones, the screen a tapestry of women in Elizabethan dress talking to a deer while a squire was in the act of encountering a nude maid who grew out of the trunk of a tree. That was late sixteenth century. (Kelly, on one half-genial occasion, had spent an evening cataloguing the items for me – 'Who knows, you may own them someday,' he had said. 'Mustn't sell them for too little.') There was a harpsichord giving off the high patina of a snake; a carved and gilt side-table with four golden alligators for legs; a rug covered the floor with a purple-red landscape of trees and garden which glowed like a fire of permanganate. There was a looking-glass frame: ormolu cupids, scallop shells, wreaths, and pearls of flesh climbed up the sides of a pondlike mirror and formed a crest at the top. It was eight feet high. So might a mouse begin to study the privates of a queen.

There was more: a Lucchese bed with a canopy encrusted in blood-velvet and gold; next to it, a Venetian throne. Golden mermaids twined up the arms to the shield at the head. The sculpture was delicate, but the throne seemed to grow as one regarded it for the sirens and cupids slithered from one to another like lizards on the vines of a tree: in the high silence of this room there was all but the sound of vegetation working in the night. Kelly sat down on the throne, leaving me to sit in some uncomfortable but exceptional antique of a chair, a small inlay table of Chinese ivory between us, and since there was almost no light in

the room, just the small glow from the fire, and the illumi-
nation of a small lamp, I could see very little, the room
was suspended about us like the interior of a cave. I was
feeling wretched, twice wretched, in some rack of exhaustion between apathy and overstimulation. Nothing seemed
here and present, not Deborah's death, nor guilt, nor his
suffering – if he felt any – nor mine: I did not know if I
was real any longer, which is to say I did not feel connected
to myself. My mind brought too much fever to each possibility. I felt once again as I had felt on entering the Waldorf,
that I was in some antechamber of Hell where objects came
alive and communicated with one another while I sank
with each drink into a condition closer to the objects. There
was a presence in the room like the command of a dead
pharaoh. Aristocrats, slave owners, manufacturers and
popes had coveted these furnishings until the beseech-
ments of prayer had passed into their gold. Even as a
magnet directs every iron particle in a crowd of filings, so
a field of force was on me here, an air rich with surfeit
and the long whisper of corridors, the echo of a banquet
hall where red burgundy and wild boar went down. That
same field of force had come on me as I left Deborah's body
on the floor and started down the stairs to the room where
Ruta was waiting.

'Do you mind if I get some drink?'

'Please help yourself.'

I was out of the room and to the bar in the next room,
and having filled a tall glass with many cubes and several
inches of gin, I drank deep, the gin going down like a
cleansing fire. There was something wrong but I could not
place it: I felt particularly unarmed. And then remembered.
There was Shago's umbrella. It was in a corner of the
first closet I searched, and the handle came into my palm:
grasping the umbrella I felt stronger now, like a derelict
provided with a cigarette, a drink, and a knife. Thus
braced, I went back. He saw me with the umbrella. I made

no attempt to hide it, sitting with the stick laid over my knee.

'Comfortable now?' he asked.

I nodded.

As though testing the plumps of a breast, he palmed both hands about the snifter, then looked off into the darkness. I became aware of a log still going in the fireplace, and Kelly got up this time and threw a new log on and poked the first with an intimate jab, as if he were waking an old stubborn hound.

'Bess tell you about her romance with me?' he asked.

'She said something about it.'

'Due to Bess, I lost the upbringing of Deborah.'

'Deborah never told me.'

'I've never talked about myself to anyone,' Kelly said. 'I detest that. It's spilling the seed. But I have wanted to talk to you. You see Deborah used to give me a hint of your beliefs. I was taken with your declaration – did you really make it on television? – that God's engaged in a war with the Devil, and God may lose.'

Oppression stirred again. An idea came to get up, make farewells, and depart, simple as that. The room, however, was a weight on my will. 'I'm not up to a discussion,' I said. And I wasn't. Tonight I had a terror of offending God *or* the Devil.

'Of course.' But there was contempt, as if the real mark was to chat at the cliffside of a disaster. 'Well,' he sighed, 'it's all in curious taste, I know, but I like teasing the Jesuits with your idea. I get them to admit that the Devil in such a scheme has to have an even chance to defeat the Lord, or there's no scheme to consider. Of course the off-shoot of this hypothesis, I point out, is that the Church is an agent of the Devil.'

He looked up as if to call for a question and I, to be polite, answered, 'Do I follow you?'

'Since the Church refuses to admit the possible victory

of Satan, man believes that God is all-powerful. So man also assumes God is prepared to forgive every last little betrayal. Which may not be the case. God might be having a very bad war with troops defecting everywhere. Who knows? Hell by now might be no worse than Las Vegas or Versailles.' He laughed. 'Good Lord and gravy, does that put a Jesuit's nose out of joint. I must say they can't come back too hard with their legendary counterattack, because I have money to dangle. One of them, however, got brave enough to say, "If the Church is the agent of the Devil, Oswald, why in damnation do you donate so much?" and of course I could not keep from replying, "Well, for all we know, I am a solicitor for the Devil."'

'But you really think so.'

'On occasion, I'm vain enough.'

We took a pause on this.

'Do you never think of yourself as a good Catholic?' I asked.

'Why should I? I'm a *grand* Catholic. Much more amusing. Then I'm hardly typical. My Kellys came from North Ireland. Oswald derives from Presbyterians. It wasn't until the question of marrying Deborah's mother came up that I decided Paris was worth a Mass. Certainly was. Kelly converted and climbed the stairs. Now, I've got stories,' he said. 'Once you're located where I am, there's nothing left but to agitate the web. At my worst, I'm a spider. Have strings in everywhere from the Muslims to the *New York Times*. Just ask me. I've got it.'

'Got the C I A?'

Put a finger to his lips at the directness of the remark. 'Threads.'

'And Mr Ganucci's friends?'

'Lots of knots,' said Kelly.

The fire blazed in a back-draft, and he looked at me. 'Ever realize how carnivorous the winds get here? Mountain winds.' I made no answer. I was thinking of the parapet. It was conceivable he was thinking of it as well. 'Rojack, I'm not as powerful as you think,' said Kelly. 'I dabble. It's the hardworking fellow at the desk who has the real power. The career man.' He said this with easy candor, ready to laugh at me, but whether for believing him, or whether for not believing him, was precisely the little difference I could not detect.

'Are you altogether comfortable?' he asked.

I shifted in my seat.

'Not much of my story is pretty,' he said. 'But then I've warned you. Look,' he added, 'it's a full warning. I'm putting a weight on you. I think everyone must tell his real little buried story sooner or later. He must pick out somebody to tell it to. But I didn't know who to tell it to. Tonight, as you came in the room, I knew. Suddenly I knew. You're the one.' He looked at me. A hint of gray ice in a river came out of the core of his heartiness. 'With your permission.'

I nodded. I had become aware again of the darkness. We sat like two hunters in the midnight of a jungle. Kelly's voice, however, was genial. 'You know I was a simple young man when I was young,' he said. 'Grew up in Minnesota, youngest child in a large family, worked on farms, grocery store after school, all of that. Deborah ever tell you?'

'Others have.'

'They couldn't know the details. We were poor as rats. But my father had pretensions, *North* Irish Kellys, after all. We even had a coat of arms, hurrah. Gules, a child proper. Can you conceive of a shield with nothing but a naked babe in it? That was us. I managed to take the child and slip it into the mouth of the Mangaravidi's serpent when I decided to consolidate the arms. Leonora was ready to have a fit. She tried to fight it clear across the seas to the College of Arms. But then of course by that time Leonora and I had been at war for years.'

'Deborah never talked about any of this.'

'Well. I won't bore you too much. I'll just say I had three thousand dollars in capital after World War One – the savings of my entire family. My father used to keep his green in an old cheesebox in a locked drawer. I got hold of that package and went to Philadelphia, hopped all over the place in Army Surplus. Blew up the three thousand dollars to one hundred thousand dollars in one year, not saying how. Gave my family five thousand back since they'd been nice enough not to scream for the sheriff. Then in two years on the market, I poked the ninety-five thousand up to one million. Explode a miser like my father and you get a mad genius like me. No explanation for my gift, my investments weren't brilliant, you see, they just kept winning. Scared me stiff. I was just a poor hick Presbyterian.'

A change had come over him. It was obvious he loved to tell a story. His voice rounded into humors, his manner became embracing yet impersonal as if he were the master for an exceptional treat which soon would be offered you.

'Well, then I met Leonora. I was set up in business in Kansas City. Grain futures, owned divvies on a movie theatre, put up money with a bully who was starting an interstate trucking concern, and still kept running a wild streak on the market, skipping from one teeter-totter of margin to another. Got into something with Leonora's father. There was a gent! Sicilian aristocrat, raised in Paris. Now marooned in Kansas City. Poor bastard had been penniless, you gather, when he married into the bullion. So even though he was just about the grandest item in the Gotha, the Caughlins shipped him out to K.C. to run their meat-packings, British money in Midwestern meat then – well, this may be going on, I know, but I can't dive at once into the center of this little tale – it's too rough.' He threw me a quick hard look. 'At any rate, Signor and I got along very well, thank you, and he came up with the idea of marrying me to Leonora, a great surprise, for he was ferociously snob, but it was his revenge, I would bet, on the Caughlins. They looked for nothing but the grandest with their granddaughter. So, too, I'm sure, did Mangaravidi, but he was able to convince himself that Oswald's Kellys were grafted stock of the Windsor vine. I didn't try to unconvince him that I was no royal bastard.

'On the other hand, I didn't take altogether to Leonora. She was a devout. Pretty girl, but completely spooked. Used to wear a perfume made, I swear, of linseed oil and camphor balls. Kept a saint in every pocket. A bacchanal for a young man, wasn't she just! But I had learned the first thing about mazuma. There are dollars which buy a million's worth of groceries, and dollars which have influence. The Caughlins had the second kind of grabbings, I had the first. So I paid court to Leonora for a year, and captured her with my conversion. In marrying me, she felt she was bringing a soul to the Church. Her little view of marriage. We did it. And I discovered myself up to here in a dank tank. I didn't know marbles about sex, I just knew something was damn bloody wrong. Why, we hadn't been married a year before our mutual antipathy was so perfect a room was spoiled if the other had been in it five minutes before. On top of that, Leonora could not conceive, so it seemed – I had nightmares the Romans would give her an annulment. No need to polish the details, you must appreciate a few yourself; I needed to be married to her long enough to lay out a thorough circuit of connections. Without her, I was upstart, whereas with her – I adored the life she opened, Leonora's friends were the patch for me. Money which cannot buy into the most amusing world is cabbage, stinking stifling cabbage, that much I knew at twenty-three.' He took another sip. 'Well, B. Oswald Kelly said to himself, "Napoleon, the armies must occupy the womb." And we did. My troops made one do-johnny of a march. On a given night, in an absolute eczema of flesh, whipping myself up with the fancy I was giving a poke to some poor flunky, I drilled my salt into her, I took a dive deep down into a vow, I said in my mind; "Satan, if it takes your pitchfork up my gut, let me blast a child into this bitch!" And something happened, no sulphur, no brimstone, but Leonora and I met way down there in some bog, some place awful, and I felt something take hold in her. Some sick breath came right back out of her pious little mouth. "What the *hell* have you done?" she screamed at me, which was the only time Leonora ever swore. That was it. Deborah was conceived.'

There was no answer I could give. I knew his story was true. The umbrella lay like a sleeping snake across my thighs.

'I've read a bit about the saints,' said Kelly, 'you'd be surprised. If a saint has his vision, he is next bothered with devils. The Devil's first joy is to pick up a saint — at least that's what I would do. And the return payment, I expect, is that the Lord's first attention is toward us little devils. I can only testify that I was never so fond of Leonora as during that pregnancy. "Oh, God," I used to pray before sleep, "have mercy on this child growing in her womb, for I have damned the creature before it began." And there would be times when I would put my hand on Leonora's belly, and feel everything which was best in me pass through my fingers into that creature sleeping in her mother's waters. What do you think came out? An absolute marvel of an infant. Almost died in birth. They had to slice Leonora nearly in half to spring the baby, but Deborah had eyes which took you on a trip through real estate!' — he laughed — 'right through glens and dells her eyes took you, and a corps de ballet of elves and spirits to take nips of your vision as you went in. That child would laugh like a fifty-year-old beer drinker, brawny little thing, laugh the devil right back at you for trying to see into her. I

never adored anything as I adored that infant. Excuse me,'
he said, 'for not obeying the pact,' and began to weep. I
all but reached over to touch his arm, but he got up as
though to avoid such a gesture and moved toward the fire.
A minute went by.

'Well,' he said over his shoulder, 'you strike a bargain
with the Devil, the Devil will collect. That's where Mephi-
sto is found. In the art of collection. Trust me: Leonora
was in bad shape after the birth, gutted, all of that. I didn't
care, I had the infant – that was my connection to good
luck. But we thought we might go to the Riviera while she
mended, and I had friends enough I wanted to make on
that glorious piece of coast. So I tidied up my affairs in
Kansas City, took a back seat in the trucking firm – which
incidentally I've still got; it became an enormous firm,
thanks to the bully – sold for a loss here, grabbed a profit
there, and we were off. I knew enough to know the pots
to be investigated. And I made a piece of that, yes, I did,
first time I ever did business with blue water and smell of
sun in the nose. Tastes pop up in you on that Mediter-
ranean. Everybody is looking for their very special little
pleasure and I wasn't ready to find all my joys in the
infant, I wanted a bit more, damn sure I was entitled to
more. Then along came Bess, the Devil's little gift. She was
in from New York to spend a season in her villa – at the
time I thought it was the most stunning house I'd ever
seen – she owned a Raphael, that sort of nonsense.

'Actually the house was a groaning display, too many
floors put down in marble, Burne-Joneses lit with candles,
homosexual sculpture – fat little cupids with pointy little
pricks and bottoms like a chorus girl – froufrou in her
bedroom, lily pads in the pond, obscene rubber trees. Even
a scorpion she kept in a glass cage. She had no taste. But
she was grand, grander than anything I'd ever seen, and
I was petrified of her. She was all of forty, though she
didn't look it a bit, and I wasn't twenty-five. She had an

awful reputation, four marriages, three children, lovers in every corner, anything you wanted, from an Egyptian with a cellar full of whips to a young American racing car specialist. And unbelievable stories about her, way off my spectrum, for Bess was petite, just as lovely as an orchid. Very elusive of course, you could turn to get a drink and she'd disappeared from the room, but her air was exquisite. She had a delicate humor. I couldn't digest the awful stories about her, but I had to swallow some part of them, because Bess was in communion with something. You didn't have amour with her, you had some species of interplay. Messages went back and forth — it was the first time I ever understood there is a hocus-pocus of the cells. Something astral in her, or whatever, was avid to snatch up bits of me. I couldn't stop the process. She kept stealing my pigeons, so to speak. Then afterwards she'd fly them back — the loan was returned — but something had been added, something foreign. I felt as if I now too was in touch with forces I would just as soon have left alone. Mangaravidi had a bit of that — I always believed he was a hussar of the ghosts, but Bess was queen of the spooks. Never met anyone so telepathic. If there hadn't been Marconi she would have been the one to dream up the radio. I remember one time we were in her garden and she asked for a five-franc piece. Soon as I gave it to her she zipped into her bag, pulled out a nail scissors, and clipped a couple of hairs from my head. Then she bent down, scooped up a stone from the bottom of a rubber tree, set the five-francker on top of the hairs and put back the stone. "Squeaks," she said, "I might be able to hear you." Well, I tried to be ha-ha about it, but it wasn't that funny — the tree stood there like a statue. And now Bess began to have a way of telling me all about private conversations I'd had with Leonora, or worse: she'd tell me some of my own little thoughts. Given that damn tree, I was directly in her power. I thought myself a competitive fellow, just consider — I had to be nearly as

supersensational with sex as I was with *dinero*, and Bess
and I gave each other some glorious good times in a row;
up would climb the male ego; applause from Bess was
accolade from Cleopatra; then swish! she'd vanish. Gone
for a day or week. "Had to, darling," she'd say on her
return, "he was irresistible." Only to tickle my ego up
again by confessing I was *more* irresistible, ergo she was
back. Or to the contrary, she'd leave me pulp; she'd say,
"Well, he's gone, but *he's* unforgettable." I was like a
hound halfway through a steak, have it snatched from him.
She got me to the point where I could be in the middle of
doing my work and all of a sudden I'd think, "Bess is off
with somebody." My brain would scoot out of me just as
fast as feeder ants from a piece of carrion that's just been
kicked. I *was* carrion. I was in her damn grip. Intolerable.
I was afraid of her. More afraid of her than I'd been of
anybody. Each time we got together I felt as if I were an
open piggy-bank: had to take whatever she would drop
into me; her coin was powers. My nose for the market
turned infallible. Lying in bed I could feel the potential of
a given stock as much as if I were bathing in the thoughts
of a thousand key investors. I could almost hear the sound
of the mother factory. It was like soaking up a view. Then
I would be left with the final impression, "Artichokes is
going up tomorrow, Beethoven is going down." Whatever!
I was spoon-fed on expert opinion, of course, I was just
about a clearinghouse for tips, but this went a distance
beyond that, I promise you. And there were other spooker-
ies. One time a bugger started to give me a hard time,
pompous little promoter. As he was walking away, I said
to myself, "Drop, you bugger," and he had epilepsy right
at my door. Wondrous sort of power.

'Well, *poco a poco*, I started to trundle along on Bess's
extra ventures. They were *wows*. Had to talk my way out
of a bad place or two – Bess was incorrigible. Only one
thing could make her put on the brakes. She had a niece

— her sister's daughter — nineteen, virgin. Lovely girl. Bess adored her. Only thing she really cared about. The niece came for a visit and before you knew it the two women were up to the elbow. Inseparable. The stickiest attraction between them. You can imagine how this put Bess at odds. A parting of the seas in her overcharged libido. Like Moses, I kept taking one nimble step after another into the Red Divide. I headed right for the heart of the problem, as if the way to get thumbs on Bess was to make her girl fall in love with me. I did not even know if I did this at Bess's bidding, or against her will, but we certainly came closer and closer all of us to the jewels. Then, one night, one more or less pregnant night in Bess's boudoir, the three of us sat about for hours. Bess was drinking a little, I was drinking a lot, this girl was sipping champagne. The longer we tried to make small talk, the more powerful became the itch to set off an earthquake. After awhile, we all got silent. There was gunpowder in the nostrils. And a whiff of something ghoulish. As if we breathed a winding sheet to and fro. I've never been so excited in my life to make the move, and yet my bones were soup — look,' said Kelly, holding up his palm, 'let me give the truth: the girl was not a niece but a daughter, Bess's little girl whom she had lost by divorce years ago. I had the feeling that to say a word would strike a match, and yet to quit the game at this extraordinary moment would deprive me of my strength. Afraid to go on, afraid to quit, we just sat in a furnace. And dear Bess melted first. She gave me the wink. I got up on the spot, it was too much, she had suggested it five minutes too soon. I bolted. Ran downstairs to have a drink by myself. Made a vow I'd give Bess up. Started to leave her house. But on the way through the garden, I thought of that rubber tree, and knew I couldn't go away while Bess still kept her little ear beneath the stone. So I started to pluck it up. "Don't you dare," I heard Bess say clearly, even though she was nowhere about.

'"Damn you," I said back, and picked up the stone, stuck the franc piece in my pocket, kicked the hole with the toe of my shoe to scatter the bits of hair, and off I went. I hadn't taken five steps before I knew I'd never make it, I'd pass out. So back plunged Kelly, took the first bathroom he could find on the ground floor, and proceeded to get sick as a boy with his first bottle of whiskey. There on my knees at that moment, pinching the five-franc piece as if it were all the riches I had, in slavery to the plumbing, I heard, clear across town, a sound of Deborah screaming. What screams! I saw flames as clear as a movie film on Bess's bathroom wall, flames licking at Deborah's crib. My house was on fire, I was convinced. Well, I got out of that bathroom fast, and got across town as ever fast I could, I don't know if I've ever driven so fast, and what do you think? Our house was perfectly all right. It was only the house next door which was on fire. A total conflagration. No one knew how it started, either. And Deborah was screaming in her crib.

'That was warning enough. I sat down with Leonora to make a complete confession. And she — I should have known it — went into hysterics. Next morning was disaster. Bess's daughter had a breakdown in the night: she carried on. The servants heard a bit of it. Result: Antibes heard all of it. We were *shunned*. You can make any kind of splash you want in that world, but keep the water clear of mud. Leonora took off and left me. Took Deborah with her. Forbid a divorce, forbid all right to the child. I was not allowed to see Deborah again until she was eight, and then for an hour. I never really saw her until she was fifteen.' He took a breath and stared at the fire. 'I had a lot to think about. I'd never been so tempted in my life as I was that night. I kept being bothered by the thought that if I had taken a chance, I would have had the opportunities of a president or a king.' He took a deep pull of his brandy. 'I decided the only explanation is that God and the Devil are very attentive to the people at the summit. I don't know if they stir much in the average man's daily stew, no great sport for spooks, I would suppose, in a ranch house, but do you expect God or the Devil left Lenin and Hitler or Churchill alone? No. They bid for favors and exact revenge. That's why men with power sometimes act so silly. Kaiser Wilhelm, for example. There's nothing but magic at the top. It's the little secret a few of us keep to ourselves, but that, my friend, is one reason it's not easy to get to the very top. Because you have to be ready to deal with One or the Other, and that's too much for the average good man on his way. Sooner or later, he decides to be mediocre, and put up with the middle. I know I was ready. Incest is the gate to the worst sort of forces, and I'd had my belly-full early.' Kelly sighed. 'The experience put me off sex for years.'

'That's not your reputation.'

'I have a late reputation,' said Kelly. 'But I was a good boy for quite a period. Very good I was. Then I got custody. Know why?'

'Why?'

'Leonora was broke. *Figure-toi.* All that bloody Catholicism. She couldn't take a deep breath until the saints were put to bed; nonetheless, she lost almost half of her inheritance in the market, that idiot! Suddenly, she was obliged to live on principal. She'd never taken a cent from me, but now she needed the stuff. Turned out Leonora loved cabbage more than morals. In return for a large piece of cash, I got full custody of Deborah. In fact the girl and her mother couldn't bear each other. Leonora had stashed her in a convent. Now Deborah and I had a home.'

'Then what?' I asked.

'Happy times,' he said. He looked away. 'Of course one does well not to talk of that. Not tonight. But I was happy until Deborah got married to Pamphli. Mind you, I did like him, Pamphli was a bit in the style of Mangaravidi.

But he was much too old for her and ill. Well, let's not talk about bad parts.'

'Deborah told me Pamphli was a fine hunter.' I was making conversation – I was uneasy. I did not know if the story were finished or half-begun.

'Pamphli had been a good hunter once. And he did actually take her all the way over to Africa for the honeymoon, but Deborah did most of the bush work with the guide. They weren't out long. Pamphli was too sick. Besides, Deborah was having a damn sick time with Deirdre.'

'Then she was pregnant when they married?'

'Afraid she was.' He shifted irritably. 'Now what the hell do you want to know?' he asked. He was about to shut down on the British accent.

'Who Deirdre's father might be.'

'You don't suppose Deborah advertised every last little fling, do you?'

But in saying this, her death opened again between us. 'All right,' he said, 'there's a little more of the story. Can't conceal it from you, can I?' He threw me a look, almost a jeering look. 'You see, by the time Deborah came to live under my roof, I had hardened up. You don't live alone for years devoted to nothing but soul and business without getting fairly rich. I didn't smoke, booze never. Let me tell you, boy, in a situation like that, it's hard not to keep making new boodles. On the one hand, you're clearminded. On the other – you would have to hurt a great many people's feelings not to fall on another buried treasure every six months, because they're begging you to take it, take their money, take their invention, take their export license, take their wife, slip it up grandmother, they are sordid with eagerness. You get bored. A rich man cannot afford that – his boredom is infinite in its dimensions. So I looked for diversion. Bought into a news magazine, I think you met the fellow who's supposed to run it. He doesn't. Some of *us* run it. We leave the praying to him. Mousy fellow. He's just a missionary on the capitalist highway of life.'

The only sign Kelly gave of being the least bit drunk: he now smiled at his own remark.

'Yes,' he said, 'well, the magazine got me interested in what we call "the problems of governments" and governments got interested in me. London's the only place to have headquarters for anything like that – what a wicked place it is. You take all of Europe and America – I suppose I was one of the hundred most important fellows around. Which is more than I could say today. Today, *everybody* is important. Well, boom, Deborah landed in all that. Fifteen years old. Full of force, all untouched, a sweet wild thing, plump, green Irish fire in her eyes, all those Mangaravidi graces. She hadn't been in the house two days before she brought home three young Bolsheviks – students at Oxford, Communists. They had palpitations when they saw me, I was the great villain, never been more seductive in my life. "You were marvelous with them, Daddy," Deborah said afterward.'

'Kelly, it's getting more and more difficult to listen to this.'

'Then don't keep me waiting. You can hardly enjoy hearing what she was like at fifteen. I don't want to go on. I just want to hear you say you're going to be at the funeral, aren't you?'

I could feel the pressure of his motive but could not name it. To fill the pause I took another half-inch of gin and caught a sniff of my lungs. They were like the air in a subway at midsummer. An imperative came through my drunkenness: I had the certainty I must not leave Kelly's suite until I went out to the terrace and walked around the parapet, around all three sides of the parapet. *All* three sides. I began to tremble very quietly at the force of this desire.

'You're going to be at the funeral, aren't you?' he repeated.

I felt as if I were now going out to do war with him in an alley. 'You haven't made it clear to me,' I said, 'why you waited so long for Deborah . . .'

'Yes?'

'And then put her back in a convent.'

'Well, I did.'

'You got her back after fifteen years, and gave her up again?'

'Not instantly. She stayed in my London house for a year.'

'Then she went to the convent?'

'The war had just started and I was traveling a bit. I thought she'd be safer there.'

'I see.'

'Look, Stephen.'

'Yes.'

'If you have something on your mind . . .'

'It seems unusual to me,' I said.

'Well,' he said, with a profound sigh as though relieved I had forced him to go on, 'you've guessed. There *was* something unusual. Listen to this: I couldn't even bear for Deborah to spend the night away with one of her little girl friends, I had to call the parents at one A.M. to check on her health. If the poor child went out to a concert with a boy, I had the horrors. Thought it was because she was fresh out of a convent and I was worried about her innocence. Good God, I was more jealous of that child than I'd ever been of Bess. Then one night the pigeons came home, every last one. Deborah came back twenty minutes late from a supper dance. I was so furious I was ready to fire the chauffeur. Took her upstairs, started to scold her, she tried to talk back, I slapped her. Whereupon she burst into tears. Whereupon I grasped her, kissed her, put my tongue on hers' – Kelly's tongue peeped out of the corner of his mouth – 'and then thrust her away. I thought I'd have a heart attack – she came up to me and kissed me back. Accept that for a horror?' But there was not exactly a horror between us. It was more like the tension provided by a joke which is likely to reveal some truth about the man who tells it or the man who listens, but just whom is not yet certain. Kelly looked at me and said, 'I walked away from her. Locked myself in my room. I had all kinds of thoughts. Suicide. Murder. Yes, I thought of killing her. First time I felt unbalanced in fifteen years. And then I felt an awful desire to go to her room: my teeth were literally grinding, my belly was a pit of snakes. It was as if the Devil had come into the room at that instant and was all over me, I tell you I could smell him, he smelled just like a goat, it was horrendous. "Deliver me from all this, O Lord," I cried out to myself. Then I felt a powerful impulse to go to the window and jump. That was the message I seemed to receive.' Kelly paused. 'Now, I was up on the second story, and the ground floor was gracious in its proportions. So, say the jump down was as much as sixteen feet, or a little more. Nothing fabulous. Worst, I suppose, was that I would break a leg. But if it had been Heaven there waiting for me at the bottom, I didn't have the nerve to jump. Look,' he said, 'I had played knees under the table with a lot of people who could cut your throat, that didn't bother me, good even nerve I've had most of my life, but I was – do you know that phrase of Kierkegaard's, of course you do – I was in a fear and trembling. I stayed at that window for an hour. I was almost blubbering at my inability to take that simple jump. And the goat kept coming back. "She's down the hall," said the goat, "she's on her bed, it's there for you, Oswald." Then I would reply, "Save me, Lord." Finally, I heard a voice say quite clearly, "Jump! That will cool your desire, fellow. Jump!" The Lord, you see had a bitch of a humor about me.

'"Lord," I said at last, "I'd rather give Deborah up."

The simple thought came, "Let me send her back to the convent." The moment I said that, I knew I'd give up having her in my house. And the compulsion disappeared.'

'And Deborah went back to the convent?'

'Yes.'

'You gave up your daughter?'

'I did. Don't you see now why you've got to come to the funeral? It has something to do with her forgiving me, I know that. Good God, Stephen, can't you see I'm suffering?' But he didn't seem to be. His eyes were a bright green, his skin was flushed, he had never seemed more like a big animal. A flush of greed came off the air about him.

'Look here,' he said when I did not respond, 'do you know why Ganucci came by tonight?'

'No.'

'Because he was in a losing position with me. Italians are clever. They understand the amnesty which is possible when there's a death in the family.'

That was clear enough. 'But do I choose to grant *you* amnesty?' I said.

I had finally reached his anger. His eyes gave a hint of murderous bad weather. 'Extraordinary,' Kelly said, 'you never come to the end of knowing Italians. It took forever before I understood that when an Italian says somebody is crazy, he means the man has no sensitivity to fear, so he will have to be killed. Now if I were Italian, I would call you crazy.'

'I'm too full of fear.'

'You do odd things for a man with fear. What was that nonsense on the terrace?'

'A private expedition.'

'Something to do with my story, could it be?'

'It could be.'

'Yes, Deborah once explained how you would like to blow up poor old Freud by demonstrating that the root of neurosis is cowardice rather than brave old Oedipus. I always say it takes one Jew to do in another. Mother of God, were you doing field work on the balcony? Did the experiment check out a winner, Stephen? Are you now ready to take a *stroll* around the parapet?'

I could hear Deborah's tones in his voice: they pushed me to answer too quickly. 'Yes, I could do it,' I said, and had said too much.

'Could you?'

'Not right now.'

'Why ever not?'

'I've had a lot to drink.'

'You wouldn't do it?'

'Not unless there was something at stake.'

He held his brandy glass and looked down into it as if the quiver of light in the liquid were the entrails of a sacrifice.

'What if there is something at stake?' he said.

'There couldn't be.'

'I'm going to have more brandy,' he said.

But as I turned my mouth to my own drink, the liquid leaped up with a lurch of my elbow off the arm of the chair, and a splash went on my cheek. It could have been blood, that small streak of Deborah's blood left as I embraced her in a full false embrace as she was lying on the street, and the sensation of something wet on my face divided me now from reason. I had a horror of being forced to walk the parapet – there was no confidence I could do it at all; yet the room fixed me in a mood I did not dare to break as if there would be a toll on my flesh, some new penalty of nausea, waste, and disease if I shattered the force which lay on us now by getting to my feet, by leaving him. Besides I did not know where his power ended. Maybe he had only to pick up the phone and some automobile could cut me down at an intersection. Everything contained its possibility. I only knew that I was in some difficult all but inextricable situation in which he would succeed to push me further, and then further again, like a chess master nursing his victory, until I would be forced to admit the inevitable necessity of going out on the terrace. And that I could not do.

'All right,' said Kelly, 'let's really talk, Rojack. Let's put the pistols on the table. There's one reason why you won't go to the funeral, isn't there?'

'Yes.'

'It's because you did kill Deborah?'

'Yes.'

The silence had no air left. Now the messenger arrived. It all came in at once. 'Yes, I killed her,' I said, 'but I didn't seduce her when she was fifteen, and never leave her alone, and never end the affair,' and I leaned forward to attack him, as if finally he were mine and I was free of waste and guilt and gutting of the earth, and looking at him knew this was exactly what he had wanted me to discover, what he had spent this night in developing until even I could not miss it, and a smile came off him, a sweet smile, the loveliest smile he possessed, it twinkled about Kelly like a harbor light: come here, the mermaids were saying, you have taken our queen and we have captured your king, checkmate, dear boy, and I slipped off the lip of all sanity into a pit of electronic sirens and musical lyrics dictated by X-ray machines for a gout of the stench which comes from devotion to the goat came up from him and went over to me. I no longer knew what I was doing, nor why I did it, I was in some deep of waters and no recourse but to keep swimming and never stop. Disaster would be on my body when I came to rest. Something stirred in the room. Perhaps it was the vat of liquor in my gut, but I had the sensation something of me was passing through a corridor and a breath, an odium, came up over my face as if finally I had blundered through a barrier. Kelly was near to that violence Deborah used to give off, that hurricane rising from a swamp, that offer of carnage, of cannibals, the viscera of death came from him to me like suffocation. I was going to be dead in another minute; all Deborah's wrath passed now through him, he was agent to her fury and death set about me like a ringing of echoes in ether, red light and green. I waited for Kelly to attack – he came that close – I had only to close my eyes and he would go to the fire, pick up a poker – his stopped-up violence fired the room. We could have been sitting in smoke. Then this suffocation passed, was replaced; on the beat of the silence, feeling his pulse as if it were my own, hearing his heart like the electronic wind in a microphone, I floated out on the liquor to a promise of power, some icy majesty of intelligence, a fired heat of lust. His body gave off the radiation of a fire, there was heat between us now the way there had been heat between Ruta and me in Deborah's hall; suddenly I knew what it had been like with Cherry and him, not so far from Ruta and me, no, not so far, and knew what it had been like with Deborah and him, what a hot burning two-backed beast, and I could hear what he offered now: bring Ruta forth, three of us to pitch and tear and squat and lick, swill and grovel on that Lucchese bed, fuck until our eyes were out, bury the ghost of Deborah by gorging on her corpse, for this had been the bed, yes, this Lucchese had been the bed where he went out with Deborah to the tar pits of the moon. Now, he had a call to bury her raw. Desire came off Kelly to jump the murderer of his beast, and unfamiliar desire stirred in me, echo of that desire to eat with Ruta on Deborah's corpse. 'Come on,' Kelly murmured, sitting on his throne, 'shall we get shitty?' and went on in a voice so low his tongue and teeth were almost in the speech, I was in that vacuum where silence is stored and the reek of murders still unconceived.

Then the umbrella slipped from my knee and the near-empty echo of its drop to the carpet went past my ear like a beating of wings, a death passed between us like a beating of wings, and I was scored with a vision of Shago knocking on Cherry's door, and she opening to receive him, opening her wrapper, opening the heart of her thighs, the lips, the hair, the picture as clear in my mind as the burning house Kelly had seen in the bath at Antibes. I would never forgive her for Kelly, and with that thought, dread came in, I was certain Shago was with her now, it was in the balance of things, he was there with her just so soon as I was here with Kelly. Or was a man being murdered in Harlem at this instant – the picture in my mind was broken with shock – did I feel a broken sawed-off bat go beating on a brain, was a man expiring, some cry (should it have been mine?) going out into an alley of the night, carrying across the miles to the thirty stories of this room – was a murderer running and caught in the patrols of the gods?

Then I was caught. For I wanted to escape from that intelligence which let me know of murders in one direction and conceive of visits to Cherry from the other, I wanted to be free of magic, the tongue of the Devil, the dread of the Lord, I wanted to be some sort of rational man again, nailed tight to details, promiscuous, reasonable, blind to the reach of the seas. But I could not move.

I bent to pick up the umbrella, and then the message came clear, 'Walk the parapet,' it said. 'Walk the parapet or Cherry is dead.' But I had more fear for myself than for Cherry. I did not want to walk that parapet. 'Walk it,' said the voice, 'or you are worse than dead.' And then I understood: I saw cockroaches following the line of their anxiety up the tenement wall.

'All right,' I said to Kelly, 'let's go to the terrace.'

I said this clearly, I must have expected Kelly to beg we remain in the room – I had never felt a sex so manacled to its desire as the desire which had passed across the table from him – but his discipline was steel: he had not won what he won for nothing. He nodded now, and managed to say in the clearest of voices, 'By all means. Let's go to the terrace.' And a confidence came off him that he would have what he wanted some other way. A fear broke loose in my body like the wobble which comes on a child when he is forced into a fight he does not want. It was a very bad fear. I looked at him – I do not know with what look – but it must have been some appeal for mercy, as if he had only to say, 'Well, let's stop the nonsense, it's gone far enough,' and I would be reprieved. His eyes were neutral, however, and nothing came from him. I could not talk anymore. Like a terminal patient whose faculties leave him one by one, so my voice went silent in my throat: I understood the final moments of a man condemned to a firing squad, and had envy for that man – his death was certain, he could prepare himself, but I had to get ready for I did not know what – that seemed worse than any certain knowledge of one's end.

We went through the French doors of the library out into the air. It was raining harder now, and the smell of wet grass came through the night, riding the wind from the Park. I did not know if I could get up on the parapet, I had no strength. The thought of using the deck chair was now ambitious beyond my means. I had rather begin at the wall, near the French windows. Neither of us said a word. Kelly came along modestly, like a chaplain accompanying a prisoner.

But it was easier now, at least that we were moving. I had left my life behind me. Just as a man in dying might have a moment when he passes into the mantle of some great cloud, and helpless, full of fear, knows nonetheless that he is in death already and so can wait for it, so my force ceased, and again I felt death come up like the shadow which is waiting as one slips past the first sentinels of consciousness into the islands of sleep. 'All right,' I thought, 'I guess I am ready to die.'

When Kelly saw I was going to get up on the parapet, he said, 'You'd better give me your umbrella.'

And I was annoyed, the way a dying man might be bothered in his last reverie by a doctor injecting him with a needle. I did not want Kelly near me, I wanted to be alone; it seemed desperately unfair in a way I could not name to give up the umbrella, but even worse to discuss it, as if I would use up something vital. So I handed the umbrella over. But that left a loss, and again I was afraid to get up on the parapet. Indeed, there was no easy way to mount. I would have to raise my foot uncomfortably high, bring my knee up almost to my shoulder, and then clinging with my right hand to the groove of mortar in the wall of the building I would have to take a quick vertical step up just as if I were springing into a high stirrup, and if I came up too hard, I might go over. But, at least, my voice came back. 'Have *you* ever done this?' I asked.

'No. Never tried,' said Kelly.

'Yes, but Deborah tried,' I said suddenly.

'Yes, she did.'

'Was she able to go all the way around?'

'She got off midway.'

'Poor Deborah,' I said. Fear was back in my voice.

'You're not the one to pity her,' he said.

That provided me with just enough to take the high step. My fingers scraped on the wall, one nail broke and came half off, and I was up, up on that parapet one foot wide, and almost broke in both directions, for a desire to dive right on over swayed me out over the drop, and I nearly fell back to the terrace from the panic of that. I stood there, pure cowardice again, my right hand shivering out of control as I took it from the wall, and stood naked, supported by nothing. It was impossible to take another step. My will slipped away from me, and I stood motionless, trembling and a blubber. I might have wept like a child if I were not afraid even of that. And then I felt some hard contemptuous disgust of my fear. 'Every cockroach has the memory of a revolting failure,' muttered something, somewhere, whether in or without my mind I hardly knew, I was soaking wet, but I took one step, one full step, my foot like a forty-pound boot of lead, and brought my rear foot up to meet it, and took another step forward on the same heavy foot like a child climbing the stairs with the right leg always in advance; then I took a third step and stopped, and felt the huge sleeping bulk of the hotel, the tower behind me, and walls still rising to right and left across the chasm of the drop, and down below, walls falling down to ledges and other walls and falling again in a waterfall of stone. But I felt no longer so exposed – the act of balance seemed less precarious, as if the walls offered hints to my ear of a vertical line my body could obey. I took a step; and another step; and realized I had not taken a breath and now took one, and stole a look down the fall and pulled myself back from the impulse to go out like an airplane in a long glide. And my trembling came back. It took a minute before I could move but then I took a step, and took a breath, took a step, and took a breath: this way I took ten steps along the twelve-inch width of the parapet which extended before me like a long board.

There were ten more steps to the point where the parapet made a right-angle turn to the left and went parallel to the street. I made it by telling myself I would get down once I reached the angle. But when I came to the turn I could not get down – I had to go around all three sides of the terrace. So I had accomplished only the first part of three separate parts. Now I hung at the first turn. I had caught a glimpse of the street below, and the fall seemed twice as far, and then opened again like a crack in the earth, which deepened as I looked into it and fell away and opened out again bottomless.

A gust blew up behind me, a slap of wind. As I swayed in it I took the turn and kept going two, three, four, five steps, I was almost halfway around. But the rain was icy cold – the temperature had dropped five degrees coming around that turn. I was somehow more exposed now. I took a step; and another step. I was no longer walking with one leg dragged behind the other, but now my body kept leaning toward the terrace – I had a panic of standing straight as though that might trick me into looking down the fall. It was exhausting. I had come a little more than halfway around and was as used up as a sailor who has been tied for hours in the rigging of a four-master beating through storm. The rain came in sharp as pins. Then the wind started up suddenly with a long screech of pain, a crack in my ear, and buffeted me to right and to left, blew me back almost to the terrace and then caught me the other way, leaned me out, my foot slipped an inch at that instant, and I had a view again of the street. I just stood in place, knees quivering, and listened to the wind whose cry came in from every angle. Something in the air was lacerated to make that cry. Then I almost fell to one knee for a blow came at me from nowhere, a fist on my back, and yet Kelly was ten feet away. I had to keep moving, everything was getting worse the longer I stayed still, but my feet were bad again. I pushed one forward; then the worst gust of wind came – Deborah's lone green eye flew into my eye. Hands came to pull me off, her hands, I smelled a breath – was it real? – it was gone. I took two more steps and reached the second angle. I was on the way back to the wall. But the wind came up again. My vision began to go – which is to say the narrow walk of the parapet began to shift – it swayed to the left, it swayed to the right, the stone was swaying, no it was me, I was swaying, my vision faded, came back again, faded, came back. I had a desire to leave the balcony and fly, I was certain I would succeed. I would fly out on some nerve, and out, and then my mind went out to a place on the edge, as close to going as an exhausted driver on a highway is close to sleep, and I said to myself, 'Get off now. You can hardly see.'

But something else said, 'Look at the moon, look up at the moon.' A silvery whale, it slipped up from the clouds and was clear, coming to surface in a midnight sea, and I felt its pale call, princess of the dead, I would never be free of her, and then the most quiet of the voices saying, 'You murdered. So you are in her cage. Now, earn your release. Go around the parapet again,' and this thought was so clear that I kept going down the third leg; and the wall came nearer to me; my limbs came alive again; each step I took, something good was coming in, I could do this, I knew I could do it now. There was the hint of when I would finally be done – some bliss from infancy moved through the lock of my lungs. As I approached the wall, ten feet away, eight feet away, six feet away, Kelly came near, and I stopped.

'It looks like you'll make it,' he said, walking up to me.

I did not care to tell him I must do it again, back the other way.

'You know, I didn't think you would make it,' Kelly said. 'I thought you'd get down before.' Then the sweet smile came off him. 'You're not bad, Stephen,' he said, 'it's just' – his smile was pleasant – 'I don't know that I want you to get away with it,' and he lifted the tip of the umbrella to my ribs and gave a push to poke me off. But I turned as he pushed, and the tip was diverted, turned just enough to grip the umbrella as it went by, which brought me back from going off, and I jumped down to the terrace even as he let go, and struck him with the handle across the face so hard he went down in a heap. I almost struck him again, but if I had, it would have been again and again, I was in a rage I could not have stopped, and in relief, some relief, wrong or right, I did not know, I turned and hurled the umbrella over the parapet – Shago's umbrella was gone – and went to the French doors, and through the library and through the bar and was almost at the door to the hall outside when I realized that I had not made the trip back along the parapet, and saw Deborah's green eye again in my mind. 'Oh, no, oh no,' I said to myself, 'I've done enough. By God, I've done enough.'

'It's not enough. It goes for nothing if you don't do it twice,' said the voice.

'Damn you,' I thought, 'I've lain with madness long enough.' And went through the door even as I caught a glimpse of Ruta coming out of a room. She had transferred herself to a negligee. But I was out and in the hall, and took the fire stairs this time, running down four flights, five, six, seven, and came up breathless at the eighth to switch to the elevator. I waited ten seconds, twenty seconds, at war with the impulse to go back to Kelly's and take the parapet again, and knew that if the elevator did not soon arrive, I would be up the stairs. But the cage came, it took me down the flights in one long sigh, to the entrance on the street where the policemen had been. And there was a cab waiting. There was a cab. I gave Cherry's address; we were off. The light, however, was red at Lexington, and dread came back again – against all my desire, like the return of disease, dread came back again. 'The first trip was done for you,' said the voice, 'but the second was for Cherry,' and I had a view of the parapet again and the rain going to ice, and was afraid to go back. 'Let's get on,' I said to the driver.

'Red light, buddy-boy.' Then it changed, and we worked down Lexington Avenue, twenty-two miles an hour down the staggering of the lights. I could not bear to be in the cab after four more minutes. 'What time is it?' I asked.

'Quarter to four.'

'Out here.'

I got into a bar before the closing, and had a double bourbon, the liquor going down like love. In a few minutes I would be close to Cherry again, and tomorrow we would buy a car. We would travel for a long time. Then, God and the gods willing, return for Deirdre. I could steal her from Kelly. There might be a way. And felt the beginning of a heart of happiness at being with Cherry — there was promise at the center of the thought. Hoisting the drink on this lilt, I looked into my mind — the memory of Deborah now like a scroll which must be read from back to front — and thought, 'You've gotten off easy,' and gagged on the drink, for dread came up like a wave. In my mind, I saw a fire in a tenement on the Lower East Side. And heard the wail of a fire engine. But it was a real fire engine; sixty seconds later it went by the bar in a red shriek and sword.

I was up and out, and tried to get a cab. Nothing followed however but the sense of sleep disturbed and people whispering in double beds. The city was awake. There was a beast in New York, but by times he slept. Other nights New York did not, and this was a night for the beast. Suddenly I knew something was wrong, something had gone finally wrong: it was too late for the parapet now. And three blocks away I heard the yawp and whoop of a gang. My stomach felt severed from me as on those long nights in this last year when Deborah took still another step away into the dark of our separation. A woe came riding down the wind. Then a taxi.

Just before Gramercy Park we turned from Lexington over to Second and continued south, down into the Lower East Side and over on Houston Street to First. But as we came north on First, the road was blocked. Three fire engines took up all but one lane, and a crowd of people had gathered, even at this hour. The fire was in a tenement a block and a half from the house where Cherry lived, far enough away for no-one to notice that a police car was stopped in front of her door, and an ambulance. There were no witnesses on the street, only faces at every window, and then my cab stopped and I paid it off. Still another police car came up, and Roberts stepped out, and seeing me, took a quick step and caught me by the arm, 'Rojack, where were you tonight?'

'Nowhere,' I said, 'nothing criminal.' The whiskey brought up a ball of bile.

'Have you been to Harlem?'

'No, I spent the last two hours with Barney Oswald Kelly. What's going on in Harlem?'

'Shago Martin got beaten to death.'

'No,' I said. 'God, no,' and had an intimation. 'What was the weapon?' I asked.

'Somebody broke in his head with an iron pipe in Morningside Park.'

'You're positive?'

'It was lying beside him.'

'Then why are you here?' the words came out as if they had been printed on paper. 'Why here?'

Now he could begin to pay me back. He spoke slowly. 'We were dipping down to see what Shago's ex might know. Then something came in on the box. Not ten minutes ago. Report of a boogie going ape in her room. That's all we heard. The Puerto Ricans were screaming.'

But now the street door to the tenement came open. Two orderlies worked a stretcher through the hall door and the street door. Cherry was on the stretcher. She was covered with a blanket and the blanket was wet with blood. The orderlies set the stretcher on the pavement and went to open the ambulance doors. A detective tried to move me away. My voice said, 'She's my wife, officer.'

'We'll talk to you later,' he said.

Cherry opened her eyes and saw me and gave the smile she had sent to me across the room in the precinct. 'Oh, Mr Rojack,' she said, 'you're back at that.'

'Are you . . . all right?'

'Well, sir,' she said, 'I really don't know.' Her face was badly beaten.

'Get out of the way, mister,' said an intern. 'Nobody comes near this patient.'

I held to the handgrip on the stretcher, and the intern looked away for someone to assist him. I had another moment or more.

'Come near,' she said.

I bent over.

'Don't tell the fuzz,' she whispered. 'It was a friend of Shago's. He got it all wrong – so dumb.'

Now mysteries were being exchanged for other mysteries.

'Darlin'?'

'Yes.'

'I'm going to die.'

'No,' I said, 'you'll be all right.'

'No, baby-pie,' she said, 'this is *very* different.' And as I reached out to her, Cherry gave a look of surprise, and died.

And Roberts took me to an after-hours joint, and kind as a mother, fed me whiskey, and finally confessed that on the night before, returning home to Queens after interrogating me, he had awakened an old mistress for a drinking bout – first time in three years – had drunk the morning in, beaten the mistress up, and still had not called the wife. Then he asked me if I had anything to do with Shago's murder, and when I said no, Roberts explained it was not his mistress but his wife he had beaten up last night, just why he did not know, had Cherry been a good piece of ass, and when I looked up with outrage at that appetite for the treacherous which rides the Irish like a leper, he said, 'Did you know she did some work for us?' – said it in such a way I would never know for certain, not ever, there was something in his voice I could not for certain deny; and Roberts said, 'If you don't like it, rat fink, take it out on the street,' and when I with all the courage of the ashes said yes, let's go to the street, Roberts said, 'Do you know what frustration is to a cop? Why, that's how we lose it,' he said, 'our standards, our quality . . .' and his features began to reef, and Roberts began to cry. The Irish are the only men who know how to cry for the dirty polluted blood of all the world.

EPILOGUE

The Harbors of the Moon Again

On the way out West, driving through the landscape of Super-America, there was a stopover in southern Missouri, a time out from the duals and freeways, motor lodges, winged motel inns, the heated pools and America's hot highway. I stopped off to see an Army friend, a doctor now, and he had read my book, *The Psychology of the Hangman*, and laid down a challenge from the bottom of the bottle. 'You write so much about death, Rojack, let this trooper show you some.' Which he did. Next morning at nine, with five hours of sleep and some booze from the night before being processed still in the vats of my metabolism, I saw an autopsy. There was no way to avoid it. The man had been dying of cancer, but he went out overnight from a burst appendix and a peritoneal gangrene; the smell which steamed up from the incision was so extreme it called for the bite of one's jaws not to retch up out of one's own cavity.

I remember I breathed it in to the top of the lung, and drew no further. Pinched it off in the windpipe. After half an hour of such breathing, my lungs were to ache for the rest of the day, but it was impossible to accept the old man's odor all the way in. After the autopsy, my friend apologized for the smell, said we had bad luck, said this was the worst smell he encountered in the last three years. I must not judge from this what a body is like, he went on to say, because healthy bodies have a decent odor in death and there is a bounty in the sight of our organs revealed. I was ready to agree — there had even been bounty in the excavation of this old man's horror; there was also the smell. I kept getting a whiff of the smell for the next two days, all along the trip through the dried hard-up lands of Oklahoma, northern Texas, New Mexico, on into the deserts of Arizona and southern Nevada where Las Vegas sits in the mirror of the moon. Then for weeks I never lost the smell. In the beginning the dead man came back at every turn, he came back from phosphate fertilizer in every farmer's field, he rose up out of every bump of a dead rabbit on the road, from each rotting ghost in the stump of a tree, he chose to come back later at every hint of a hole in emotion or a pit of decay, he offered the knowledge this was how your organs would look when you had exploited them that far. The cadaver had been crowned with the head of a good-looking old man; a stern waxlike face looked back as the tubers were revealed. It could have been the face of a man who owned his own farm or had been the local banker. It was lustful and proud, much hate in it, but disciplined. A general could have been cousin to that face. Maybe the discipline did him in; all that desire and all that compression of the will clamped on one another in some spew of the private states, the pressure continuing into that instant when the dissecting knife went into the belly. A sound hissed, the whistle of still another ghost released, pssssssssssss went this long sound like an auto tire in the instant before it blows, eighty miles an hour, and rubber all over the highway. Then the smell came up. Madness in it. It was a maniacal smell.

In some, madness must come in with breath, mill through the blood and be breathed out again. In some it goes up to the mind. Some take the madness and stop it with discipline. Madness is locked beneath. It goes into tissues, is swallowed by the cells. The cells go mad. Cancer is their flag. Cancer is the growth of madness denied. In that corpse I saw, madness went down to the blood – leucocytes gorged the liver, the spleen, the enlarged heart and violet-black lungs, dug into the intestines, germinated stench.

It was bad to mine into that cavern. More than the odor of madness went into the chest; some of the real madness went into me. The stink of the dead man went along the dry lands of Oklahoma and northern Texas, through the desert bake of New Mexico, Arizona, on into the valleys of the moon.

I got into Las Vegas at five, after twice ten hours of driving across a night of heat, July heat in the month of March, black and full of waves. The lights were on in town. The Fremont was one electric blaze, the Golden Nugget another, the sky was dark, the streets were light, lighter than Broadway on New Year's Eve, the heat was a phenomenon. Was it ninety degrees at nine minutes to five, five in the morning now? The car took a ride down the Strip in the dawn, carburetor smelling the burned-out air, madnesses forming, madnesses consumed. A small fist of the large fear which is saved for eternity formed like a stone in the pipe. Smell of death in the nose, I found a hotel, unpacked the dusty baggage. The bedroom was cold, seventy degrees, a cellar, a tomb, an air-conditioned chill. Sank into unconsciousness through vortices of road, blast furnaces of heat and currents of Las Vegas which carried me on a nerve-strung sleep to New York, where I was moving from friend to friend to find the money to buy a car. I had gone to a funeral after all, but it was Cherry's. And wanted to go to another, but it was Shago's, and let it pass. I did not want to face the Chinese Negroes who would be waiting at the door.

It was March, near the beginning of April. The heat wave held. I went into two atmospheres. Five times a day, or eight, or sixteen, there was a move from hotel to car, a trip through the furnace with the sun at one hundred and ten, a sprint along the Strip (billboards the size of a canyon) a fast sprint in the car, the best passenger car racing in America, driving not only your own piece of the mass production, but shifting lanes with the six or seven other cars in your field of collision. It was communal living at its best, everybody ready for everybody else, and then an ace's fast turn off the Strip to land in the parking lot of the next hotel, lungs breathing up the bellows of the desert, that hundred-and-ten air, hotter than hot flannel on the lining of the throat, and once again it was hopeless to know whether one could go to the end, or if in two hours, four hours, six, or six-and-twenty, the heat would swell some hinge of the brain, and madness would burn up out of that rent in the hinge. But for five or ten minutes the desert air was nothing to endure, a sport, one hundred and ten and going up, half-conducive the way the entrance to a sauna is half-conducive — that heat, that desert bake, hot as the radiation from a hard-wood fire. But then always into a hotel where the second atmosphere was on, the cold atmosphere, the seventy degrees of air-conditioned oxygen, that air which seemed to have come a voyage through space as if you were in the pleasure chamber of an encampment on the moon and fortified air was brought in daily by rockets from the earth. Yes the second atmosphere had a smell which was not the air conditioning of other places: the hollow sucked out by the machine left a hole which was deeper here. You caught the odor of an empty space where something was dying alone.

Lived in this second atmosphere for twenty-three hours of the twenty-four — it was life in a submarine, like in the safety chambers of the moon. Nobody knew that the deserts of the West, the arid empty wild blind deserts, were producing again a new breed of man.

Stayed at the dice tables. I was part of the new breed. Cherry had left a gift. Just as Oswald Kelly once went to sleep knowing which stocks would be on the rise by morning, so I knew the luck in the hands of each man who came to the table, I knew when to go down on the pass-line and when to bet the Don't Come. I was flat with the dice on my own, I dropped them quick as I could, but I kept an eye for the losers and worked up the fortune there. In four weeks I made twenty-four, paid my debts, all sixteen plus the loan for the car, and got ready to go on. There was a jungle somewhere in Guatemala which had a friend, an old friend, I thought to go there. And on to Yucatán. The night before I left Las Vegas I walked out in the desert to look at the moon. There was a jeweled city on the horizon, spires rising in the night, but the jewels were diadems of electric and the spires were the neon of signs ten stories high. I was not good enough to climb up and pull them down. So wandered farther out to the desert where the mad before me had come, and thought of walking into ambush. Eyes had been on me four full weeks, eyes collecting more and more – the news was out of who I was and verdicts were waiting. But I was safe in the city – no harm would come to me there – it was only in the desert that death would come up like a scorpion with its sting. If anyone wished to shoot me, he might have me here. But no-one did, and I wandered on, and found a booth by the side of the empty road, a telephone booth with a rusty dial. Went in and rang up and asked to speak to Cherry. And in the moonlight, a voice came back, a lovely voice, and said, 'Why, hello, hon, I thought you'd never call. It's kind of cool right now, and the girls are swell. Marilyn says to say hello. We get along, which is odd, you know, because girls don't swing. But toodle-oo, old baby-boy, and keep the dice for free, the moon is out and she's a mother to me.' Hung up and walked on back to the city of jewels, and thought before I left the spires, might go out to call her one more time. But in the morning, I was something like sane again, and packed the car, and started on the long trip to Guatemala and Yucatán.

Provincetown,
New York,
September 1963–October 1964

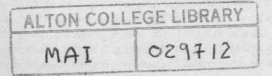